PRAISE FOR *GODZILLA*™ *2000*

"PULSE-POUNDING! Cerasini's knowledge of military hardware is astounding....Godzilla's fans can count themselves fortunate....Random House's flagship Godzilla series couldn't be in better hands."

—J. D. Lees, *G-Fan* magazine

"A DELIGHT! In *Godzilla 2000,* Marc Cerasini has managed to bring a new sense of appropriate gravity to the legendary monsters. Before him, the myth had gone rotten, the behemoths being reduced to cartoon characters. Now they are what they once were: embodiments of apocalyptic doom and dread."

—Robert Price, *Crypt of Cthulhu #97*

"Marc Cerasini has done it again, with a Godzilla book that's a cross between a techno-thriller and Old Home Night for Japanese monsters. **THE ACTION NEVER LETS UP,** and you'll have millennial fun reading it!"

—John J. Pierce, science fiction critic and historian

"EXTREMELY ENTERTAINING...A FAST-PACED PAGE-TURNER! The only problem with this novel is that you really can't hold it and eat a nice big bucket of popcorn at the same time. Cerasini has put all the fun of a Saturday matinee into this one!"

—Joe Mauceri, *World of Fandom* magazine

PRAISE FOR *GODZILLA*™ *RETURNS*

PRAISE FOR GODZILLA™!

"As a proud graduate of Yokohama High School, I've always had more than a little fondness for the big green guy. Long may he stomp!"

—Mark Hamill, actor

"Godzilla is the hero for our times....He has been mine for all time!"

—Bob Eggleton
Hugo Award–winning artist

"Godzilla is more than a National Treasure of Japan; he's evolved into one of the world's. A modern myth and part of contemporary consciousness, Godzilla has become the most popular and successful of all movie monsters. His film series spans nearly two dozen authorized titles—so far—more than that of any other monster character made by a single studio. A combination of appealing design, size and strength, personality and style, Godzilla truly holds the title of 'King of the Monsters.'"

—Donald F. Glut, author
Dinosaurs: The Encyclopedia
The Empire Strikes Back novelization
and over 30 works of fiction and nonfiction

MORE PRAISE FOR GODZILLA™!

Lifetime Achievement Award.

—MTV

"He's beloved by millions the world over. In this business of stars and superstars, it would be no exaggeration to say that he is the biggest."

—Patrick Stewart, actor

"Tarzan, Sherlock Holmes, Superman, Mickey Mouse...Godzilla...There are only a handful of fictional characters who have achieved the status of worldwide icon. And of these, only Godzilla has had the range to play both villain and hero, harbinger of nuclear doom and prehistoric savior of the modern age. Is it any wonder we love him?"

—Randy Stradley
creative director, Dark Horse Comics

"Godzilla is one of the most important icons of the post-atomic age."

—Alex Cox
director of *Repo Man* and *Sid and Nancy*

"Go, go, Godzilla!"

—Blue Oyster Cult

GODZILLA™

2000

by Marc Cerasini

Random House 🏠 New York

Library of Congress Catalog Card Number: 97-66656
ISBN: 0-679-88751-2
IL: 10 and up
First edition: November 1997

Special acknowledgment: "Go, go, Godzilla," from the song
"Godzilla" by Donald Roeser. Copyright © 1977 Sony/ATV
Tunes LLC: All rights administered by Sony/ATV Music
Publishing, 8 Music Square West, Nashville, TN 37203.
All rights reserved. Used by permission.

Printed in the United States of America
10 9 8 7 6 5 4 3 2 1

*In the year 1999, in the seventh month,
from the sky will come a great King of Terror...*

—Nostradamus, *The Prophecies,*
Century 10, Quatrain 72

PROLOGUE
IMPACT!

Deep space, a long time ago...

For a billion years, a swarm of asteroids sped across the universe, propelled by the momentum of a galactic catastrophe.

For a long time, the chunks of rock, ice, and debris traveled through space, unaffected by the celestial bodies around them. Finally, the swarm fell into an enormous elliptical orbit in a galaxy at the edge of the universe.

Part of that orbit included a small solar system with ten planets, many moons, and an unimpressive yellow sun.

Time passed. The asteroids circled in their immense orbit. Every sixty-five million years or so, the swarm of rocks and ice would cross the orbit of the little ten-planet solar system.

On one such pass, a huge asteroid in the swarm struck the system's fifth planet, annihilating it utterly. Some of the debris from that collision drifted into a set orbit around the yellow sun, forming a belt of asteroids.

Most of the swarm, however, remained unaffected. It continued in its immense elliptical orbit, speeding away from the little solar system once again.

*   *   *

Another sixty-five million years passed, and the swarm returned to these same planets once more. There was another collision. This time a huge asteroid struck the third planet from the sun.

Before the collision with the asteroid, the planet was a verdant world covered by living oceans and land thick with jungles, swamps, plains, and thousands of species of reptilian creatures of all shapes and sizes.

Although life on the third planet was not eradicated completely, the changes caused by the impact were such that evolution there took an entirely new direction.

The reptiles were all but destroyed. A new breed of warm-blooded creatures took their place as the preeminent life form on this blue-green planet.

Meanwhile, the rest of the asteroids swept out of the solar system once again. The swarm of rocks would not return for another sixty-five million years.

And life on Earth continued...

GODZILLA™

1
DANGEROUS
GAMES

Friday, October 30, 1998, 1:23 P.M.
A video game arcade
Los Angeles, California

Kip Daniels stepped from the sun-dappled sidewalk into the dim video arcade. He blinked his blue eyes, waiting for them to become accustomed to the gloom. Although this place was only a few blocks from the campus of the University of Southern California, there were no students here.

Today the arcade was practically empty. That was lucky. Very lucky.

Kip had risked the coach's wrath by cutting gym class. It was the only way he could beat the after-school crowd and claim his favorite video game. There was only one BATTLEGROUND 2000 machine in Los Angeles, and competition for it was fierce.

Playing BATTLEGROUND 2000 was worth any punishment, as far as Kip was concerned, and it was *especially* worth missing gym class. Kip wasn't good at baseball, basketball, or football. He hated push-ups and sit-ups. He couldn't even swim very well, and for a kid who lived in California, that was kind of an embarrassment.

But here at the arcade, Kip was the champ. All because of BATTLEGROUND 2000.

Kip pulled a five-dollar bill from his baggy jeans, stepped around a man in a black suit who was loitering near the door, and headed for the change machine. He turned his paper money into quarters, then went straight to the back of the arcade. Kip's heart raced when he saw the familiar blue-and-violet glow of the BATTLEGROUND 2000 machine.

Unfortunately, his hopes of claiming the game for himself were instantly crushed. A trio of Latino kids from another school had beaten him to it. Even worse, the teenagers were wearing gang colors.

Gangs were another part of life that Kip just couldn't get used to. He'd been living in Southern California for three years, but he couldn't stop comparing L.A. to Grand Rapids. He'd never had to deal with street gangs back in Michigan.

Warily, Kip eyed the gang members. Two of them were watching a third, who had a hair design displayed on his shaved scalp. Pretending disinterest and praying for invisibility, Kip checked the score in the right-hand corner of the screen.

Baldy's not doing so good, Kip thought with some pride. *I can usually reach 250,000 points with my first Bullettchopper. This loser's on his third!*

The two Latinos who stood behind their friend were also unimpressed. "Why're you so stupid?" the tall one cried, smacking the player on the back of his head. The blow broke the player's concentration and he lost his third and final Bullettchopper.

The blue lights on the game changed to red and an alarm went off, announcing the end of play.

The kid with the designer head got up, and his friend pushed him out of the way. "Lemme show you, man!" the tall kid cried. "Gimme a buck."

But as the bald guy rose from the cockpit, he spotted Kip, who quickly averted his eyes.

"Hey, kid," the guy called. "You wanna play?"

Kip's face flushed. He didn't know what to say. At school, these were the type of kids who tormented him. But to Kip's surprise, there was genuine admiration on the Latino's face. "Come on, man," he called. "I watched you play yesterday."

The tall kid objected to Kip taking his turn at the game, but the other two silenced him.

"Wait till you see this kid play," Baldy insisted. "He's a terror, man!" He turned to Kip again. "Come on, kid," he called. "I ain't gonna hurt ya."

Kip nodded, then hesitantly approached the game. The tall kid moved aside and let him by. As he sat in the familiar cockpit and reached for the control stick, Kip drew some quarters out of his pocket. But to Kip's surprise, the Latino kid fed the machine with his own change.

"Go, man," he said, standing back and crossing his arms over his chest, watching as if Kip were a champion boxer and he was Kip's proud manager. The other two gang kids stepped back to watch, too.

Kip swallowed hard. He pressed the button marked PLAY and the blue-and-violet lights flashed. The eerie ultraviolet glow seemed to reach out and envelop him like a soft blanket. It was always this way when he played BATTLEGROUND 2000. It felt satisfying, predictable, even comforting—maybe because he was doing something that he was good at. Kip didn't know. Or care. He just wanted to play!

His hand gripped the control stick. Instead of shoving or jerking it, the way a lot of players did, Kip smoothly eased it from side to side, safely guiding the Bullettchopper through computer-generated valleys and mountain ranges. Even at high speed, Kip easily avoided the obstacles thrown at him.

Soon, he knew, things would become much more complicated. He didn't have to wait long.

First a gigantic bird swooped into his path. This surprised him. Usually the Spider-Robots attacked first. But despite the shock, Kip managed to dodge the Swooper's attack and fire back. He took the bird out cleanly.

Kip glanced at the screen. His first thousand points were displayed in the upper right-hand corner.

Good, he thought, remembering a quote from his favorite movie. *"Our first catch of the day."*

After the Bird-monster—or Swooper—was duly dispatched, the attacks came fast and furious. The Spider-Robots, the Buzz Bees, the Razor Wasps— they all descended on Kip's little Bullettchopper. These were just some of the denizens that swarmed the cyber-world of BATTLEGROUND 2000.

As he concentrated, Kip barely noticed the gasps of awe and surprise that came from the gang kids behind him. The Latinos began to duck in time with the perils that appeared on the game screen. Their whoops and hollers got louder and more enthusiastic as the game progressed.

Kip was in top form today. Usually he had to play two or three times just to warm up. But today, for some reason, he was scoring better than ever.

Maybe it was the audience, he decided.

Suddenly, the score reached 500,000 and the game jumped to the second level. For a moment, the action eased. Kip permitted himself a breather. He noted with pride that he had never before reached the second level with his first Bullettchopper. He usually lost at least one along the way.

The game lights dimmed and flashed, and he was off again.

The second level—set against a cityscape of towering skyscrapers and street-spanning bridges— added a whole new set of obstacles. The occasional Swoopers, and the swarms of Buzz Bees and Razor Wasps were more numerous than ever.

But added to the mix were the Laser Bats and the deadly Flying Toads. The bats were tough to shoot down. And they shot back. Initially, Kip handled their threat deftly, easily downing the first three who came at him before they could fire a shot. He even managed to take out a swarm of Razor Wasps, too—*before* they could disperse and surround his Bullettchopper.

Then, unexpectedly, a virtual shadow fell over the Bullettchopper. Faster than Kip could possibly react, the Flying Toad slammed down on his fighter, crushing it to pieces.

Releasing the control stick, Kip watched help-lessly as the debris fell to the virtual streets below. He glanced up at the scoreboard. He was nearly at the 700,000 mark, and he still had two Bullett-choppers left.

Kip was still ahead of the game. The lights dimmed and flashed, and he was quickly back in the war.

He heard oohs and aahs behind him, but he ignored his audience. Kip was too focused on the game to notice that more and more gang members were gathering around the BATTLEGROUND 2000 machine—and getting more and more excited.

Kip cried out in frustration when he lost his sec-ond Bullettchopper—again to a Flying Toad. But this time, he took the toad with him, reaching a total score of 950,000.

Kip exhaled in astonishment. He had never scored 900,000 before. It actually moved him to a *third* level. He hadn't even known a third level existed!

Kip's hands were sweating on the control stick, and his heart was racing. Usually he relaxed and got into the game. But as he moved to this new level, he felt an ominous sensation of someone watching him—and not the gang kids who contin-ued to mill around and shout their encouragement, either.

Kip shook off the feeling and forged ahead. As play resumed, he got his first glimpse of the third level's playing field.

It, too, was a cityscape. But this one was wrecked, as if a war had been fought among the towering skyscrapers. Some of the towers were demolished and leaned to the side, creating obstacles. Bridges were broken, and the tops of several of the tallest buildings were blown off.

Virtual smoke billowed from the wreckage. As Kip flew into it, he was temporarily blinded. His vehicle emerged in time to be attacked by a swarm of Laser Bats. He fired rapidly, dispatching all but one of the creatures.

The final Laser Bat took up a position behind Kip's vehicle, and he had to use all of his skills to dodge the beast's destructive rays, even as he raced through the virtual canyons of the ruined city.

Time and again, as Kip outran the Laser Bat, he had to defend himself against other creatures. Buzz Bees, Spider-Robots, and Razor Wasps threw themselves at him. He managed to dodge each attack and destroy every adversary.

But still the persistent Laser Bat dogged him.

Finally, in a desperate move, Kip deliberately flew into another billowing cloud of smoke. In the middle, he changed direction suddenly. When his Bullettchopper emerged once again, it had turned around and now faced the Laser Bat.

The audience cheered. Kip fired, and the bat exploded. But even as it did, a Flying Toad dropped out of the sky, its shadow covering the hovering Bullettchopper. Kip dived and turned—and two more Flying Toads were facing him.

Kip depressed the button, and his chopper spit fire. Two toads exploded. Kip stood his vehicle on its tail and fired upward, eliminating the third toad.

Behind him, people whooped, but he shut out the sound. All of his attention was focused on the game.

As the minutes flew by, Kip seemed to slip into a trance. He became a one-man virtual destroyer, easily and effortlessly dispatching each and every virtual being that came his way.

Finally, his heart slowed and his heartbeat and breathing dropped to normal. His every move was economy in motion. He eased the stick right or left, eliminating each threat as it appeared. It became second nature to him, and each time he fired, he knocked down another threat.

The scoreboard kept jumping up and up, surpassing the million mark. Kip kept firing, oblivious to everything but the game.

Finally, after Kip smoothly knocked down two more Flying Toads, something appeared in the virtual city ahead of him. He pushed the stick forward, rushing to meet this new foe.

But to Kip's surprise, the enemy did not swerve to avoid his attack. Instead, it came toward him at an amazing rate.

Kip's eyes opened wide. And he froze.

A wedge-shaped, feral head of charcoal black hurtled toward his tiny Bullettchopper. Its red eyes seemed to burn into Kip's soul.

As the monstrous head filled the screen, the creature's mouth opened so wide that Kip could see its double rows of sharp teeth and a dark tunnel as black as hell's gate, leading to the beast's stomach.

Kip watched helplessly as the creature's jaws

snapped shut. The monster gulped and swallowed Kip's third and final Bullettchopper.

The blue lights turned to red and began to blink. A siren blared, signaling the end of the game, and the final score flashed on a readout above the screen: 1,375,000.

Kip Daniels had surpassed every previous record.

For a few seconds, he was unable to move. He was still paralyzed by the terrifying power of the game's final image.

It was Godzilla, realized Kip. The reptilian monster that had destroyed Tokyo only a few months before.

At that moment, Kip suddenly noticed the silence all around him. He turned. The gang members were standing in one corner of the video game parlor.

A man in a black suit and a severe, military-style haircut was pointing a handgun at them.

Suddenly, two strong hands gripped Kip's shoulders. "You're coming with us, son," said a second man in black as he lifted Kip from the BATTLE-GROUND 2000 cockpit.

The stunned teenager tried to resist, but it was no use. The men effortlessly hustled Kip out of the arcade and into a waiting car.

With a squeal of rubber on pavement, the sedan with U.S. Government plates swerved down the street and disappeared into the rush-hour traffic.

GODZILLA™

2
TOP SECRET

"They grabbed him too soon," United States Air Force General Jake Taggart complained loudly. He ran his hands through his iron-gray hair, then continued berating the younger officer in front of him. "We had a golden opportunity to evaluate this kid *before* we pour a million bucks into his training. But your boys grabbed him too soon!"

The general punctuated his comments—and his disgust with this miserable turn of events—by dropping the hastily assembled personality file onto his crowded desk.

The file was an expensive document, gathered in the last twenty-four hours with the full resources of the United States government. But General Taggart pointed to the thick bundle of papers as if it were so much garbage.

"That file is absolutely useless!" Taggart cried, emphasizing the point by scattering the pages across his desk like autumn leaves. "What I really need to know isn't going to be found in any personality file Dr. Markham dreams up," he continued. "What I really need to know is if this Kip Daniels has the Right Stuff. Get it, Colonel? Do you know what that means?"

"Yes, sir, I do," the younger man replied stiffly. Colonel William Krupp, the Air Force officer charged with recruitment for Project Valkyrie, had just endured the full force of the general's wrath. Now that Taggart was winding down, the colonel faced his commanding officer.

"Don't blame the intel boys," Krupp insisted with quiet authority. "The kid was surrounded by gang members, two of whom were armed with automatic weapons. One of *those* punks was wanted for questioning in a drug-related homicide."

General Taggart frowned. Then, after a tense moment in which the colonel was sure that his commander would explode again, Taggart visibly relaxed.

"I know, Bill. I know," the general muttered at last, shaking his head. "Sorry I blew up, Colonel."

The two men stood in silence for a moment, clearing the air.

"Hell, they probably did the right thing," General Taggart admitted. "But the kid was so close to the end of the game."

Taggart paused, then looked at the other officer. "And don't forget what one of the Air Force Intelligence agents said at the debriefing," he reminded the colonel. "The kid froze when he saw the image of Godzilla coming at him on the screen."

"But, General," the colonel argued. "That was at the *end* of the game. He may have been distracted when the retrieval team went in to grab him; he may have been tired. Hell, this kid's so good, he may have just been *bored*."

The general nodded, which, to Colonel Krupp, was an indication that it was *his* turn to push. "This kid hit—then breezed by—the one-million mark. He earned the highest score ever, and it wasn't luck. This Kip Daniels beat Pierce Dillard's highest score—and Dillard only hit a million *after* two months of intensive training here at Nellis."

"I know," General Taggart acknowledged. "But if Daniels freezes in combat, then he's no good to us, the Project, or his country."

"So I should just send him home?" Colonel Krupp asked. "Send the kid back to Los Angeles, to a school full of gang members, and, of course, to his loving mother…" His voice trailed off meaningfully, and the general understood the other officer's concern.

"No, Colonel Krupp," Taggart replied softly. "If his papers are all squared away, then Kip Daniels is in. But only if he *wants* to be."

A look of relief crossed the younger man's chiseled face. Then Colonel Krupp smiled for the first time that day. "I'll go notify the Intelligence team," he announced.

The colonel turned to leave but paused. "When do you want to meet him?" Krupp asked.

Taggart sighed. "Give me ten minutes or so to look over his evaluation."

Krupp nodded, then saluted.

Taggart returned the salute, then sat down into his chair as the other officer departed, leaving the general alone in his tiny office, with his troubled thoughts. As he slumped in his chair, he gathered the scattered pages on his desk. The Project was everything right now. He'd given the past year to it—a year that should have been spent in quiet retirement.

But my country called, and I answered, one last time, he thought bitterly.

Taggert sighed. The problem wasn't in serving his country, the problem was the mission itself.

I spent my life training to defend America from foreign enemies, he reasoned. *I trained to fight men, not monsters.*

The Soviet threat was gone. In its place was a new menace and a new mission. Now the combined might of the armed services of these United States was retooling—to go into the pest-control business.

General Taggart snorted with contempt as he thought back to the events surrounding the reappearance of Godzilla months before, and how an obscure article he wrote in the 1980s for a strategic studies journal had returned to haunt him.

Taggart had boldly written how certain weapon systems could be modified to defend against the unlikely reappearance of Godzilla, or another monster like him.

Of course, Taggart reminded himself, *nobody really expected Godzilla to show up again.*

But Godzilla *did* show up again, just ten years later. And just when Taggart was ready to retire to his house in California, some pencil-necked adviser to the President of the United States remembered his obscure little article.

"Well," Taggart reminded himself, repeating the familiar words—his personal mantra—"you knew the job was dangerous when you took it." And Taggart had taken it. Truth to tell, he had *jumped* at it.

He was bored after the first six months of retirement, and the call from the Pentagon sounded awfully good.

Taggart recalled the uphill battle he had fought through the corridors of power in the nation's capital. It had been tough convincing his superiors that his crazy plan was sound *and* sensible. His reputation convinced the military men of his ability to find and lead the perfect team to accomplish the difficult—some said impossible—assignment.

After three months of working on the project, General Taggart was beginning to envy Colonel Krupp. Nobody would blame the colonel if things went wrong. And right now, it seemed, *everything* was going wrong.

Their weapons weren't ready. Their aircraft weren't ready. Their budget wasn't approved. Hell, they didn't even have office space. *Well*, Taggart reminded himself, *what did you expect? Catered meals and a cheery fireplace?*

The President of the United States and the boys up on Capitol Hill wanted Taggart to get the job done, but nobody wanted to spend more of the taxpayers' money doing it, even though the public was clamoring for protection against monsters—or *kaiju,* the Japanese term for "giant monsters," which the scientists were calling the creatures.

So, after they took the trouble to hire him for the

job, General Taggart was forced to go to the Oval Office personally to negotiate a budget with a president he didn't like, and hadn't even *voted* for.

"And why should the nation invest even a tiny percentage of defense spending to fight monsters?" the president asked.

Taggart supplied all the stock answers. *We're the only superpower left. If we don't do it, who will?... It's our duty to be prepared for any threat against the people of this nation. Who knows what type of creature might yet emerge?*

They were all sound arguments, and Taggart almost believed them. In the end, though, the president needed a photo op, and the guys building Raptor-One and Raptor-Two were good, card-carrying union men and supporters of the president's party. So Project Valkyrie was born.

All it took was the president's signature, a special dispensation by the House Intelligence Committee, and a billion-dollar black budget from the CIA, the National Security Agency, and the Air Force combined.

And *that* was only the beginning.

Maybe my idea is *crazy,* he thought. Many people expected him to fail—maybe even *wanted* him to fail.

If that was the case, then Project Valkyrie was the rope, and Taggart was about to hang himself. *And only a bunch of teenagers can save me, the Project, and maybe even this country, if it should ever come to that.* Taggart shook his head. *I pray that it never will...but just in case...*

The general refocused his eyes on Kip Daniels's

personality file. As he skimmed the psychological profile, school records, family history, IQ tests, and medical records, the general wondered if he was wrong—if maybe Project Valkyrie wasn't exactly what some of his enemies in the Pentagon called it.

Taggart's Folly.

Of course, General Taggart couldn't take *all* the credit for this crazy scheme. It was Colonel Krupp and Dr. Markham who developed the video game called BATTLEGROUND 2000. "The perfect way to find the brightest and the best candidates for the Project," Dr. Markham stated.

Taggart had to admit that the psychiatrist had been right, too, because try as they might, Taggart could never train even the best pilots the Air Force had to offer to operate the complicated weapons systems of Raptor-One effectively.

"You can't teach an old dog new tricks," Dr. Markham had insisted. "They're too old. Running the simulator is like learning a martial art. And to learn a skill like that, the younger an individual starts, the better he or she will perform."

That, in a nutshell, was the reasoning behind BATTLEGROUND 2000. Taggart had to admit that it worked. The video game had found seventeen possible candidates—all in their mid-teens—who scored above 800,000 on the game. Each machine was designed with a chip that notified the command station here in Nevada when someone scored above the programmed mark.

These candidates were unknowingly photographed and fingerprinted by the game machine itself, and this information was transmitted by satellite to the Project's massive computers. Each potential candidate was then targeted by Air Force Intelligence for observation and evaluation. Those who displayed past criminal, behavioral, or psychological problems were eliminated.

None of those rejected were even aware that they had been tested, or that the government had completed an extensive background check on them, their parents, teachers, friends, and associates. Only those with a high probability of success were finally selected as candidates for Project Valkyrie.

Which left them with only six potential candidates so far. Six candidates who were summarily drafted.

Oh, the Air Force and the Pentagon liked to call it "voluntary conscription," but that polite phrase covered a multitude of sins. The truth of it was that the best and brightest were conscripted—if need be, against their will. The problem was *that* pressing, the situation *that* serious.

So far, conscription wasn't necessary. All of those who'd been offered the chance to join took it—with their parents' or guardians' consent. Indeed, the candidates welcomed their selection for a variety of reasons.

For some, it was an opportunity to get out of a bad situation. For others, Project Valkyrie was a call to adventure, or to duty. Most of the recruits were high achievers in other areas. They were highly motivated and smart enough to recognize a golden opportunity when they were offered one.

Unfortunately for Kip Daniels, his situation fell in the first category. If he took the job, it would be to escape his disturbing and chaotic life.

Kip was what social workers called a "troubled" teenager who came from a "stressed environment." A child of a broken home, Kip never knew his father, who was doing fifteen years in a Michigan correctional facility for forgery and grand larceny.

His mother was no better: A drug addict who dragged her son from the Midwest and then summarily dumped him into a rough city school system with the worst sort of punks and malcontents— despite the boy's phenomenal IQ and his amazing hand-to-eye coordination.

"If we draft this kid, we'd be doing him a favor," the general muttered aloud. *But the kid froze,* Taggart reminded himself. *And, anyway, the decision is Kip Daniels's to make, not mine.*

The officer glanced at the BATTLEGROUND 2000 readout again. *Nearly a million and a half points in a single game.* The general whistled in amazement. *The kid's performance was phenomenal. The best so far.*

Taggart knew that time was running out. If the scientists were right, Godzilla was still alive, and the monster could rise out of the sea and return at any moment.

Time was running out.

GODZILLA™

3
THE BOX

"Okay, you're clear to move in a little closer, Raptor-One," Air Combat Controller Lori Angelo radioed from the cockpit of Raptor-One's sister ship, Raptor-Two.

Kip Daniels monitored the air combat controller's—or "Air Cap's"—commands through the headphones in his flight helmet. His gloved hands gripped the stick of the weapons control system. His eyes were fixed on the view outside the cockpit windows, searching for the elusive target still ahead of them.

"Moving in," Pierce Dillard, the pilot of Raptor-One, announced. As he spoke, Pierce's eyes squinted with determination and he struggled with the joystick. The Raptor's controls seemed stiff, and he fought to maintain aircraft stability. The erratic and unpredictable updrafts from the huge buildings below were causing the problem.

No matter what he did, Pierce could not seem to tame the Raptor's violent shaking.

"The controls are sluggish," Pierce announced.

At the co-pilot's station, to the left and slightly below the pilot seat, Martin Wong scanned his HUD—head's-up display. The huge color monitor offered countless readouts, informing the co-pilot/flight engineer of the Raptor's condition, inside and out.

"We have primary computer failure on the star-board tilt-engine motor," Martin announced calmly. Then he quickly punched up a program from the computer files.

"Backups coming on-line...now," he said.

The vibrations slowed, then all but ceased. The Raptor was moving smoothly once again.

"Raptor-One, watch out for those towers at your three o'clock," Tobias Nelson, the pilot of Raptor-Two, warned Pierce. Toby's deep, booming voice surprised Kip. *Lori should have been the one to warn us,* he thought. *She's the combat controller.*

Pierce eased back on his stick, and Raptor-One's advance through the steel, glass, and concrete canyons of downtown Chicago slowed. As the Raptor hovered at a virtual standstill over the city, gusts of wind continuously buffeted the aircraft.

Well, Kip reasoned, *that's why they call it the Windy City.*

The Raptor began to drift toward a round glass tower, and Pierce had to move the control stick to compensate.

Tobias Nelson, at the controls of Raptor-Two, also hovered in a stationary position, but he was far, far above the city, and Raptor-One. Raptor-Two's job was air combat control, and for that they needed a bird's-eye view of the battlefield.

"Raptor-One, move into attack position," Lori Angelo commanded from her combat control station in Two. "I want you to circle the Sears Tower…" Lori paused for effect. "That's the tall building on your left, *Dillard*."

Pierce's face remained stony as he listened to Lori's instructions. But the crews of both ships could hear Toby chuckling.

"After you pass the building, make a sharp right," Lori concluded. Pierce nodded, then clicked his mike to acknowledge her command. Cautiously, he moved the joystick forward, and to the left. The panoramic vista outside the cockpit windshields tilted and changed as Raptor-One gracefully swept around the towering, glass-walled skyscraper. Chicago sprawled below them.

"Your target *should* be in sight," Lori cautioned.

"Roger, Air Cap, got it on screen," replied Tia Shimura from her station behind Martin. Tia was Raptor-One's navigation and communications officer, and the youngest member of the team.

Raising her eyes from the monitors, Tia gazed through the huge, cathedral-like windows of the cockpit. Like the rest of the Raptor-One crew, she wanted to be the first to lay eyes on the enemy.

As One sped past the Sears Tower, the aircraft dipped and then leveled off. Suddenly, their target appeared ahead of them—a black silhouette that stood out starkly against the cluttered, smog-bound city.

"I see him!" Pierce cried. He pushed the stick, and the Raptor surged ahead. The monster loomed larger in the windshield. So far, Godzilla seemed oblivious to their approach.

Even over the drone of the Raptor's engine, the

crew could hear the echoing roar as Godzilla bellowed his rage at humanity. Kip watched in fascination as the creature moved slowly, ponderously through the city. As he walked, Godzilla waded through the structures at his feet, callously cutting a swath of destruction through the heart of Chicago's business district.

Thick clouds of black smoke and red fire billowed into the afternoon sky in the creature's wake. As they watched, an immense skyscraper tumbled to earth in a cloud of dust and smoke.

Despite himself, Kip gasped. He immediately regretted the outburst, and hoped that none of the others heard him.

"Quiet, Wizzo," Pierce rebuked him, using Air Force shorthand for "weapon systems officer." Kip's mouth snapped shut and his face burned with embarrassment. He was glad his station was far ahead of the others, at the very front of the Raptor's huge cockpit. *And* that his back was turned to his teammates.

"Prepare for final approach." The radio didn't mask the tension in Lori's voice.

"Moving in," Pierce replied coolly. The Raptor moved closer to the rampaging monster. Then Lori, from Two, cleared them for action.

"You may attack Godzilla at will, Raptor-One," she declared.

Kip's sweaty hands gripped the weapon's control stick. At his station in the very front of the cockpit, he felt totally alone and far removed from the rest of Raptor's crew.

But their lives depended on him, nonetheless.

He looked up from his heads-up display, and through the windshield. Almost simultaneously, Godzilla's neck twisted, his feral head turned toward the aircraft.

The creature seemed to stare right at Kip, who immediately felt a surge of panic. Sweat trickled down his back under the olive-drab flight suit.

"Prepare to relinquish control," Kip finally said, with much more confidence than he felt. His heart raced and he prepared to take over control of Raptor-One.

As the weapon systems officer, it was Kip's job to take complete command of the aircraft while they were in attack mode. He not only selected and fired a multitude of exotic weapons at Godzilla, but he also piloted the aircraft.

Being the "wizzo" was the hardest job in the cockpit...and a job everybody had fought for. Kip still didn't understand why *he* had been chosen. He was probably the only team member who *didn't* want the task.

Kip swallowed hard and focused on the mission.

"Weapons officer to take command of the aircraft at the count of three," he announced, his voice tight.

"Three. Two. One...mark!"

Pierce felt his control stick go slack. He loosened his grip and sat back in the pilot's chair. His job was done. He was just a passenger now. Dead weight. *I hate this part,* he thought. Pierce felt frustrated and helpless as the rookie moved the Raptor into attack position.

"Watch out for the buildings at three o'clock," Lori warned from Two. Kip slowed his lateral movement and moved forward again—still dangerously close to the skyscrapers on their right.

Martin and Pierce exchanged worried glances.

"You're too close to the buildings, Kip," Tia warned him. "And you're too low. Watch out for Godzilla's tail."

Kip eased the stick back, concentrating on his targeting computer, which was in the process of locking on to the monster.

Kip chose to lead the attack with cadmium missiles. He touched the appropriate keys on his pad. They opened the shielded missile bays on the Raptor's wings.

But Godzilla wasn't waiting for the Raptor to make the first move. The creature's eyes never left the oncoming aircraft. As the Raptor neared Godzilla, he became more agitated. The creature's lips curled and a low rumble erupted from his throat. Instinctively, the *kaiju* recognized One as a threat.

Suddenly, Godzilla's head reared back and his eyes narrowed. Blue electricity danced along his three rows of dorsal spines.

"He's going to fire his radioactive rays!" Lori cried from Raptor-Two. Godzilla was about to utilize his most terrible weapon—the powerful radioactive fire that originated in pockets of radioactivity in his chest and burst from his mouth.

Kip heard the warning, but he reacted a split second too late. Godzilla's maw yawned, and superheated blue rays spewed forth. The radioactive fire enveloped the Raptor's cockpit windshields, fuselage, and wing surfaces.

"Wing damage!" Martin announced, scanning the readouts. As he watched, two sets of warning lights flashed. Then the alarm klaxon announced that there was a fire on board the Raptor.

"The cadmium missiles are exploding in the missile bays!" Martin cried, his fingers flying across his keypad.

Damn! Kip thought, instantly closing the missile bay blast shields, though he knew full well it was too late for that. Kip cursed himself. *I opened the missile bays too early,* he realized.

While Martin activated the emergency fire system, Tia handled damage control. Pierce reached out and gripped his control stick again, ready to wrest control of the aircraft away from Kip as soon as he could.

Meanwhile, Kip tried to move out of Godzilla's line of fire. But the torrent of radioactive breath kept on coming at them. Not even the Raptor, which was coated with the same material that protected the space shuttle from the heat of re-entry, could withstand this kind of punishment for long.

Kip quickly shifted to hover mode, then moved the Raptor backward and to the left.

Pierce tore his eyes away from Martin's damage assessment display and sneered openly when he realized what Kip was doing. *This had better work,* he thought bitterly.

Fortunately for Kip, it did.

The wizzo managed to slide the Raptor backward, then deftly moved the aircraft to the side, ducking behind the Sears Tower.

All the while, Godzilla focused his radioactive fire on the retreating aircraft. As the Raptor slipped behind the huge skyscraper and out of Godzilla's line of sight, the building took the full brunt of the monster's fiery fury.

As the crews of Raptor-One and Raptor-Two watched in amazement, the middle of the Sears Tower exploded outward, raining shattered steel beams and deadly glass shards down on the city below. Then one of the tallest buildings in the world lurched precariously and split in two. While fire and smoke engulfed the lower portion of the building, the upper half tilted to the right and plunged onto the smaller structures below.

"So much for keeping casualties down to a minimum," Martin muttered.

"Pull back, Daniels!" Pierce commanded, staring through the windshield. At the same time, both Toby's and Lori's voices cried out over the radio.

"Your aircraft is taking hits from ground fire!" Lori cried. But Kip couldn't make out Lori's frantic warnings among the other confused voices that screamed in his ears.

"Pilot taking over control of the aircraft," Pierce announced.

Immediately, Kip released control of the Raptor, and the aircraft began to ascend rapidly. Pierce, in a vain attempt to avoid the debris that was flying up from the destruction below, was taking Raptor-One higher.

But Kip had initiated the attack at a low altitude—too low, in fact. He'd exposed Raptor-One to Godzilla's chief weapon—his fiery breath—as well as residual damage from the fire and explosions rising up from the ground. The two mistakes combined, finally, to bring the mighty Raptor down.

More klaxons began to sound throughout the cockpit, spurring the crew on to more frantic action. Martin and Tia began reciting a litany of system failures—any one of which had the potential to shut down the Raptor for good.

Kip stared helplessly ahead, his eyes still locked on the rampaging creature called Godzilla. *I caused this,* he realized, a sick feeling in the pit of his stomach. *I made mistakes, and I killed my friends!*

Suddenly, the whole cockpit shook violently. Kip's teeth rattled as the Raptor seemed to shake itself apart around them. He expected to see fire sweep through the cockpit at any moment, even though he knew that was impossible.

"The starboard engine has exploded!" Martin cried. Kip didn't think he'd ever heard so much emotion in the young Asian-American's voice before. Then Tia's frightened screams echoed throughout the cockpit.

With an abrupt lurch that made them all queasy, the cockpit tilted precariously to the left. The cityscape outside the windows tilted, too.

The buildings below seemed to reach up for them. Gravity pulled Kip to one side, wrenching him against his seat belts. He yanked his helmet off so he wouldn't have to listen to Tia's cries.

"Eject! Eject! Eject!" Pierce shouted so loud that Kip could hear him even without the radio.

Kip's hands reached behind his head and grasped the yellow-and-black-striped handles that activated his McDonnell-Douglas ACES II ejection seat.

But before he could yank the emergency handles the picture outside of the cockpit transparencies faded and blurred until it was only a kaleidoscope of colors. The flashing lights, klaxons, and even the HUDs and computers, all went off at once. The cockpit—or, rather, the "mockpit"—froze in place.

Then, with the grind of unseen machinery, the deck slowly began to level itself. Kip used this lull in the exercise to regain self-control. He made an effort to slow his breathing and heartbeat.

Remember the exercises Dr. Markham taught you, he reminded himself.

Finally, the mockpit was level again and locked into position. "Clear?" Pierce asked, releasing his safety belts.

At his side, Martin took a deep breath. "Clear," he said, smiling. Martin's calm demeanor was instantly restored.

"Clear," Tia called, pulling off her helmet and laughing at her panic just moments before.

Kip lowered his arms from the ejection seat handles. "Clear," he said hollowly as his seat automatically turned around, bringing Kip face-to-face with his disappointed teammates. Suddenly, the double doors at the rear of the cockpit opened, and Kip's heart sank.

General Taggart strode onto the deck of the Raptor-One mockpit, one of two Raptor simulators at Nevada's Nellis Air Force Base.

His bearing was stiff, his posture erect. He looked formal and impressive, even though he wore a battered olive-drab flight suit just like the rest of them. His hard gray eyes scanned the mockpit crew, but they seemed to avoid Kip.

"Well, ladies and gentlemen," he grumbled. "You lost Raptor-One, destroyed the Sears Tower, and you're all *dead.*"

He paused, glowering at them.

"Best of all, you never even fired a shot!" The general scanned the downcast faces around the mockpit with barely concealed contempt. Only then did he glance in Kip's direction.

Hastily, the youth lowered his eyes.

"Just how in the hell am I going to explain your miserable failure to the *taxpayers?*" the general asked.

In the simulator of Raptor-Two, a similar scene was being enacted. But it was Colonel Krupp doing the scolding, and it was Lori Angelo and Tobias Nelson who were bearing the brunt of his anger.

"You didn't give Raptor-One adequate or specific warnings when the aircraft moved in too low."

"I warned him!" Lori argued, pulling off her helmet and running her hands through her short-cropped dark hair.

"Too little and too late, Angelo," Krupp barked back. "The story of your life, I might add."

"You *might,*" Lori muttered.

But if the colonel heard Lori's insubordination, he didn't acknowledge it. Instead, the officer turned and faced Toby. "And you—" he sputtered.

"I know, Colonel, I know," Toby said, nodding. Though he was only seventeen, Toby's deep, rich voice reminded everyone on the team of another African American—the actor James Earl Jones, voice of Darth Vader.

"I confess that I did it again," Toby continued. "I just can't seem to keep my big mouth shut."

"*Lori* is the one in the combat control chair, so she does the talking," Krupp reminded the pilot. "Unauthorized radio chatter is both distracting *and* confusing—especially during combat. You are *both* guilty of that!"

Toby nodded in agreement. But he smiled, too.

Lori figured he had the right. Toby was about the only one who *hadn't* screwed up big-time in today's simulation.

With one final look of contempt, Krupp turned and walked out of the mockpit. "Simulator training is over for today," he announced over his shoulder as he departed.

The simulator session is over, Lori mused. *But the "screw-up" lecture from Taggart is guaranteed to go on all night!*

Lori was quite familiar with those little "talks." She'd been the focus of many of them. As she unbuckled her seat belts and climbed out of her command chair, she reviewed the exercise in her mind. It was clear who had really messed up.

Poor Kip, she thought sadly.

4
LUCKY ACCIDENT

Monday, May 3, 1999, 1:15 P.M.
Robinson Laboratory
Department of Astrophysics and Astronomy
California Institute of Technology
Pasadena, California

With a shaky hand, Carl Strickler signed for the two thick Federal Express envelopes. His nerves began tingling with excitement when he saw the return address—NASA's Hubble Data Retrieval Center.

The lanky graduate student ran up the stairs to his cramped and cluttered office. In less than a minute, he'd reached his tiny cubicle on the third floor. The office also doubled as his bedroom.

Even though he had a real bedroom in the dorm just a few blocks away, there were many nights when he didn't sleep there. Strickler had lost a *lot* of nights' sleep planning for—then worrying about—the contents of the packages he was now carrying.

Fumbling with his keys, Carl unlocked the door. For luck, he brushed his hand across the worn plaster busts of Galileo and Isaac Newton that he'd bought the year he'd begun his doctoral studies in astronomy and orbital mechanics.

After dropping the packages onto his desk, Carl plopped into his chair and activated his computer.

His mind whirled. Years of working, planning, and theorizing suddenly distilled themselves into the contents of two thick envelopes.

I passed up job offers and broke up with Amy all because of those, he thought bitterly, staring at the envelopes. *I only hope it was worth it.*

Carl was not the kind of person to focus on the negative for long. His natural optimism kicked in and he tried to look on the bright side.

With this data in hand, I can finish my doctoral thesis in weeks instead of months…and I just might make history in the process!

Finally, Carl tore open the first envelope, which contained the data printouts. The bundle of paper contained millions of bits of raw data condensed into a computer code, then translated into numbers. Carl called up the copy of the Hubble program he'd designed. Then he turned his attention to the hard copy from the NASA scientists.

For three minutes, he studied the data on the printout versus the data stored in his computer. At the end of that short space of time, he knew that something had gone horribly wrong.

Instead of focusing on a section of space far beyond the orbit of Pluto, the Hubble had taken photographs, electromagnetic readings, and other images of a point in space that was much closer to Earth, in relative terms. A section of space between the fourth and fifth planets—Mars and Jupiter.

Carl found the error he'd made after a few more minutes of comparisons. It was, he discovered, a simple, stupid, incredibly basic mistake that he should have caught months before he even forwarded the instructions to NASA. He had juxta-posed two numbers. The error had pointed the Hubble Space Telescope at an empty area in space.

There goes my career, Carl thought bitterly, the magnitude of the mistake finally sinking in. *I wanted to be discoverer of the unknown tenth planet of our solar system, the one beyond Pluto. Instead, I sent a multimillion-dollar piece of scientific equipment on a wild-goose chase.*

Numbly, without thinking, Carl reached out and picked up the second envelope. Distractedly, he tore it open and pulled out the photographs.

Oddly, there was a note attached to the top picture. The letterhead read FROM THE DESK OF DR. JACOB BERMEISTER.

He's the new head of the Hubble program, Carl realized. With a dry throat, he read the note.

Congratulations on your discovery. Do you think it is a comet cluster, or a group of asteroids? In any case, let me know what you find after you've studied all the raw data. And please tell me when you intend to go public. I look forward to meeting you, Doctor *Strickler.*

The note was signed *Dr. Jacob Bermeister.*

Thoroughly puzzled, Carl Strickler began to examine the pictures. He saw what the older scientist was referring to almost immediately. There was a black mass blocking some of the star clusters. The mass appeared in each and every photograph. In some of them, Carl noticed two smaller masses as well. According to his measurements, the objects were very close to Earth.

An hour later, the awestruck graduate student

quickly gathered up the printouts and the photographs and threw the bundle into his battered duffel bag. He glanced at his watch.

I hope Dr. Dawson's having a late lunch at the Atheneum, Carl thought. *Maybe he can help me verify my findings.*

As the young scientist rushed out of his office, he was overwhelmed by the importance of what he had discovered—by accident. Of course, if his initial estimates were correct, then the people of the world had a *big* problem. And Carl would have one, too.

Yes, he'd earn his doctoral degree; and, yes, he'd be famous for making a grand discovery. But he'd also have to announce that the total annihilation of all life on Earth was only a few months away.

It turned out that Carl Strickler's name did not loom so large in the scheme of history. A week before Carl received his data, two other scientists had discovered and photographed the same celestial bodies from their observatory on Earth.

Dr. Ramon Reyes and Dr. Chandra Mishra, both from the Lowell Observatory, had been mapping asteroids for several months. Technically, they discovered the asteroid swarm first.

Carl, with the help of the Space Telescope, was able to determine the speed and trajectory of the objects, but he was not credited with the discovery.

Further observation, using the VLA (Very Large Array) Radio Telescope in New Mexico, gave the scientists a clear picture of what they were dealing with.

The objects were asteroids, not comets. They were made of rock, not ice. And there were three of them. The largest asteroid was shaped like an hourglass and measured about three kilometers across. It looked almost delicate in the computer-enhanced radio telescope images. The smallest asteroid was less than a kilometer across, the middle one a little larger.

It was also determined that there would soon be a measurable increase in the amount of meteors striking the earth's atmosphere over the next several months. Whether or not these smaller objects belonged to the same swarm as the larger asteroids was debated inconclusively.

Due to the impressive nature of his work, Carl Strickler accompanied a group of eminent astronomers, astrophysicists, and space scientists to a top-secret briefing with the President of the United States. The briefing also included Doctors Ramon Reyes, Chandra Mishra, and Jacob Bermeister of NASA.

Everyone agreed that the stunning news should be handled carefully. The president asked them to wait twenty-four hours. The scientists reluctantly agreed, but everyone knew that news of this magnitude could not be kept secret for long.

To his surprise, Carl Strickler was chosen as a spokesperson for the group of scientists. They felt he knew as much about the phenomenon as any of them, and he was the man who had discovered the trajectory—and the target—of the asteroids.

So Carl found himself on the podium when a momentous press conference was held at the National Aeronautics and Space Administration's Kennedy Space Center on Monday, May 10, 1999.

Because someone had leaked part of the story to a reporter for the Sunday *Washington Times,* curiosity was high. The event was aired live and became the most-watched NASA program since the conference following the *Challenger* disaster.

And it was Carl Strickler who informed the world that he had discovered the exact day, date, and time of doomsday.

"I have news that will affect every living creature on the face of this planet," Carl stated without visible emotion.

"On Saturday, July 31, at 7:16 P.M. Eastern Standard Time, an asteroid will strike the eastern seaboard of the continental United States. This initial strike will be followed by two others within the next few hours. The impact will release energy equal to that of two thousand hydrogen bombs. The results will be catastrophic.

Carl paused, and his voice caught. "It is likely that this asteroid, and the two others in its wake, will cause the extinction of all life on this planet."

At that moment, Dr. Bermeister stepped up to the podium and touched Carl's shoulder. As Carl stepped away from the microphone, Bermeister announced that there would be no questions. Rather, the president would address the nation in two minutes.

The chief executive's statement was brief.

The news was real, the president said. All the

scientists who had studied the data concurred with the results. The governments of the world had all been informed. The military had been put on alert. The National Guard had been activated. The authorities were doing everything they could.

The scientists had a plan, the president said with a politician's smile. The details would be announced within twenty-four hours. But, first, there was to be a debate at the United Nations.

Most important of all, the president asked the citizens to stay calm. He urged Americans to turn to their families, their friends, or their churches in this time of trouble. "I ask you, as your president, to maintain the peace and order in your communities."

Three hours later, there were riots on the streets of Cleveland, Dallas, Baltimore—and Washington, D.C.

The day after the president's address, the news was reflected in the national press headlines.

A TRIO OF ASTEROIDS TO STRIKE EARTH IN TWO MONTHS! the *Los Angeles Times* proclaimed.

COULD THIS BE THE ASTEROID THAT KILLED THE DINOSAURS? asked *Time* magazine.

SCIENTISTS CALCULATE IMPACT OF ASTEROID ON LAST DAY OF JULY, the *New York Times* announced soberly.

USA Today and CNN conducted a joint poll, starting with the question: "Do you believe that an asteroid will destroy the Earth this summer?"

In the days that followed, the riots ended and calm was restored. People returned to their lives, many doubting that the end was near. Scientists, after all, had been wrong before. And if they *were* correct? Well, scientists had solved problems before. Surely they would solve this one.

On the other hand, even if a solution were found, could it be implemented in time? No one knew. There were only two things that the scientific community agreed upon: The asteroids were heading toward Earth, and they would be called the Reyes-Mishra Asteroid Swarm, after the two scientists who first photographed them.

Privately, Dr. Reyes and Dr. Mishra had offered Carl a chance to have his name attached to the discovery. The young graduate student had declined.

Carl had seen the tape of his announcement being replayed every hour of every day.

I wanted to go down in history as the man who discovered a new planet, thought Carl sadly. *Not the prophet who announced the end of the world.*

Carl Strickler had earned his doctorate. But he didn't crave fame. Not anymore.

It wasn't long before a tabloid television show discovered a passage by the sixteenth-century French astrologer Nostradamus that began:

> *In the year 1999, in the seventh month,*
> *from the sky will come a great King of*
> *Terror…*

With gleeful relish, the reporter reminded his viewers that Reyes, the name of one of the discoverers of the asteroid swarm, was a variation on the Spanish word for *king*.

KAMACURAS™

5
MEETINGS

Wednesday, May 19, 1999, 8:55 P.M.
Project Valkyrie headquarters
Nellis Air Force Base, Nevada

When he heard the knock, Kip looked up from the textbooks, graphs, and schematic charts that were spread across the top of his desk.

"Come in," he said anxiously.

The door swung open and Tia Shimura, looking relaxed in her off-duty uniform, smiled at him.

"Are you coming to the lounge?" she asked. "There's another news conference about the asteroids. Everyone will be there."

"I'm not sure…" Kip hesitated. "I'm not done yet."

Tia stepped into his room and closed the door. It was against regulations to have another student in your quarters, but like Lori, Tia liked to ignore regulations.

She sat down and stared at Kip.

"What?" he demanded.

"You can't just hide in your room, you know."

Kip closed a book and looked at her. "Why not?"

"Listen," Tia replied. "Everybody screws up. You're not alone. Look at Lori, look at Toby, look at me!"

"But *seven* times, in seven straight simulations?

That's got to be a new record," Kip snapped back. "Nobody messes up that much, and stays in the program for long. Krupp said so himself!"

"Krupp isn't in charge," Tia argued. "Taggart is—"

"I *know* I've let him down," Kip interrupted. "He took a big risk signing me up. Have you heard that Dr. Markham was against letting me in the program? Said my childhood was too unstable."

"Don't worry about Dr. Markham. The lady shrink has gotten into *all* of our heads at one time or another, and she can be pretty harsh."

Kip sighed. "Maybe Dr. Markham is right. Maybe I'm not cut out for this Project."

"Just what is *that* supposed to mean?"

Kip's eyes avoided Tia's. "I'm not sure we're doing the right thing..."

Tia stared at him, puzzled.

"I can't...I can't bring myself to think of Godzilla as the enemy. Every time I see him, in the simulator, on film, and in our classes, I see an animal. Confused. In pain. But just an animal. So I just freeze..." Kip looked up, finally meeting Tia's eyes. "Godzilla isn't evil," he whispered. "And I can't force myself to believe he is."

"That's ridiculous!" Tia cried. "You saw the films of Tokyo. You know what kind of destruction Godzilla brings with him! Thousands died in the past, millions more could die in the future if Godzilla shows up again."

"I know," Kip replied a little too defensively. "But when I see him, a voice in the back of my mind says we're doing the wrong thing. I can't bring myself to pull the trigger. Even in the simulators."

Kip's voice faded away. Tia gazed at him.

"So *that's* the problem," she said.

Kip nodded, and Tia shrugged her shoulders. "Quit then," she said simply.

Kip stood up and crossed the room. He stared out the window at the stars shining down on the barren desert of Nevada. The silence stretched on.

Finally, he spoke. "I don't want to leave. I've found a home here."

Tia sighed. "Then don't forget that what we're doing is important. The scientists will save the world from asteroids. Our job is saving it from Godzilla, or whatever other monster crawls out of the woodwork. We're fighting the good fight, Kip."

Kip nodded "I know that, but…"

"Forget your doubts," Tia insisted. "The Project needs you, and *you* need the Project."

Kip nodded but said nothing. He still had primal doubts about his mission, but he decided he would not share them again. With anyone.

Tia hopped to her feet. "Come on, Kip," she said, taking his hand. "Let's go watch the press conference."

"Earth is too fragile a basket to keep all of humanity's eggs in," Dr. Jacob Bermeister announced to the assembled journalists and the millions who watched the conference on television.

As the astronomer spoke, the newspeople crowded around the podium. The journalists were packed together like sardines in the jammed auditorium at Kennedy Space Center.

"The Reyes-Mishra Swarm stretches from near

Earth's orbit to a part of space millions of miles away," Dr. Bermeister continued, pointing to a map of the solar system with the asteroid cloud highlighted in red. "But only the three large asteroids in the center of the swarm pose a real threat to human life. The rest will provide a colorful show when they burn up in our atmosphere, nothing more.

"However," Bermeister warned, "a strike by any one of the three large asteroids could mean the end of life as we know it. That is why Operation EarthFirst is being implemented."

"Dr. Bermeister!" a reporter cried out, much louder than the rest. "What are the chances of success?"

Cameras flashed, and cameramen vied for position before the half-dozen scientists on the stage as Dr. Bermeister considered his answer.

"With the help and cooperation of all the member countries of the United Nations, we have formulated a plan. The United States, Canada, Russia, Japan, France, and Great Britain have already begun the work necessary to implement that plan—"

"But what are the chances of success?" the journalist interrupted rudely.

"It has a good chance of success," Dr. Bermeister declared.

"Can you give us a mathematical probability?" another journalist demanded.

"No," Bermeister replied curtly. "I'm not Jimmy the Greek." A chuckle rippled through the room.

"Is it true that Operation EarthFirst will involve

nuclear weapons?" a French television anchor-woman demanded hostilely.

"The plan *does* involve the use of nuclear weapons, yes," Bermeister stated. Before he could continue, the room erupted in chaos, with a hundred questions being shouted at once.

Finally, Dr. Chandra Mishra rose from his chair. The journalists quieted, waiting for the co-discoverer of the asteroid swarm to speak.

"Ladies and gentlemen," the dignified Indian scientist said, "there are no guarantees in science. We have checked and rechecked the calculations and used every resource available on this planet, as well as our satellites in space.

"As far as we can deduce, these asteroids can be vaporized by using nuclear warheads delivered in a precise sequence while they are still far away.

"To accomplish this task, Operation EarthFirst will use the Russian Mir space station as an orbital base of operations. The shuttle *Atlantis* will carry the nuclear warheads into orbit—"

A young journalist stood up. "But isn't it dangerous to take nuclear weapons into space? And aren't there international laws against doing that?"

Dr. Reyes rose to the challenge. He defended his colleague and the plan. "The United Nations has agreed to suspend the laws against nuclear weapons in space for the duration of this crisis."

"But, Dr. Reyes, Dr. Mishra," another journalist demanded, "isn't there a danger that the bombs will do nothing more than break up the asteroid into smaller parts—pieces that could still pose a significant hazard to life on Earth?"

Dr. Mishra nodded. "That is a possibility," he agreed. "But it is a remote one. We have carefully estimated the density of each of the three asteroids and have concluded that they can be almost completely vaporized by the nuclear warheads."

"So the smaller pieces won't be dangerous?" asked Nick Gordon, a young science correspondent for the Independent News Network.

Dr. Mishra shook his head. "No, Mr. Gordon," he replied, recognizing Gordon from his award-winning science reporting over the last few years. "The real danger lies in doing nothing."

"Yes," Dr. Reyes agreed. "After all, hundreds of smaller asteroids—we call them meteors or shooting stars—strike our planet every day. Most of them burn up in the atmosphere; a few even reach the surface of the planet. But compared to the menace the human race faces from the asteroids, the smaller meteors pose almost no danger..."

Several hours later, the very tip of the Reyes-Mishra Asteroid Swarm crossed Earth's orbit. Small space rocks began to enter the atmosphere.

Over the midwestern United States and Canada, the meteor shower lit up the night sky for thousands of miles. Millions of North Americans gathered on hillsides and rooftops to witness the celestial show of bright lights and brilliant colors.

True to the scientists' predictions, the vast majority of meteors that fell in that night's shower burned up in the Earth's atmosphere. The meteor shower continued for three hours, then ceased.

Only a few fist-sized space rocks actually made it

to the surface of the Earth. One struck deep in a Kansas grain field with enough force to shake loose a dozen green apples from Oswald Peaster's fifty-year-old trees, a good two miles away.

Farmer Peaster never noticed what had been delivered to his property. Nor did anyone else in the little rural town of Natoma, Kansas.

But they would soon take notice.

Very soon, in fact, the eyes of the whole world would be on this sleepy American town—or, more precisely, what would remain of it.

VARAN™

6
BACK FROM
THE GRAVE

Sunday, May 23, 1999, 1:12 P.M.
Fifteen miles northeast of Mérida, Mexico
On the Yucatán Peninsula

Robin Halliday gazed through the helicopter's window at the rough, deep blue and aquamarine waters of the choppy Gulf of Mexico far below. She gripped her microphone with a sweaty hand as she waited for her cue from the director. Below her, Robin spotted a group of long-necked pink flamingoes flying gracefully in formation over the green canopy of the rain forest.

As the helicopter climbed into the brilliant blue sky, Robin peered farther along the coast of the peninsula. Through the late afternoon haze, she could barely make out the tower of another one of the massive modern resort hotels that dotted the white beaches all along the Yucatán Peninsula.

Not a bad place to be when the world ends, she thought.

"Thirty seconds," she heard the director say through her headphones. Robin hoped that her long, dark hair covered them and the thin electronic wires that ran down her blouse. Robin didn't want to look "wired up" on camera.

This is my first report on live television, she thought, tingling with excitement. It had taken a lot of work to get this far, though she knew she'd impressed her boss with her audition tape.

And flirting with him didn't hurt, either.

Now Robin Halliday, of Avalon, Pennsylvania, was in a helicopter over the Mexican coast, waiting to do her first ever network news story.

Pretty good for an almost-eighteen-year-old intern, she thought proudly. Today's live report was a lucky break for her career, and it only happened because her boss, Nick Gordon—chief correspondent for the *Science Sunday* program on the Independent News Network—got the chance to cover an even better story at the last moment. So while Nick went off for a one-on-one interview with Dr. Ramon Reyes in Mexico City, Robin got this plum on-camera assignment over the Yucatán Peninsula.

Luckily, there was no one else around to do it.

Robin suspected ulterior motives for Nick's last-minute change of assignments. *Gossip at the bureau says he hates helicopters,* she recalled with a smile. *If it's true, then thank goodness for airsickness!*

"Twenty seconds," the director announced.

The cameraman, sitting on the seat opposite hers, lifted the heavy camera and focused it on her face. The technician who operated the satellite link gave Robin a thumbs-up, then turned the tiny monitor so that she could watch herself on-camera.

Here goes, she thought, her heart racing.

"Ten seconds," the director warned, holding up the clipboard with Robin's lines printed on it in big, bold letters.

"Five...four...three...two...one...action!"

Robin Halliday smiled at the camera and lifted the microphone to her perfectly made-up face. "This is Robin Halliday, special correspondent for INN *Science Sunday,*" she began smoothly.

"Below me is the breathtakingly lovely Mexican coast of Yucatán, a resort mecca for tourists from the United States, Canada, Europe, and Japan.

"As the twenty-first century dawns, this is one of the most natural, peaceful settings in the world."

The director switched to a camera mounted on the exterior of the helicopter. The viewers were treated to a bird's-eye view of beautiful white sand beaches, even as Robin's voice took on a more ominous tone.

"But sixty-five million years ago, this part of the world was very different..."

The director cued the special effects, and back at the INN studios in New York an animated segment began. As Robin spoke, she watched the images on the satellite monitor, images of a computer-generated asteroid hitting the Mexican coast.

"This area was the site of the most destructive event in the history of our planet. Right below us, buried under the sand and sediment of eons, lies the original impact crater left behind after the asteroid that destroyed the dinosaurs struck Earth—with a force equal to every nuclear weapon ever built..."

The director cued the cameraman, and Robin's face filled the monitor once again. "Some people call this crater the Graveyard of the Dinosaurs."

The director signaled for her to speed it up as he

flipped the page on the clipboard. Robin skimmed the words as she picked up the pace.

"Scientists estimate that the asteroid that killed the dinosaurs was twice the size of the largest one now heading toward the earth."

Again, Robin modulated her voice to sound grim and portentous. Again, the director signaled her to pick up the pace.

This time, Robin ignored him.

"It took nature millions of years to recover from that first cataclysmic asteroid impact...millions of years to restore the rain forests below and the varieties of animal and vegetable life that abound all around us."

For dramatic effect, Robin turned and looked out of the window as if she were meditating on the fate of our puny planet.

"How long will it take nature to restore Earth if another asteroid should strike the planet in the next two months?" she asked dramatically.

The cameraman never wavered, though he wanted to burst out laughing at the director's obvious annoyance with the intern's theatrics.

Fortunately, the segment was winding down.

"In the next half-hour, INN's Nick Gordon will pose these questions to Dr. Ramon Reyes, the co-discoverer of—*oh my God, what's* that?"

The director ripped off his headphones and almost choked. Luckily, the cameraman was on top of things. He shifted the camera and focused in the direction Robin was pointing.

Through the lens, the cameraman saw an immense dark green blur in the blue waters of the

Gulf of Mexico. Hastily, he tried to focus.

As the cameraman worked the lens, the director whistled in amazement and the pilot dipped the helicopter lower. The pilot was also a seasoned journalist, and he knew when to chase a story.

Suddenly, the image on the monitor sharpened, and the astounding vision was revealed to the viewing public on live, nationwide television.

Science Sunday had just been interrupted by the appearance of a giant prehistoric monster swimming in the Gulf of Mexico!

"Keep talking!" the director screamed through Robin's headphones. The intern snapped to attention, then turned away from the creature in the water, to stare, wide-eyed, at the camera. She looked like an idiot.

Fortunately, the camera's eye was focused on the creature swimming in the surf far below.

"Talk!" the director shouted again.

Suddenly, Robin Halliday regained her composure and began to report on what she was seeing. As she spoke, Robin was able to summon up a measure of calm, poise, and professional detachment, much to the director's surprise.

"As we watch, a gigantic animal is moving through the Gulf of Mexico toward the resort complex below…"

The director fumbled with his headphones. As he put them back on, he nodded encouragement to the intern, who continued to speak.

"Though I can't make out the details of the creature from this distance, I think I can say with some certainty that this animal is a totally new species.

This creature is *not* a whale, and it is *not* Godzilla…"

The helicopter swooped over the monster, and the cameraman switched to a wide-angle lens so that the creature was clearly visible to the television audience. More and more details of the astounding monster were unveiled.

Pleasure boats swept past the creature, fleeing its path. A speedboat, pulling a water-skiing couple, capsized in the churning waters. The monster swept the sinking boat and the floundering swimmers aside as if they were toys bobbing in a bathtub.

As Robin described the event, the creature emerged into shallower waters close to the white, sandy beach. More details about the leviathan's anatomy were revealed.

"The creature looks like a long, thin iguana," Robin observed, "though its legs are arranged more like a toad's. It has very long legs and a leg joint below thick thigh muscles. I believe that the claws and feet are webbed.

"The head is round, not wedge-shaped, and the mouth seems frozen in a perpetual sneer. The jaws are lined with irregular teeth. I would describe its overall color as brown and gray, but there are blue and green splotches on its back and sides.

"The eyes are large and narrow, and seem to follow movement…"

As Robin Halliday spoke, the monster pulled itself onto the beach, directly in front of a twelve-story glass and steel resort hotel. Frantic vacationers on the beach fled in terror as the mysterious creature approached the hotel.

The pilot began broadcasting a general warning in Spanish over the radio while maneuvering the helicopter deftly. The aircraft was hovering to the right of and above the strange monster. Robin continued to describe the creature to her viewers.

"The reptile has a prominent line of translucent, bony spikes that run in a straight line from the crest of its head to the end of its long tail.

"There also seems to be a thin webbing, or membrane of some kind, that runs along its torso, connecting the front and back legs. The creature has a leathery layer of flexible armor plating that covers its back. This plating is covered with round bubbles or knobby bumps..."

Suddenly, the creature opened its mouth and emitted an eerie, whistling roar. The noise shook the helicopter and surprised the INN news team. A swarm of jungle birds burst from the trees below, narrowly missing the chopper's swirling blades.

"I hope you heard that sound at home," Robin said, instantly regaining her composure. As she spoke, she glanced at her director. To her shock and delight, he was beaming. Once again, the technician gave her a thumbs-up.

He was beaming, too.

Meanwhile, the monster strode onto dry land on all four legs. Its massive front claws knocked aside abandoned outdoor furniture and brightly colored beach umbrellas, some of which bounced down the beach as if a terrible wind were blowing. Sand was kicked up from the beach as well, and began pelting the helicopter blades and fuselage.

At that moment, some of the people who had taken refuge inside the main hotel building began rushing out the other side. They crossed a huge parking lot and ran in a mob toward the main ribbon of highway. And not a moment too soon...

With a tremendous roar, the amphibious creature slammed into the hotel. Instantly, every window in the structure exploded outward in a shower of sparkling shards. The roof collapsed next, spilling debris, and several screaming guests, into the huge swimming pool.

From the area of the first floor near the restaurant, bright crimson flames gushed forth as a gas main ruptured. A secondary explosion quickly followed. The force of the blast sent a geyser of flames into the bright blue sky and knocked the startled creature backward.

Robin couldn't speak fast enough to describe the amazing event to her millions of viewers. Circling over the destruction, the news team was getting remarkable footage of the devastation. But in the excitement of the moment, the pilot of the INN news chopper had flown too close to the disaster.

As the creature was rolled onto its back by the force of the explosion, the helicopter was buffeted by shock waves from the blast. As the pilot struggled to regain control of the vibrating aircraft, the helicopter's blades were struck by flying debris.

Inside the aircraft, Robin Halliday, the satellite

technician, and the director were thrown to one side. The cameraman, realizing that the satellite link had been broken, tried to load the camera with fresh videotape even as the chopper tumbled toward the earth.

Robin screamed. The director paled. The technician fainted.

But the pilot struggled on. Just when it seemed as if the chopper was going to strike the earth, the pilot twisted the aircraft around and landed it on the soft sand of the beach.

Despite the sandy cushion, it was a hard landing. The support struts instantly caved in and the chopper tilted to one side. Then the swirling blades struck the sand and dug in, spinning the helicopter around and slamming the fuselage against a copse of tall palm trees.

The blades shattered, and the main body of the helicopter leaped into the air for the last time and came to a rest in the middle of a huge, manicured garden—part of the resort hotel's luxurious grounds.

"Everybody out!" the pilot cried when what was left of the helicopter came to a grinding halt. The director kicked open the door and tugged the satellite man out by his collar.

The technician was out cold.

Robin, meanwhile, struggled to open her door. The cameraman, bleeding from a cut on his head, pushed past her and slid the door wide open. Then he jumped out, still clutching his camera.

"Hey!" Robin cried. "How about some help?"

The pilot rushed over to the shaken intern. Her

seat belt was jammed, but the pilot cut her free with his emergency knife.

As they stumbled away from the demolished helicopter, the fortunate survivors watched in awe as the monster righted itself and moved past the burning building.

Despite a mild case of shock, the director smiled. "Attaboy, Chuck!" he shouted when he saw the cameraman shooting more footage. The director turned to Robin and patted her on the shoulder.

"You did good, kid. But *that's* what I call a *pro!*" he said, pointing to the cameraman.

Just then, the monster emitted another piercing, high-pitched squeal. Robin covered her ears.

While the cameraman filmed, the rest of the team watched as the monster reared up on its long hind legs.

"It's swelling up like a blowfish!" Robin exclaimed into her dead microphone. "The creature seems to be inflating…"

As they watched in awe, the bubbles on the armor plating dotting the monster's back and sides began to expand. The entire creature seemed to swell up. Finally, it leaped into the air like some nightmarish giant toad.

As it left the ground, the creature flew right over the cowering news team. In its wake, a tremendous wind swirled around them, kicking up sand and almost knocking them down.

The wind lasted for only a few seconds, then subsided. Suddenly, the air all around them smelled very sweet. Robin sniffed the air, then she looked at the director. He was smelling the air, too.

"Look up there!" the cameraman cried, without taking his eye from the eyepiece. The pilot, who was busy administering first aid to the unconscious satellite technician, ignored the cameraman. But Robin and her director both looked into the sky. Far away now, they could see the silhouette of the monster as it disappeared into the low clouds over the jungles of the Yucatán Peninsula.

The monster's arms and legs were spread wide, and the membranes that ran along the beast's torso were stretched to the limit, so that they seemed translucent.

"He looks like Rocky the Flying Squirrel," the director quipped.

Robin nodded. Then she turned and looked behind her at the smoldering ruins of the hotel.

"But this flying squirrel is a lot more dangerous than Rocky," she whispered.

Sunday, May 23, 1999, 2:00 P.M.
Osborne County, Kansas
A grain field

A single foraging praying mantis crawled along the fertile and familiar land of Oswald Peaster. The creature was hungry, and it sensed sustenance was nearby, so its tiny legs moved forward until it reached an unnatural pit in the plowed earth.

Cautiously, the mantis approached the edge. At the bottom of the pit, there were many strange rocks. One of them suddenly popped open with a loud hiss. The movement and sound caused the mantis to retreat momentarily, until a thick yellowish substance leaked out of the still-smoldering meteorite and attracted the mantis's interest.

Once again, the mantis approached. This time it moved down into the pit to dip its mouth into the slime.

As soon as the insect's mandibles touched the substance, a violent biological reaction occurred. Even as the mantis stumbled away, it was changing, shifting, mutating.

The mantis soon attracted a female of its species. The two insects mated, and according to its instinctive programming, the female devoured the male mantis at the moment of consummation—ingesting the same toxic substance that had mutated the male.

In the days that followed, the infection spread through the entire mantis population of Osborne County and beyond.

As more insects were exposed, more radical genetic changes took place.

A voracious hunger was one of the many adaptations that seemed to ensure survival. Uncontrolled growth was another, so the creatures began to grow bigger and bigger and bigger...

VARAN™

7
ALERT!

Klaxons blared throughout the three-story concrete and glass structure that served as the living
and training area for Project Valkyrie's six-member
team of trainees.

The alert surprised everyone, because Sunday
afternoon was technically "down" time. So nobody
thought it was a drill *this* time. Their faces were
grim, serious, and reflective as they filed out of
their rooms, toward the command center.

Toby Nelson, Martin Wong, and Pierce Dillard
exchanged meaningful glances as they rushed
down the long white corridors. Behind them, Tia
Shimura walked with Lori Angelo. They were sub-
dued and pensive.

"Look, Lori," Tia whispered, pointing at the
senior Air Force personnel who were also stream-
ing toward the command center. "They don't know
what's going on, either."

Lori, who was yawning, had just awakened from
a nap. Her short hair was messed up and she was
cranky.

"Trust me," she said knowingly. "This is just
another surprise inspection or something, or

maybe another senator on a fact-finding mission…"

But Tia glanced at the hard faces of Toby and Pierce, and she wasn't so sure.

At the far end of the long corridor, a steel door flew open and Kip Daniels rushed in. He was the only one not wearing G-Force overalls. Instead, he wore battered Levis and a worn T-shirt with "May the G-Force Be with You" emblazoned across his chest. He was also flushed and out of breath.

"I was down by the flight line when I heard the beeper go off," Kip whispered to Tia when he stepped up beside her. "I ran the whole way back, so this had better be *good!*"

The team members reached the command center together and took their assigned seats.

Standing in the front of the room and behind the raised podium was General Taggart. On his right, Colonel Krupp gazed at his watch, timing the team's response to the red alert.

On the opposite side of the general, Dr. Max Birchwood, Valkyrie's resident kaijuologist, paced back and forth, muttering through his ragged beard.

Everyone could see that the scientist was agitated, even though he usually acted pretty eccentric, anyway.

Kaijuology was the youngest of the sciences, established with the return of Godzilla. Biology, biochemistry, microbiology, astrobiology, and a host of other scientific disciplines went into making one an expert in the field of kaijuology.

The few men and women who had trained in

that area of expertise were highly imaginative, brilliant, and innovative.

They were pretty weird, too. And Dr. Birchwood was no exception. Kip wondered why the professor was present. He usually skipped test alerts and visits from prominent politicians.

His presence here today was a bad omen.

When the team members were all in their seats, the alarms died as suddenly as they began. Colonel Krupp looked up from his wristwatch and faced the recruits.

General Taggart scanned the assembled team with cold eyes.

"This is *not* a drill," he announced. "We've got a *kaiju!*"

Kip felt his heart skip a beat. Tia looked excited and worried at the same time. Lori looked stunned. Pierce's and Toby's frozen features never cracked, but excitement was evident behind their calm demeanor.

"Is it—is it Godzilla, sir?" Lori stammered.

The general shook his head. "Before you start asking a bunch of questions, here's Dr. Birchwood to brief you. Doctor…"

The scientist shook his head, as if to snap himself out of a trance. Then he stepped up to the podium.

"Could we have the pictures, please?" Dr. Birchwood said to a technician in the control booth. The lights dimmed and two large panels at the front of the room slid aside, to reveal a large-screen television monitor. The monitor came to life.

Pictures of the monster in the Yucatán Peninsula of Mexico filled the screen. "This creature appeared less than two hours ago," Dr. Birchwood declared in a quiet, almost distracted voice. "An INN news team first captured footage of the *kaiju* during a routine satellite feed for a live broadcast."

The kaijuologist paused, checking his notes. "It was INN *Science Sunday*," he announced.

"Wow," Lori whispered with carefully measured sarcasm. "That's my favorite show!"

"Keep it down, Angelo!" Colonel Krupp barked.

Dr. Birchwood continued.

"The creature is amphibious, and appeared near the city of Mérida on the Yucatán Peninsula of Mexico...less than seven hundred nautical miles from the Florida coast."

Tia gasped. Toby looked suddenly grim. Even Lori became serious.

"While reports are still coming in, the Associated Press wire service has issued a story that claims that this creature can *fly* as well as swim."

Kip stared at the image of the rampaging monster on the television screen. Try as he might, he couldn't find any wings.

"Our initial estimations as to the size, shape, and nature of the creature are as follows..." The scientist looked down at scribbled notes he held in his hand.

"The creature is reptilian. There seems to be no radioactivity in the immediate vicinity of this beast, so it may not be a mutation. It measures approximately eighty to ninety meters in length—or 275 to 300 feet long. It stands about fifty meters high, and walks on all four legs, though it can rear up on its hind legs…"

He looked up from his notes once again. "We have not confirmed that the creature can fly—that sounds like mass hysteria to me—but, in any case, we are still processing information, and further reports should be forthcoming.

"I have contacted Dr. Kajiro Tanaka, the chief archivist of G-Force Japan," Birchwood informed them. "Dr. Tanaka is running a description of the monster and its behavior through his database right now. We may have an answer shortly."

The kaijuologist shuffled his feet, then turned around and looked up at the screen. "I guess that is all for now," he said, then left the podium.

General Taggart replaced Dr. Birchwood in front of the microphone. All eyes followed the scientist out the door as he hurried to his laboratory.

When the doctor was gone, General Taggart cleared his throat.

"I have spoken with the president," he announced. "The chief executive has mobilized this unit, and we are now on full alert."

Kip felt as if he was going to faint. *We're not ready!* he wanted to scream, but he bit his lip instead.

"Ladies and gentlemen," Taggart continued. "Project Valkyrie is over. G-Force USA is now *officially* a reality, by order of the president."

A stunned hush fell over the room. Suddenly, everything that G-Force had been working for had become a *reality.*

"I know you are not ready yet," Taggart added.

"God knows I told the president as much. But he has every confidence in you, and so do I."

Pierce raised his hand. "Are we going to Mexico, sir?" he asked.

General Taggart hesitated before answering. "The president and the State Department are speaking with representatives of the Mexican government right now. Something should be worked out in the next twenty-four to forty-eight hours."

"What about Raptor-One?" Toby asked.

"The president has spoken with the head of the defense company responsible for the outfitting of the aircraft," Taggart said with frustration in his voice. "Raptor-One is almost finished. We are promised delivery before the end of the month."

"So how are we going to Mexico?" Lori demanded. "By train?"

"Raptor-Two is ready to make the trip," Taggart announced, "if the Mexican government permits it. The Air Force has agreed to make a second CV-22 with some special modifications available to us, if we need it."

"We can't fight a monster with observation planes," Pierce blurted.

"No, we can't, Mr. Dillard," Taggart replied. "Our mission in Mexico, *should* we be permitted to go, will be as *observers.*"

Pierce's mouth dropped open. At his side, Toby muttered. "What are we training for, then?"

"I know you are disappointed," General Taggart said to the two pilots. "But as I said, this team is not yet ready, and its primary weapon, Raptor-One, is not yet completed. Until I am confident that we have the proper training and the right equipment, this unit will remain on standby alert."

The general scanned the room again. "That is all," he barked. Then he strode out of the briefing room with Colonel Krupp in tow.

The G-Force team members filed out of the briefing room, each one lost in his or her own thoughts. As they headed back down the long corridor toward their quarters, Tia slid alongside Lori, who was rubbing her eyes and yawning.

"Are you all right?" Tia asked.

Lori nodded. "I'm just tired. I haven't been sleeping too good lately. All this excitement."

"Well, ladies," Colonel Krupp barked, "I guess we'll just have to wake you up!"

Nobody had heard the Air Force officer approach. It was as if Krupp came out of nowhere.

"Starting tomorrow morning at 0600, we begin advanced simulator training," the colonel announced with an evil little smile. There were moans and groans from the G-Force team.

Kip, who was even more disturbed than the rest, said nothing. Anxiety welled up inside him, and he groaned inwardly.

Not the simulators again...

KAMACURAS™

8
THE SWARM

Tuesday, May 25, 1999, 5:21 A.M.
Peaster's Farm
Osborne County, Kansas

Oswald Peaster sat up in his bed and threw off the blanket. He turned and checked on his wife, but she was still sound asleep and snoring gently. He remembered that she'd stayed up late the night before, making cakes for the church bake sale.

I'd better let her sleep, he decided as he gently eased himself out of bed.

After pulling on his overalls in the dark bedroom, Oswald stumbled into the hallway and limped down the steps. As he walked to the kitchen, he rubbed his aching shoulder and knees the whole time. The arthritis in his joints was persistent now, and getting worse. It was especially bad in the mornings.

Oswald could never admit to his wife that he was suffering, however. As it was, Millie was making noises again about selling the farm.

"After all, you're not getting any younger," his wife had argued on Sunday afternoon while they drove home from church. It was not the first time she'd brought up the subject. Oswald shook his head as he fetched the coffee pot and filled it with water.

Millie just doesn't understand, he thought sadly. *This land has been in my family for generations. This part of Kansas has always been known as Peaster's Farm...and it will stay Peaster's Farm for as long as I live and breathe.*

Once again, Oswald Peaster regretted his eldest son's patriotic decision to join the Army. Instead of taking over the farm and carrying on the family tradition, First Lieutenant Michael Oswald Peaster had died on some forgotten, bloodstained jungle trail in Vietnam twenty-seven years before.

What a waste, Oswald thought as he set up the coffee to brew. *Nearly thirty years and I'm still mourning him. It's a bad thing when a father outlives his son.*

Oswald sighed and rubbed his shoulder again.

Neither of the Peaster girls wanted a life on the farm, he thought. *Not that I blame them. Farm life is harder on women than it is on men.*

Oswald thought about his two daughters. He realized he hadn't seen either of them in at least three months. He knew that Millie missed them both terribly.

Anna had married a grain dealer and lived in far-away Wichita. No children yet, but Millie was hopeful. Eleanor, still single, lived closer—she was a beautician in Russell.

Maybe we'll drive down and visit Ellie this Sunday, Oswald thought with a smile. *Millie would sure like that.*

Absentmindedly, he switched on the radio. Instead of the farm report, he found he was listening to the network news feed out of Alton. The news anchor was droning on in a flat voice.

"The creature that emerged from the Gulf of Mexico is still ravaging coastal cities on the Yucatán Peninsula. Yesterday, the monster destroyed the airport in the city of Mérida. Elements of the Mexican Army and Air Force are converging on the area for a possible confrontation…"

Oswald noticed seven cakes lined up on the kitchen table. Five of them had chocolate icing. The other two were topped with vanilla. *A piece of cake would sure go good with my coffee,* he mused.

Oswald's mouth watered, but he resisted the temptation. The cakes were for the bake sale. And anyway, his doctor had warned him off fatty food because his cholesterol level was too high.

What do they expect from an old man? he wondered. *I'm seventy-two now—how much longer do they want me alive and paying taxes, anyway?*

Finally, the coffee was done, and Oswald Peaster poured himself a steaming mugful. Then he sat down at the table and listened as the announcer droned on.

What time does Paul Harvey come on? he wondered.

"In other news, it's just sixty-six days until doomsday, and according to a NASA spokesman, Operation EarthFirst is ahead of schedule. In just ten more days, the space shuttle *Discovery* will launch from Cape Canaveral, carrying a payload of nuclear weapons into Earth's orbit. These weapons will be fired at the approaching asteroids in the hope of destroying them. In a statement issued by—"

Oswald snorted and switched over to the farm report.

The end of the world, he scoffed. *Pastor Bob has been predicting the end of time since Millie and I started going to his church.*

It ain't happened yet, and I don't reckon it will happen this time, either...

Oswald took another sip of his coffee, still eyeing the freshly baked cakes spread out in front of him. But as he reached over to scoop up a fingerful of vanilla icing, the electricity suddenly went off.

"Damn," Oswald muttered.

Setting down his cup, Oswald heard his two hunting dogs barking. They sounded loud and frantic, even this far away from their kennel behind the barn.

Then the six cows in the barn joined the chorus. They began to moo in fear and panic. Even the passel of chickens Millie kept in the yard began to squawk. Then Oswald heard another sound, a faraway rumbling, like distant thunder.

"What the hell?" Oswald muttered cantankerously.

With a grunt, the old man rose and rushed to the back door. As a precaution, he pulled down his double-barreled shotgun from the rack on the wall. He cracked the shotgun open and loaded both barrels with buckshot.

"Ozzie...Ozzie...what's all the noise about?"

Oswald heard his wife call to him from the bedroom. Her voice was still thick with sleep. The old farmer ignored her call. He hefted his weapon and stepped out onto the back porch.

The morning sun had just risen, and dew still covered the flowers and grass. Everything appeared normal, but almost as soon as he stepped outside, Oswald heard the rumbling again.

No sign of a storm, he thought, looking at the morning sky.

He stepped to the edge of the porch and stared off into the distance, where a copse of century-old oak trees stood. As Oswald watched, the branches on the trees began to sway and shake, though there was no wind.

Then he felt a stirring under his work boots. He took two steps backward as the ground under the old house began to quake like jelly.

In the barn, the cows grew even more fearful, and the dogs redoubled their frantic barking, which became shrill with fear.

Oswald stared in the direction of his barn and silo as the earth continued to shake.

Suddenly, the rumbling grew louder. It filled the air. It sounded to Oswald like the stampeding feet of a thousand impossibly huge creatures. And the noise seemed to move closer to him with each passing second.

Oswald Peaster's blood turned cold.

Quickly, he rushed back into the house.

"Millie," he cried. "Get down here! Something is wrong. We have to leave!" Then the farmer went back outside.

Again, he stared off in the distance as the thunderous rumbling increased in intensity. He heard a crashing sound. He turned toward the barn.

As he watched in terror and disbelief, the tall silo with PEASTER'S FARM painted on its side fell to the ground and splintered into fragments with a loud crash.

Then the barn itself seemed to explode. Wooden boards flew outward, bouncing across the barnyard and scattering the terrified chickens. Oswald raised his arm to cover his face even as a nail struck his elbow, bringing tears of pain.

As pieces of the shattered barn bounced against his farmhouse, the old man looked up again.

Oswald Peaster watched, awestruck, as the fields around his house began to *move*. The entire farm, and the land around it, was crowded with gigantic roving insects. They looked like impossibly huge praying mantises. The largest of the creatures—a shiny green insect at least fifty or sixty feet long— knocked down the last section of the barn that remained standing.

As the structure collapsed, one of the cows broke free from its pen. The terrified animal burst from the ruins as another insect crawled over the shattered silo and instantly snatched it up with its huge, curved claws.

The giant insect lifted the cow to its mandibles, and they snapped closed, biting the cow in two. The head and front legs flopped to the ground, the cow's eyes still alive and rolling. Almost instantly, another rampaging insect snatched it up and devoured the carcass.

"Oh, my gawd…" Oswald moaned.

He rushed back into the farmhouse and slammed the door behind him. He locked and bolted it.

"Millie!" he screamed. "We got to get out of here!"

But it was already too late for Oswald and Millie Peaster.

Before the old man reached the stairs, the house began to rock violently. Plaster dropped on Oswald's shoulders, and a beam fell from the ceiling, smashing the kitchen table.

Millie Peaster's cakes smashed on the linoleum floor.

Again, the house shook as the huge insect slammed against it. Oswald tumbled backward and bounced against the sink, dropping the shotgun.

When he bent down to retrieve his weapon, he slipped on splattered icing and fell to the floor. Upstairs, he heard his wife's horrified screams and the sound of walls shattering.

"Millie!" he cried, struggling to his feet. "I'm coming!"

Clutching his shotgun, Oswald rushed to the steps. But when he looked up, instead of the upstairs hallway, he saw daylight. The creatures had ripped off the roof and part of the second floor! Oswald heard his wife scream again. But this time, her cries were cut off—as if Millie had been swept away in a tornado. Oswald remembered the cow and gagged.

"Millie…" Oswald moaned as he staggered up the stairs. When he reached the top, the house quaked again.

A shadow fell over Oswald Peaster, blocking the daylight that streamed through the hole torn in his roof. The old man raised his head and stared upward—right into the multifaceted blue-green eyes of one of the gigantic monster insects.

"Get away from my farm!" Oswald shouted, his legs spread wide. Despite the crumbling house all around him, he stood his ground and aimed the shotgun at the slavering, snapping mandibles of the insect monster.

"I *said,* get off my farm!" He squeezed the trigger and fired both barrels at point-blank range, but the shotgun blast didn't even slow the creature. The insect closed its gripping claw around the old man's waist. Under the crushing pressure of its grip, Oswald finally gave up.

The useless gun dropped from his limp hand as the man was lifted high into the air. The last thing that Oswald Peaster saw was the insect's dark, looming, gigantic maw as the bony mandibles snapped shut, crushing the life out of him.

Within three hours, the swarm of gigantic insects, which numbered nearly a thousand, had swept across Osborne County. The ravenous creatures devoured everything in their path. Fields of grain, storehouses of feed, livestock, poultry—and even people—were consumed by the marauding insects.

By noon, the authorities had been alerted to the danger. The National Guard was sent to investigate the destruction, and military units moved from Fort Leavenworth toward the insect swarm. But for many, it was too little, and far too late.

Rural communities had been destroyed, their citizens devoured without any warning whatsoever. No one knew where the mysterious creatures came from, or where they were headed.

By late afternoon, dazed refugees with faraway stares and tales of horror began arriving in the surrounding towns of Russell and Alton. At first they came in a trickle, their faces pale with shock. Later on, as word of the monstrous swarm spread via the Emergency Broadcast Network, the trickle became a flood.

Cars, trucks, buses, even tractors and horse-drawn wagons, jammed the few highways out of Osborne County.

At sunset, a National Guard unit arrived in the largest town near the epicenter of the invasion, a town called Natoma. As three Blackhawk helicopters, fully armed and carrying a complement of troopers, flew over the beleaguered town, the National Guardsmen could not believe what they saw below them.

Natoma was in ruins.

Houses, churches, and businesses had been destroyed, and there was absolutely no sign of life. Even the trees had been stripped of their leaves, and many had been devoured whole. Only splintered stumps remained.

The commander of the guard unit ordered his troops to search the shattered streets in an attempt to find possible survivors who might be trapped in the rubble. At ten-thirty that night, they were rewarded for their trouble. One of the soldiers thought he heard a baby crying. Within thirty minutes, the National Guardsmen had spread out and located the source of the sound.

The men frantically dug through the smashed remains of a two-family house until a little baby girl was finally pulled from the wreckage.

Despite the destruction, the child was unharmed.

No other survivors were found. Though the soldiers searched through the night and into the next morning, they never even found a corpse.

The giant insects had eaten everything—and every*one*—in Natoma, Kansas.

GODZILLA™

9
ARMED CONFLICT

Thursday, May 27, 1999, 12:01 P.M.
The auditorium of Fort Hays State University
Hays, Kansas
Joint Services Military Command Headquarters
press conference

On the banks of Big Creek, between the town of Hays and the natural wonder called the Cathedral of the Plains, an emergency command headquarters was established to deal with the crisis.

The command center, established in less than thirty-six hours, was charged with the task of halting the advance of the swarm of mysterious insect giants that had appeared overnight and decimated a good portion of Osborne County.

So far, the troops in Kansas were undermanned and undersupplied for the battle ahead. But that was quickly changing. Route 70, which cuts horizontally through the center of Kansas, was jammed with military vehicles coming from both directions. Trucks, tanks, personnel carriers, Hummers, and mobile artillery choked the highways running into Ellis County.

The airport in Hays, a town of less than 20,000 souls, had been taken over by two A-10 attack fighter wings.

Miles away, the municipal airport in the city of

Hutchinson also had been commandeered by the military for air supply and support. McConnell Air Force Base in Wichita had been tapped to supply fighter and bomber cover when and if needed. It was the largest military operation conducted inside the borders of the United States since the Civil War.

The U.S. military forces were being helped by unseasonably cool temperatures in Kansas. Kaijuologists conjectured that the species of gigantic insects—dubbed Kamacuras—evolved in much warmer conditions. Hence the creatures were dormant in cold weather.

A civilian adviser and animal behaviorist dissented. She suggested that the creatures just weren't hungry anymore.

But whatever the reason, after the initial decimation caused by the marauding swarm, the insects had halted their advance.

Surveillance photographs taken by Air Force spy planes and satellites in Earth's orbit showed that the swarm—which numbered over a thousand individual insects, each measuring between one and two hundred feet in length—now rested between Plainville and the banks of the Saline River.

No communication had been established with Plainville, or nearby Codell, since the crisis began. The authorities assumed that these towns were completely destroyed and their citizens devoured.

However, as General Burt Selkirk noted in his opening remarks during the first televised press conference, this information *was* conjecture.

General Selkirk was the overall commander of

the joint military operation. A short, stocky man who had risen to prominence by commanding an armored division in Desert Storm, Selkirk was a no-nonsense fighting man who spoke his mind. He had little patience with civilians, especially members of the press. But the press didn't feel the same way about the general. Selkirk was colorful, and the media loved him.

On this cool, sunny afternoon, the auditorium on the campus of Fort Hays State University was filled to capacity. Reporters from all over the world listened to the general outline his plan to destroy the Kamacuras. On the stage with Selkirk was Dr. Max Birchwood, of G-Force USA, and Dr. Chandra Mishra, the co-discoverer of the Reyes-Mishra Asteroid Swarm.

After opening remarks, General Selkirk turned the proceedings over to the two scientists.

"As far as we can determine, the swarm of Kamacuras is of extraterrestrial origin," Dr. Chandra Mishra announced to the stunned journalists.

"The seeds of these creatures were deposited on our world mere weeks ago, during the violent meteor storm that appeared over North America," Dr. Mishra continued.

"We have found evidence of a kind of parasitic alien DNA in meteorite fragments discovered in a farmer's field. We think that DNA somehow bonded with that of a praying mantis, and the alien infection spread to create the creatures we call Kamacuras."

"The horde of gigantic insects has an extraterrestrial origin, unlike the creature now rampaging through Mexico," Dr. Birchwood interjected, "which is of *terrestrial* origin—"

"Do you mean Varan?" Peter Jimson of ABC News interrupted, shouting from a front row.

Dr. Birchwood nodded and scratched his dark beard. "We've studied blood and tissue samples of the creature *you* call Varan, obtained after a failed attack by the Mexican Army. From these samples, we have concluded that the *kaiju* in Mexico evolved right here on Earth—"

"Wait a second," Jimson interrupted again. "Are you asking us to believe that a giant flying reptile evolved *naturally?*"

"Well, first of all, Varan doesn't fly," Birchwood corrected. "We speculate that it can somehow separate the oxygen and hydrogen in water. The creature then expels the oxygen and pumps the hydrogen molecules into sacs along its torso. So you see, Varan actually *floats,* or *glides.* It does not fly. Of course, this is all speculation."

The scientist paused before continuing.

"As to your second question...nobody said that Varan evolved *naturally*. We think that chemical and industrial pollution on the Mexican subcontinent may have contributed to the monster's creation—"

But General Selkirk cut the scientist off. "That information can be supplied later," the general announced. "I have a lot of work to do, so let's get to the business at hand."

General Selkirk rose and stood before a detailed map of Kansas.

"At 0600 tomorrow morning, we are going to

attack the Kamacuras from the air," he announced. A hush fell over the chaotic assembly as he pointed to the map.

"Originally, the Air Force planned to carpet-bomb the swarm from high altitudes, using B-52 bombers. It was felt that this would eradicate the horde before it moved again and before the creatures began their reproductive cycle.

"But because there is still a chance that survivors may be hiding in the area and unable to flee, the joint command has decided to try a surgical strike first, using A-10 Thunderbolt II attack aircraft. Employing their 30mm cannons, along with air-to-ground missiles and high-explosive incendiary bombs, these low-flying 'Warthogs' will cut a swath of destruction through the swarm."

A buzz rose among the audience, but the general ignored the reporters.

"As you know, the A-10 'Warthog' is a tank killer, and we feel sure that its armor-piercing cannons will easily penetrate the thick exoskeletons of the Kamacuras."

"But what if the swarm starts to move again!" Nick Gordon, INN's award-winning science correspondent, demanded.

"We have tanks and heavy artillery surrounding the swarm. At any sign of movement, they will be deployed, and heavy bombing will commence from the air, despite the risk to any survivors."

General Selkirk's plan was reported on television and in the press. The controversy began immediately.

Some military analysts thought that the risk was too great to worry about possible survivors in an initial attack. They advocated bombing by B-52s, thinking it would be more effective than a low-level attack by slow-moving A-10s.

Others went so far as to suggest the use of nuclear weapons, but ultimately, no one wanted to go on record with *that* opinion.

In the end, the administration went along with Selkirk's plan. If it failed, more drastic steps could easily be taken later.

But not too *much* later.

Meanwhile, at the secret testing facility in the Nevada desert, another general was mulling over his own problems.

With mounting dread, General Jake Taggart read the report filed by Project Valkyrie's physicians and psychologists, and a second report from the project's training coordinator, Colonel Krupp.

He didn't like what he saw.

The good news was that Raptor-One would be delivered tonight, two months ahead of schedule. *Looks like the Pentagon boys kicked some butt,* the general thought with satisfaction.

The massive weapons platform, constructed with the cooperation of all the major American defense contractors, was designed to be the ultimate weapon against Godzilla, or any other monster. The completed and fully tested Raptor-One would be flown into Nellis Air Force Base tonight, in total secrecy, under the cover of darkness.

That was the good news.

The bad news was that General Taggart had no crew to man the Raptor. His team was still not ready, despite a new and intensified training regimen. Worse than that, according to the project's psychiatrist, Dr. Irene Markham, the stress was starting to wear down his teenage recruits.

Lori Angelo had been the first to crack. Lately, she had been having nightmares, and she even experienced a sleepwalking episode. If her psychological state deteriorated any further, Ms. Angelo would have to be pulled from the program.

Tia Shimura, the other female member of the team, was faring much better, despite the fact that she was the youngest. General Taggart had no reservations about Tobias Nelson, Martin Wong, or Pierce Dillard.

But Kip Daniels was also a problem.

He still exhibited more raw talent and potential than any of the others. He had beaten the simulator—finally—on the ninth try. And he hadn't been beaten by the computer simulators since. But Kip had never really flown the Raptor, and none of the G-Force team had yet fought in real combat.

This led to General Taggart's third and final problem. *Public relations.*

If G-Force had to go into action now, it would be a public relations disaster. How can we justify sending teenagers into combat—and ill-prepared teenagers, at that?

The G-Force team was supposed to be ready by 2001, when all of its members would be well past their eighteenth birthday. Unfortunately, Varan and the giant insects weren't following the timetable.

Fortunately, Varan is a problem for the Mexicans, and the conventional forces can probably take care of the bugs.

As long as Godzilla doesn't show up, we might still have enough time to kick G-Force into shape...

Meanwhile, in the middle of the South Pacific, in the bowels of an ultramodern, high-tech Japanese research vessel, Dr. Emiko Takado was reviewing the reams of data gathered by the ship's deep-sea robotic bathysphere.

We've found Godzilla, realized the eminent kaijuologist. Her emotions were in turmoil over the discovery. On the one hand, she should have felt pleasure. After all, she and the other scientists aboard the hydrofoil *Kongo-Maru* had been searching for Godzilla for the last six months. Now they knew the location of the creature that had destroyed Tokyo and given birth to a new science.

But Dr. Takado felt no pleasure, no thrill of discovery. Instead, she was haunted by the memory of her mentor, Dr. Hiroshi Nobeyama, the father of the nascent science of kaijuology, and she felt crushed by the magnitude of the terrible knowledge that she alone possessed.

It seems Dr. Nobeyama's sacrifice has been in vain, she thought. It was that Japanese scientist, along with Admiral Maxwell B. Willis, who formulated the plan to lure Godzilla away from the Japanese mainland. Together, they flew the aircraft that accomplished the mission—until it expended all of its fuel and crashed into the Pacific.

Now Dr. Nobeyama and Admiral Willis were both lost. *But Godzilla has survived,* Dr. Takado thought sadly. As she studied the printouts, she hoped that she was mistaken, that her data was flawed.

But in the end, Dr. Takado's hopes were dashed. The data confirmed it. *Godzilla is still alive,* she realized, her heart racing. *And it looks as if he's awakening…*

Far beneath the hull of the *Kongo-Maru,* Godzilla lay in uneasy hibernation. Over the last twenty-four hours, his heartbeat had begun to increase. Electronic monitors placed by the *Kongo-Maru*'s undersea robot had recorded this change, along with the rise in his temperature.

Soon, the most powerful *kaiju* of them all would rise from the sea again, and there was absolutely nothing that mankind could do about it.

Emiko Takado was torn by indecision. The world was already faced with a host of terrible new menaces, each of them threatening human extinction.

According to a report Dr. Takado had received that morning from Dr. Martin Birchwood of Project Valkyrie, the giant insects that were now ravaging America's heartland were caused by the asteroids that threatened to strike the earth in two months.

Meanwhile, Dr. Chandra Mishra had forwarded to her a secret report of his own. Dr. Mishra's data suggested that the asteroids were not what they seemed. According to Dr. Mishra's theory, the largest of the celestial bodies heading toward Earth was hollow, and might contain the seeds of a creature more destructive than the Kamacuras.

And there was still the monster ravaging Mexico to deal with, the one the press called Varan. *A mutated reptilian species that can actually fly,* Dr. Takado marveled.

Now there was evidence that Godzilla could rise from the depths at any time.

Dr. Takado knew what her government wanted her to do. She was supposed to inform the government, which would digest and disseminate the information as they saw fit.

But she feared that the Japanese prime minister and the Diet would hold back the information, possibly until it was too late.

Should I share this information? Or should I only tell my government and withhold the data from General Jake Taggart of G-Force USA?

Dr. Takado had to ask herself whether all the nations of the world had a right to know what she knew. In the end, she did what she thought was right.

That is what Dr. Nobeyama would have done, she concluded. Her decision made, Emiko Takado activated the satellite radio.

KAMACURAS™

10
THE CALM BEFORE THE STORM

Friday, May 28, 1999, 4:41 A.M.
Hays Municipal Airport
Hays, Kansas

The population of Hays would have doubled in the last three days, except that most of the civilian population had been evacuated from the town the day before. Now the 15,000 men and women in Hays were either military personnel or civilian reporters selected from a press pool and brought to the front.

One of those press crews was even now interviewing members of Captain Jerry Tilson's A-10 squadron in the municipal airport's tiny terminal. Fortunately, Captain Tilson managed to avoid them.

Tilson stepped out of the terminal and into the cold morning air. The sun had not yet risen, but the promise of dawn was visible in the eastern sky. He took a deep breath.

The plains of Kansas smell sweet, he thought. *But not as sweet as the Pennsylvania hills.* Tilson, an Air National Guard pilot who had only been called up two weeks before, missed his home and his wife, Sandy. She waited for him back in Allentown.

Sandy always kidded him about staying in the National Guard. She said that he liked playing soldier because he had never grown up, and that being a "weekend warrior" gave him the chance to get away with the "boys" a couple of times a year, fly fast planes, and shoot off some ammunition.

Honey, if you only knew, he thought, wondering how he and his fellow pilots would fare today.

In a way Sandy was right. Tilson liked flying military aircraft—even an ugly clunker like the Warthog—but he stayed in the Air National Guard mostly because of the flight pay. You didn't make much money as the manager of a Laneco store. Not enough to support a family, anyway. And now Sandy was pregnant, and would probably have to give up her job soon.

Tilson accepted a clipboard from a young woman in dirty overalls. He scanned the flight check, signed it, and handed it back to her.

Then he approached his aircraft.

As he crossed the tarmac, the whine of twin General Electric turbofan engines cut the air like a knife. The squadron's A-10 FAC—forward air control—taxied to the primary runway. The FAC would lead the attack and guide the other A-10s to the target. Tilson gazed down the runway and gauged the distance. *There shouldn't be any problem.*

Hays Municipal was a tiny airport that served privately owned light planes and small commercial commuter aircraft. The facility could never support the high-tech, high-maintenance fighters and bombers that would be the core of the United States Air Force of the twenty-first century. But it was just the right size for the A-10.

The Fairchild A-10 Thunderbolt II, affectionately

known as the "Warthog" because of its uncommon ugliness, was built to land and take off from runways less than 5,000 feet long.

The Warthog flew low and slow, which made it an easy target against modern weapons, but it was the perfect tool against the horde of giant insects. The A-10 was also known as the "flying gun" because it was designed around the GAU-8/A Avenger 30mm cannon, the most powerful rapid-fire weapon ever installed in an aircraft.

The pilots, who slept in tents and hangars around the airport, were selected to lead the first wave of the attack. They would be joined by more A-10s out of McConnell and Salina—and F-15s and F-111s, if necessary. But it was Tilson and his colleagues who would be the first to face the Kamacuras.

When he passed through the terminal after the morning briefing, Tilson heard some of the other pilots blowing hot air about the "bug hunt" to each other and to the press.

Tilson wasn't going to do any bragging. Unlike some of these youngsters, he had seen combat before. He knew that anything could happen.

He completed his pre-flight inspection—his "walkaround"—tugging on the Maverick air-to-surface missiles that hung from wing pylons and the fragmentation bombs that dangled from the wings and belly. He wanted to make sure the deadly payload was secure.

Then he checked the control surfaces, the avionics pod…and even kicked the tires. When he was satisfied with the condition of his aircraft, Captain

Tilson climbed into the cockpit.

An airman helped strap him into his ejection seat and shook Tilson's hand and wished him luck. When the ladder was withdrawn, Tilson did a final system check.

Everything looked good. He started the engine and listened to it hum as it revved up. Then he closed his canopy and taxied onto the flight line. Now all he had to do was wait.

Though it was early, even by Project Valkyrie's grueling training standards, none of the members of G-Force had trouble getting out of bed.

With the exception of Lori Angelo, the team showed up in the command center ahead of schedule. And even Lori was wide awake and watching the monitors as the A-10s prepared to lift off in faraway Kansas to do battle with the creatures from outer space.

Colonel Krupp and a team of technicians trucked over from the main complex of Nellis Air Force Base downloaded real-time images of the coming battle from satellites and surveillance aircraft that hovered in the sky above Osborne County.

Tia was thrilled by the prospect of handling all that communications technology, and she worked alongside the colonel at one of the electronic warfare stations.

"This surveillance stuff is pretty cool," Tia told Lori when the older girl arrived.

"Hey, colonel, how about some breakfast?" Tobias Nelson complained when he discovered that the cafeteria wasn't even open yet.

"So sorry for the oversight," Colonel Krupp barked. "I'll have Sergeant Harris get you some milk and cookies. We don't really *need* him here, and I'm sure he'd be happy to fetch you a snack."

Toby backed away with a frozen smile.

The colonel was cranky because he'd been up all night making sure that the downlinks worked properly. Krupp felt it was vital that his recruits see the battle, whatever the outcome.

Only one of the dozen wide-screen televisions was tuned to a commercial station. While she worked, Tia watched her uncle Brian Shimura, an INN reporter, interview a pilot before he took off. The Air Force officer seemed confident that the Kamacuras would be wiped out by nightfall.

"My uncle is so cool," Tia told Lori. "He was in Tokyo. He saw Godzilla *in the flesh!*"

Lori nodded distractedly. She tried to pay attention to the images on the monitors but couldn't concentrate.

I wish I understood the dream I had last night, Lori thought. *It was so real…it felt like someone was trying to tell me something.*

Unlike the other dreams Lori had been having lately, this one wasn't a crazy nightmare filled with images of golden dragons.

This dream was different.

Vaguely, Lori recalled a veiled figure shrouded in a diaphanous robe of many colors. There was singing in the dream, too, and sparkling motes of light seemed to surround the figure.

But no matter how hard Lori tried to recall the

dream, the images slipped away until all that remained was the uneasy feeling that something momentous was about to happen.

Sitting alone, Kip anxiously watched the monitors. During a lull in the action, he glanced at Tia and Lori, who were talking in front of a command station.

Martin Wong was busy, too. He was manning a satellite link with the help of a pretty young Air Force officer in a short skirt. Kip stifled a laugh. Martin was obviously smitten with the older woman, but Kip wasn't sure she even noticed.

Then Kip spotted Pierce Dillard. The older pilot sat staring at him from across the room. *He's been doing that for a week,* Kip realized. *Ever since I started beating the simulators.*

Dillard's furrowed brow and severe gaze gave Kip the impression that storm clouds were about to form above the guy's crewcut head.

Great, thought Kip. *First Dillard didn't like me because I wasn't any good…Now he doesn't like me because I'm too good.*

Kip suddenly frowned as he recalled his own dilemma.

How good am I, really? he wondered. *I can shoot at Godzilla easily enough now—at least I can in the simulators. But I still don't feel right about it. Attacking Godzilla still seems wrong somehow…*

Suddenly, a heavy hand descended on Kip's shoulder, and he nearly jumped out of his chair. He turned to find Toby Nelson smiling down at him.

"Hey, Toby, shouldn't you be sitting with the other aircraft commander?" Kip asked, pointing at Pierce.

"Shouldn't *you* be sitting with him?" replied the handsome African American teenager.

"I like it here," Kip declared.

"Okay," Toby said. He sat down next to Kip.

"So you've beaten the simulator seven times," Toby remarked. Kip nodded, and Toby smiled. "Not too shabby."

"Yeah, well, it hasn't helped team spirit much," noted Kip. "Dillard still won't say two words to me outside the mockpit."

Toby smiled. "How many words have you said to him?"

Kip did not reply. For a few minutes, they sat in silence, watching the monitors as the A-10s taxied onto the runway.

"You've got to understand something about Pierce Dillard," Toby finally said. "He takes his job very seriously. Maybe *too* seriously. He doesn't like things to go wrong, so he tries to control every-thing...and everybody. Not just *you*."

Kip nodded. "I've heard stories about how he pushed Lori when she first joined the Project."

"He didn't *push* Lori," Toby replied. "He tried to make her better than she was. Lori messed up a lot at first, just like you did. But she had a lot of poten-tial. Pierce took it upon himself to straighten Lori out."

"Well, I'm not messing up anymore," Kip assert-ed. "But Pierce is still riding me."

"That's because you have a very special talent,"

Toby said earnestly. "You're *magic* behind the controls of Raptor-One, Kip. I've watched Pierce work for months, from sunup to sundown, just to *match* what you've accomplished in the last few weeks. But he *can't* do it, Kip. *You* can."

Kip blinked, surprised by Toby's words. "If I'm so good, why does Pierce ride me?"

"As good as you are, Pierce knows you could be better. He knows that, for whatever reason, your heart just isn't in what you're doing. Pierce knows you're holding back."

Toby looked hard at Kip. "You could be better, Kip," he said. "And Dillard knows it."

"Your point?"

"Dillard wants G-Force to be a success. That's his entire focus. Sometimes he rides people. Sometimes he can't let go and trust the rest of us to do our jobs. But at least Pierce Dillard is focused. He's *here,* all the time. One hundred percent."

Toby paused to meet Kip's uncertain blue gaze once again.

"But you, my friend, are *not.*"

With that, Tobias Nelson rose. "Cut Dillard a little slack," he added, patting Kip's shoulder. "He can help you."

Then Toby glanced around the room and stretched. "Not much going on yet. I'm gonna go find me some breakfast."

In Kansas, Captain Tilson taxied to the end of the runway.

"Stand by, Nail Two." The flight controller's voice crackled in his ears. Tilson eased the throttle back, cutting some of the power to the twin turbofan engines. The Warthog seemed to shudder in protest, but was tamed.

Ahead of Tilson, Nail One raced down the runway and shot into the sky. Already, the blue-black canopy was streaked with the hint of dawn.

"Ready, Nail Two?" the controller asked. Tilson clicked his mike.

"You're cleared for take-off."

Tilson pushed the throttle forward and his A-10 picked up speed. Seven seconds later, Captain Jerry Tilson's A-10 left the runway and leaped into the Kansas sky.

GODZILLA™

11
MAN AND MACHINE AGAINST MONSTERS

Friday, May 28, 1999, 5:57 A.M.
Somewhere over Osborne County, Kansas

It took almost no time at all for Jerry Tilson and his squadron to fly to the target area. As the sun rose and dusty yellow light washed over the plains of Kansas, the dozen A-10s reached their destination.

Spread out below them was a huge brown area of barren earth. The Kamacuras had stripped the rich, rural landscape of Osborne County bare of all life, vegetation, and even the topsoil, leaving the land as useless as the Gobi Desert.

"Is everybody on station?" the squadron leader in Nail One, Colonel Mike Towers, asked over the radio. The pilots began to reply in numerical order, from Nail Two—Tilson—to Nail Twelve, a newbie by the name of Myron Healey.

When everybody had checked in, the squadron leader contacted the pilot serving as the forward air controller (FAC).

While they waited for the signal to attack, the A-10s flew in an easy figure-eight pattern over the ravaged countryside. Although the FAC reported he could see the monsters, the Kamacuras were still out of Tilson's line of sight.

Suddenly, they heard the voice of the forward air

controller crackle in their ears. It was laced with excitement, even a little panic.

"This is Hammer to Nail, Hammer to Nail," the FAC said. "Be advised that the creatures are moving. Repeat, the creatures are awake and moving!"

The Kamacuras were supposed to be paralyzed by the cold, the scientists said. It was cooler now than yesterday—but the swarm was still active.

So much for the best-laid plans and all the experts' predictions, Jerry Tilson thought sourly.

The FAC radioed the change of coordinates for the attack. Jerry dutifully keyed the new data into his navigational computer as the forward air controller gave the squadron a final briefing.

"The Natoma High School is just ahead," announced the FAC. "Bring your aircraft in low and fast. Pass over the school at about a hundred feet, and you should see the target area ahead. Good luck."

"Okay, form up," Nail One commanded. "I want Two, Three, and Four on my wing. Let's go bug hunting!"

Tilson followed his commander's aircraft as it dipped its nose and plunged toward the earth. At a hundred feet above sea level, the commander leveled off, and Nails Two, Three, and Four came up alongside him.

Suddenly, the ruins of Natoma High School loomed ahead. Tilson could just make out a shattered building, a torn and riven football field, and row upon row of collapsed bleachers before his aircraft flashed past the wreckage.

Finally, he saw them.

Just ahead, filling the entire screen of the head-up display, was the swarm.

Hiram Roper gazed through a crack in the storm shelter's stout wooden door. He was sure he'd just heard the sound of jet engines above his farm.

The old man shushed his fearful wife, who held their neighbors' youngest child, nine-year-old Ronette Carry, in her plump arms. The little girl had appeared two mornings before, just as Hiram was heading out to his barn to milk his cattle.

He had found the girl wandering aimlessly along the country road that ran past their farmhouse. Ronette was dirty and dazed, and seemed to be suffering from shock. Try as they might, neither Hiram nor his wife, Wanda, could get the once-talkative little girl to speak a word.

Worried about the Carry family, Hiram left the little one with his wife, hopped into his Jeep Cherokee, and headed over to the Carry home.

But he never made it.

He'd hardly pulled onto the rural route when a gigantic insect lumbered across the road, oblivious of the Jeep. Stunned, Hiram gazed through the dirty windshield and saw a dozen more of the creatures devouring the Carrys' orchard, tree by tree.

Fighting panic, Hiram rushed home. When he arrived, the electricity was already out. He tried the phone, but the lines were down, too. Then he heard the thunderous tread of the creatures approaching his own farm.

Hiram bundled his wife and little Ronette into their underground tornado shelter and door behind him. There was sufficient food and water inside, and a Coleman lantern filled with fuel. There was a radio, too, but the batteries were dead.

Hiram, Wanda, and Ronette remained huddled in the shelter for almost forty-eight hours. Little Ronette hadn't uttered a word since they found her. Hiram could imagine what the girl must have witnessed, and he took pity on the poor child.

While they hid, the creatures foraged through the countryside. Hiram heard them moving about, but he dared not open the shelter door.

Then, just minutes ago, the old farmer heard jets flying overhead, coming from the direction of Natoma. *The military has finally come,* he thought. But Hiram knew that he, his wife, and Ronette weren't out of danger yet. So far, they had survived the giant insects. Now they had to survive whatever the military had planned.

"On target!" Colonel Mike Towers announced.

Jerry Tilson watched as his squadron commander dived toward the hideous mass of squirming, swarming insects. The morning sun glinted off the creatures' shiny black, brown, and green exoskeletons. Their multifaceted eyes gleamed with a cold malevolence. There were so many of them that it appeared as if the ground itself was moving and writhing.

How could anyone be alive down there? Jerry Tilson wondered.

Suddenly, he was filled with a terrible hatred he'd never felt before, not even during Desert 'torm, when he faced a human enemy who'd brutally taken the lives of some of his colleagues.

Somehow, Tilson realized, the Kamacuras were a different kind of enemy. He wanted to exterminate these remorseless creatures before they exterminated him. The monsters had murdered thousands of his countrymen as they slept in their beds or went about their daily lives.

Tilson's gloved hands gripped the control stick as he dived his A-10 into the very center of the swarm. His eyes were locked onto his squadron commander's aircraft in front of him.

Tilson watched as Nail One released its bombs and pulled up. The high explosives detonated on a horde of the creatures. The blast rocked his A-10 as Tilson shot through the smoke and fire and dropped his own bombs on another group of crawling monsters. On either side of him, Nails Three and Four dropped their ordnance and pulled up as well.

"How's it look?" Mike Towers called from Nail One.

"It looks good!" Nail Four replied. "Some of the bugs are down, and others are burning."

Tilson felt jubilant, but there was no time for celebration.

"Okay," Colonel Towers announced. "We're going in for another pass. This time we'll use missiles. Nails Five, Six, Seven, and Eight will follow up behind us with another round of bombs."

Tilson forgot the fears and misgivings he'd felt that morning. He was transformed into a cold, calculating killing machine—a professional soldier. All he wanted to do was get back into action again and inflict more damage on the creatures.

The four A-10s circled back until they assembled over the ruins of the high school again. Then they repeated their attack pattern, this time using Maverick air-to-surface missiles.

"In we go!" Towers cried as his A-10 dived into the fire that still burned from their first pass.

As Tilson streaked through the billowing smoke, he saw the charred and tattered remains of dozens of bugs. Some were blown to bits, others lay on their backs like roaches suffering from an overdose of Raid. It gave him a rush of satisfaction to discover he could kill his monstrous, unnatural foes. He felt anticipation as he dived toward his enemies for a second time.

But as Nail One fired its Maverick missiles into the armored backs of several creatures, the unexpected occurred.

As the first A-10 passed over a huge Kamacuras, half again as long as the others, the creature opened up the back section of its elongated carapace. Huge wings popped out of the creature's body and unfolded like a fan. As Tilson looked on, the enormous insect began flapping its massive wings until they moved so fast that they blurred like the blades of a helicopter.

"They can fly!" Tilson cried. "Nail One, be advised. The Kamacuras can fly!" As Tilson spoke, the monster was rising rapidly into the air beneath his commander's aircraft.

As Tilson watched in horror, the Kamacuras flew directly into the path of Mike Towers' A-10. Colonel Towers tried to veer his aircraft out of the way, but it was too late. Nail One's A-10 slammed right into the center of the creature's head.

The airplane and the insect's head exploded simultaneously. Fuel from the shattered warplane spilled over the creature's body and instantly ignited.

There was no time for the pilot to eject. Colonel Mike Towers was gone.

The dead Kamacuras dropped back to earth, burning like a firecracker. It smashed two other Kamacuras to a pulp when it landed on them.

There was no time for Tilson to mourn his commander and friend. Now he had troubles of his own. The entire horde was sprouting wings and taking to the air. Their dark bodies blocked out the sun. Their wings dashed against the aircraft that flew, trapped, in the center of the swarm.

Tilson shoved his stick from side to side, avoiding the beating wings, groping claws, and snapping mandibles as numberless creatures lifted off the ground and took to the air all around him.

"I'm hit! I'm hit!" a terrified voice cried.

Tilson recognized Pederson. He was flying Nail Three. Still struggling with the stick, Tilson risked a sidelong glance. He saw Pederson's A-10 crumble into pieces as it was battered apart by a host of gigantic wings. Just before the aircraft disintegrated, Pederson punched out.

Tilson saw the parachute open. Then his A-10 shot past, and Tilson lost sight of the stricken pilot.

"Oh, no! *No!*" Swanson, the pilot of Nail Four, cried. "The bastards *ate* him...the bugs *ate* Pederson!"

Tilson ignored the anguished cries of the other pilot. It was all he could do to keep control of his aircraft—and he wanted to do as much damage to the swarm as he could.

A huge Kamacuras rose into the air right in front of him. Its multifaceted eye filled Tilson's display. Quickly, the pilot armed the Avenger cannon and pressed the trigger.

Tilson's A-10 vibrated as over a thousand rounds of armor-piercing depleted-uranium shells ripped into the creature's eye. Like a ripe pimple, the eye popped, spewing black ichor into the air like a fountain. Some of the oily black slime splattered onto Tilson's windscreen, limiting his vision, until the air rushing over his cockpit blew it away.

As he banked to the left, Tilson saw Nail Four open up with its cannons, and two insects blew apart in midair. Then another Kamacuras appeared in front of him, and Tilson fired again. The monster exploded, cut in half by the Avenger's killing shells.

Tilson flew through a cloud of gore. Pieces of flesh bounced against his fuselage. Tilson prayed that his turbofan engines wouldn't suck up any of the creatures' guts. He didn't want to stall at such a low altitude. If he did, there was nothing to do but eject—and Tilson didn't want to end up like Pederson. He'd rather stay on top of the food chain.

Through his headphones, Tilson could hear the excited cries of the pilots in the second string. They, too, were in the fight of their lives.

"I got one on my tail!" Nail Four cried. Tilson looked sideways and spotted the other A-10. A huge creature was flying behind it, its mandibles snapping at the warplane's already damaged tail fins.

"I got him," Tilson replied. He pulled back the stick and did a high, arching loop, barely missing a smaller Kamacuras flying above him. He came down right behind the bug chasing Nail Four.

Tilson aimed and fired. The stream of explosive shells cut the monster's wings into tatters. The Kamacuras dropped out of the sky and was dashed to bits on the earth below.

"Thanks, Nail Two." The other pilot's voice crackled in Tilson's helmet.

"Any damage?" Tilson asked. There was a pause before the pilot of Nail Four replied.

"The controls are sluggish," he radioed. "The rear stabilizers are heavily damaged."

"Let's get out of here," Tilson replied. "I'm out of ammo, and there's nothing more we can do now."

Before he turned and banked away, Tilson watched as the second wave of A-10s attacked the swarm. With each bomb dropped and missile fired, more of the ravaging Kamacuras died.

But not enough, Tilson thought bitterly. *Not nearly enough.*

Then he and the only other survivor of the first wave headed their battered and stained aircraft back to Hays Municipal Airport for refueling and rearming.

And then I'll be back, Tilson vowed.

On the banks of Big Creek, a line of M1A1 Abrams main battle tanks waited for the signal to fire. The swarm was moving toward them, and though more air attacks were inbound, the swarm would almost certainly reach the river in another fifteen minutes.

It was up to the tanks to stop them, to hold the line. If they couldn't, then the rest of Kansas, and maybe the rest of America, was doomed.

Thousands of miles away, alarms began to blare on the Japanese research vessel *Kongo-Maru*.

Still in her nightclothes, Dr. Emiko Takado emerged from her cabin and rushed onto the bridge. Quickly, she scanned the instruments. What she saw chilled her, even in the warmth of the South Pacific air.

"What's the matter?" a sleepy technician asked as soon as he reached the bridge. Without taking her eyes off the radarscope, Dr. Takado answered.

"It's Godzilla. He's fully awake now, and moving."

The crew of the research vessel immediately went to work, manning all stations.

Emiko felt as if she'd been caught off-balance. Her data had suggested that Godzilla would awaken eventually, but not nearly so soon. Nor so quickly.

"We must get clear of Godzilla—" she began, but she was interrupted by the sonar technician.

"Dr. Takado!" he cried as an image burst upon his screen. "Godzilla is rising to the surface—he's coming up right under us!"

"Send an SOS—" But Dr. Takado's command was again cut short as something rammed into the *Kongo-Maru*.

Helplessly, Dr. Takado was thrown across the bridge. The control panel in front of the sonarman exploded in a shower of electric sparks.

Then the entire ship was lifted out of the water.

A thunderous roar slammed against the crew's ears and echoed throughout the vessel. Then the ship lurched again and the lights went out. This time, Dr. Takado was dashed to the floor.

A second roar shook the entire ship. Dr. Takado pulled herself off the floor. Fearfully, she peered out through the cracked windows.

The Pacific night was lit by blue electric flashes. The water glowed as if on fire.

Godzilla comes, Dr. Takado thought, an eerie calm descending on her. *It is karma.*

Then fire ripped through the research ship as the fuel tanks ignited. Crewmen and technicians were incinerated in the terrible heat.

Finally, a tremendous blast ripped through the ship, and it split into two burning pieces that quickly sank into the dark ocean like stones.

A row of jagged, irregular dorsal spines broke the surface briefly, then sank again as Godzilla swam away.

The destruction of the *Kongo-Maru* happened so fast—and was so complete—that not even the briefest message of warning had been broadcast.

12
BIRDS OF PREY

According to the White House press secretary, the first phase of General Burt Selkirk's battle plan was a great success. The swarm was contained, many of the giant insects were killed or wounded, and the lives of dozens of civilians had been saved.

According to Pentagon insiders, however, the initial assault was an unmitigated disaster. Million-dollar aircraft had been reduced to metal fragments and a number of pilots—trained with plenty of Air Force dollars—had been slaughtered, possibly in vain, because the swarm was far from defeated.

In fact, three hours after the battle in Kansas began, it was obvious there would be no immediate victory. Contrary to the kaijuologists' predictions, the creatures had proved to be immune to cold. Now the scientists were thinking that the Kamacuras had gone dormant only long enough to grow wings.

At least the initial assault had confirmed that the creatures were relatively easy to destroy. The biggest problem the military faced now was their numbers. After the first two hours, the A-10s were recalled, and F-111 low-level fighter/bombers were scorching the big bugs with napalm.

The tanks were able to hold the creatures back. So far, none of the monsters had moved beyond Route 70 or the banks of the Big Creek, despite their ability to fly.

The bad news was that casualties were indeed heavy, and the battle was far from over. The joint military command announced that the conflict was expected to stretch on into the night.

In the meantime, reconnaissance teams were sent into areas where the Kamacuras had rampaged. Civilian survivors who'd found refuge in storm shelters, root cellars, and drain pipes were quickly airlifted out.

Tia watched the INN network feed and saw her uncle interview a farmer, his wife, and a nine-year-old girl who had survived the onslaught by hiding in a tornado shelter.

The G-Force team, along with Air Force technicians and Colonel Krupp, watched the battle in real time on the giant television screens. Over the course of the three hours, they lost their connection with one satellite after another as each moved out of range. Soon, however, another would move into orbit over the battlefield.

Tia Shimura was enjoying herself thoroughly. She took to the satellite equipment the way she took to every other technical problem thrown at her—like "a duck to water," according to Colonel Krupp.

At ten o'clock, the G-Force team broke for brunch. To Colonel Krupp's surprise, the usually solitary Kip Daniels sat between Pierce Dillard and

Tobias Nelson at the table. They didn't talk much, but at least some of the tension that had fragmented the team was evaporating. Krupp believed the change was due to the harsh lesson of the battle in Kansas.

During the meal, Lori Angelo was unusually quiet. She couldn't forget the haunted eyes of that mute little girl she saw on television, nor the troubling feeling that her dreams had been more than mere dreams.

As the meal ended, General Taggart made an appearance. He ordered them all to report to the front door of Hangar 13 at 1200. Then he left the cafeteria without another word.

All of the members of the G-Force team, including Colonel Krupp and Dr. Birchwood, were assembled in front of Hangar 13 fifteen minutes ahead of schedule.

None of them had ever been inside 13, the largest hangar at Nellis Air Force Base. It was so large that it could comfortably house a B-52 bomber.

Nellis AFB was close to an area of the Nevada desert commonly known as Dreamland, because so many strange aircraft were designed and tested there. Much of the base had been abandoned in the mid-nineties when the Pentagon realized that the activities at the top-secret base were no longer much of a secret.

The place was so famous that it had even passed into modern myth and legend. According to UFOlogists, Nellis was one of the possible locations of the infamous "Hangar 18," where the Air Force stashed the dead aliens they recovered from the Roswell "UFO" crash of 1947.

Indeed, when she first arrived, Lori was familiar with the stories. And she was disappointed to learn that there were only *sixteen* hangars at Dreamland!

When G-Force was established by a joint decree of Congress and the president, the Air Force dumped the program—called Project Valkyrie to hide its true purpose—at Nellis. By the late 1990s, even the UFOlogists had stopped hanging around.

As they stood in the hot Nevada sun, Kip noticed that Toby and Pierce both seemed to be bursting with excitement. Even the usually taciturn Colonel Krupp was smiling. Tia, Martin, and Kip all shared meaningful glances as the purpose of their visit became obvious.

There was a rumble of heavy machinery, and the huge hangar doors began to grind open. A hush fell over the group as they faced the Raptor.

Raptor-One had been designed on the same principles as the Bell/Boeing V-22 Osprey tilt-rotor aircraft. But the Raptor was twice as large, with a wingspan of 175 feet and length of over 100 feet.

Like the Osprey, the Raptor's wings seemed short for the thickness of the fuselage, and the huge turboshaft engines were mounted at the very tips of the wings. The two engines were topped with four-bladed propellers that were fifty feet long.

The Raptor lifted off the ground with the propellers in the horizontal position. Then computer-assisted controls tilted the engines forward until the propellers were vertical. The engines could be adjusted at various angles, allowing the aircraft to slow, speed forward, or hover like a conventional helicopter.

From the side, the stubby fuselage of the Raptor was thick in the front, with a mass of windows making up the entire nose of the aircraft, but tapered in the back. Like the Osprey, the Raptor had twin vertical tail stabilizers, but they were mounted on the fuselage—not on the swept-back rear horizontal wings.

The Raptor was a propeller-driven airplane, so it was not as fast as more conventional jet aircraft. But it didn't have to be. It was designed to battle Godzilla, not high-tech fighters. Its top cruising speed of 250 miles per hour was just right, because the real magic of the Raptor lay in its defensive and offensive capabilities.

Behind the cockpit, which was filled with the most advanced avionics, targeting, communications, and radar equipment, the Raptor was not much more than a huge ammunition bay. Its heavy-lifting capabilities enabled it to carry a wide variety of anti-*kaiju* weapons—from dozens of cadmium missiles to thousands of rounds of 30mm armor-piercing uranium shells for the four Avenger cannons that ran along its fuselage.

The wing pylons were designed to carry two standard cruise missiles—one per wing—and an array of smaller missiles. The cadmium missiles, Maverick air-to-surface missiles, and laser-guided smart bombs were all in armored bays in the wings themselves.

As a defense against Godzilla's radioactive

breath, Raptor-One was almost completely coated with a lightweight variation of the reinforced carbon-carbon (RCC) tiles that protected the space shuttle from the heat of reentry.

The propeller blades were made completely of reinforced carbon-carbon, and RCC was even used to cover the missile bays and the cannons, which were exposed only when they were being utilized.

The cockpit transparencies were made from double panes of a revolutionary new translucent Teflon, which repelled heat instantly. This allowed the Raptor to take a direct blast of Godzilla's breath, with temperatures in excess of 1,200°F, without suffering damage.

The overall color scheme of Raptor-One was called "cloud gray," and there were jagged lines of purple and mauve cutting across its back and sides. Scientists conjectured that Godzilla might have trouble spotting the aircraft in the sky with this jangled color scheme.

Kip stared at the fighting machine with awe. Though he'd flown the simulator dozens of times—the mockpit was an exact duplicate of the Raptor-One's cockpit—and he knew the schematics, the performance capabilities, and the dimensions of the aircraft by heart, seeing the gigantic airplane in the flesh was still breathtaking.

I'm supposed to fly that? Kip thought nervously.

Toby whistled in admiration. Pierce was so awestruck that he couldn't stop staring, despite the fact that he'd flown this very aircraft before it was armed. Tia and Martin exchanged glances, clearly impressed.

"She's beautiful," Lori whispered. General Taggart stepped up behind the astonished group.

"There she is," he announced with pride. "Raring and ready to go. I'll give you a guided tour."

"When do we take her up, General?" Kip asked hesitantly.

"0600 tomorrow morning, son," he replied.

Saturday, May 29, 1999, 1:25 A.M.
Minnow, Alaska

The aged shaman came down from a tundra village near the Noatak River in a very remote area of Alaska far above the Seward Peninsula, where the Athabaskan people still lived by subsistence and followed the ancient traditions.

He'd been moving south for many weeks, stopping in any native Alaskan village he passed—no matter which tribe the town belonged to. Shortly after he arrived in each town, the shaman called the elders together and requested that all the men build a *qasgiq*—sweat bath—and join him in a purification ceremony.

He had much to tell them, the shaman claimed, and so they should be spiritually prepared to hear his words.

The men in Minnow, a tiny village on the shore of Norton Sound, heeded the shaman. They left their comfortable wooden houses and their color televisions and their satellite dishes and constructed a low structure out of sticks, walrus bone, and seal skins in the way of their forefathers. Then the men of the village stripped off their clothes and entered the *qasgiq*.

As per tradition, the shaman presided over the ritual ceremony. He stoked the fire built in the central pit, then banked it and tossed in some green branches to create smoke.

Soon the younger members of the tribe were coughing and complaining, but the elders hushed them.

Craig Westerly, a young anthropologist from Columbia University in New York City, was also inside the *qasgiq*. He had been living among the native Alaskans—or what those in the "Lower Forty-eight" might call Eskimos—for six months. As soon as he heard about the ceremony, he approached the old shaman and pleaded with the ancient medicine man to be admitted to the *qasgiq*. To his surprise, he was granted permission immediately.

"The *inua*—spirits—want everyone to know what is coming," the old man had said.

Westerly endured the heat and the smoke without complaint, and his quiet determination impressed some of the other natives who before had only laughed at the white man who tried to understand their ways.

As the smoke filled the tiny structure, one of the elders handed Westerly a bundle of tightly woven reeds and showed him how to cover his mouth to filter out the worst of the smoke. The intensity of the heat increased, and the smoke began to sting and burn his eyes. But Westerly was happy. He was able to observe firsthand this important ancient ritual of the native Alaskans.

Soon the temperature inside the sweat house became so intense that the men's skin turned red and some of them began to roll about the floor in agony. Westerly was one of them.

When the fire finally died down and the hut began to cool, some of the men helped Westerly to the shore of a nearby lake. He screamed in shock and agony when the men threw him into the icy waters. There was no shame in this. Many of the younger native Alaskans cried out as loud when they were thrown into the lake.

When the shaman felt that the men were prepared, he led them back to the *qasgiq*. They sang songs and told stories until the sun set, at around eleven o'clock. It was May, and daylight lasted almost twenty hours.

After the villagers swapped tales, the shaman rose and finally began to speak.

"For six long months I have dreamed," the old man said in a halting voice. "The dream has bothered me."

The other men listened with rapt attention as the shaman spoke. They knew that the dreams of a medicine man were portentous, and they listened to him without question.

"Though my totem is the owl, I have dreamed only of the Thunderbird!"

The native Alaskans gasped, and Craig Westerly noted their reaction. He knew he was hearing something important, and Westerly tried to memorize what the shaman said. He had to rely on memory, because no writing implements were permitted in the *qasgiq*.

"Did the Thunderbird speak?" one of the villagers asked the shaman.

The old man nodded. "The Thunderbird told me that it is awake. That it is coming on mighty wings to the places of man, for the Thunderbird may soon be needed."

A ripple of fear swept the tiny hut as the men of the village digested this news.

"What else did the Thunderbird say?" Westerly asked in the tongue of his hosts. Slowly, the shaman turned and gazed at the white man.

"I have spoken with the Thunderbird in my dreams, lo these many nights," the shaman continued. "His spirit visits me when I sleep, and he spreads his red wings and spits fire and lightning…"

Some of the villagers began to beat their drums and chant. One elder rose and danced naked around the sweat house, mumbling an ancient invocation.

"And the Thunderbird has told me a great secret," the old man announced. "The Thunderbird has told me his name."

The men all gasped in awe and amazement. Even the dancing man stopped in mid-step. Everyone gazed at the ancient shaman.

There was great power in knowing a creature's true name, and this shaman possessed much power if he knew the true name of the Thunderbird.

"Can you—can you speak this name?" the village elder stammered.

The shaman nodded again, his eyes burning intently. "The Thunderbird's secret name is *Rodan!*"

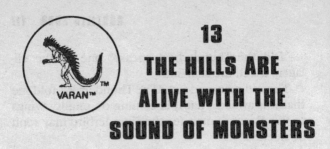

13

THE HILLS ARE ALIVE WITH THE SOUND OF MONSTERS

Sunday, May 30, 1999, 11:33 A.M.
The Sierra Madre del Sur Mountains
55 miles north of Jamiltepec, Mexico

Robin Halliday had been chasing Varan more doggedly than the Mexican government. When the creature disappeared into the vast forests of the Yucatán Peninsula, the American public's interest in the monster disappeared as well.

What Robin thought was going to be her big break—the live on-camera reports covering the monster's rampage south of the United States border—was all but forgotten by the network. Especially after the Kamacuras appeared in Kansas.

Now Robin's old boss, Nick Gordon, along with his pal Brian Shimura, were covering the attack in Kansas. She snorted in disgust as she got ready for another day chasing the elusive Varan. *It's the good ol' boy network,* she thought. *But at least that story is pretty much over.*

Robin brushed her long dark hair in front of a dirty, flyspecked mirror. She sighed as she gazed at her reflection.

Look at me. I've only been out of the shower— or what passes for a shower—for fifteen minutes and I'm already sweating.

She glanced hopefully up at the ceiling fan, but the machine was already going full blast. The blades turned in lazy circles, barely stirring the air in her sweltering hotel room.

It's no better than every other town I've been in the last few days, she thought miserably. *Nobody in rural Mexico seems to have heard of air conditioning.*

Actually, there was plenty of air conditioning, and soft beds, and sunny beaches, just 150 miles away.

But Acapulco ain't where the action is, she reminded herself stubbornly. *I'm here for a story…and I've already got a lead.*

When Robin was satisfied with her makeup, she donned her Banana Republic khaki shorts and hiking boots. Then she went to fetch her camera "man."

Robin left her room and stepped into the narrow, uncarpeted hallway. There was an almost cool breeze flowing through the corridor from open windows on either end of the hallway.

Robin went to the next room and banged on the door. She heard Linda mumble something from the other side of the room.

"It's me, Robin," she said. "Open up."

The door swung open and Robin saw her cameraperson, Linda Carlisle, still wrapped in a towel.

"I got up late," Linda mumbled. "Be ready in a couple of minutes…"

Robin rolled her eyes as she stepped into the

other woman's hotel room. "Come *on*, Linda!" Robin whined. "We don't want to miss anything."

Linda turned and faced the younger girl. "Listen, kid," she barked. "We've been chasing that monster for a week with no success. Trust me, this "lead" of yours is just another wild-goose chase. Varan's probably disappeared for another million years!"

"No way, Lin!" Robin protested. "I got this story from official sources."

"You mean Colonel Huerta?" said Linda dubiously. "He just wanted to get the *gringa* drunk and take advantage of her."

"Which reminds me," Robin said. "When I'm interviewing a news source, don't drag me away. It's embarrassing!"

"You're not even eighteen, Robin," Linda argued. "And you were in a *bar,* talking to a *soldier*…"

"Jeez, Linda," Robin sighed. "You're only twenty-five yourself. And you are *not* my mother, so stop acting like her. Anyway, I only wanted to be social."

Linda pulled some comfortable clothes out of the closet. *No, I'm not your mother,* Linda wanted to say. *But somebody has to look after you. You're too young and headstrong to watch out for yourself…*

"Where's Mike?" Linda asked instead as she pulled on her shorts.

"He's gone out to find some transportation," Robin answered as she checked herself in the mirror again. Linda had to elbow the girl aside to comb her own hair.

Worst case of Diane Sawyer disease I ever saw!

Linda thought sourly. There was another knock at the door.

"Linda," a man's voice called from the other side. "Is Robin in there with you?"

"Yeah, Mike," Linda replied. "We'll be right out."

Ten minutes later, Robin, Linda, and their producer/director, Mike Timko, stood in front of the rickety hotel waiting for the rest of their team to show up.

Five minutes later, Tony Batista skidded his battered Land Rover to a halt in front of them. Pete Hamilton, the sound man, was in the front seat next to him. From the way Pete looked, it was obvious he had been up partying all night with Tony.

Linda had to admit that Batista, the young INN liaison officer for Mexico, knew his way around the country. *And* he knew all the hot spots, too. It gave Linda a good idea of the kind of journalists Tony Batista was used to escorting around.

Once again, Linda wondered why she was even in this stupid business. *I wanted to be a documentary filmmaker once,* she remembered. *Before I realized I would have to make a living.*

Now she was far from her Ohio home, traveling with two party animals, a workaholic director, and a teen princess. Worst of all, they were chasing a big *lizard*.

Well, at least the countryside is nice...

Everyone loaded up their stuff and climbed aboard the Land Rover. Then Tony raced through the narrow streets of Jamiltepec. To Linda's surprise, the usually jammed boulevards were practically empty—until they got near a splendid stone cathedral. The plaza around it was packed with townspeople.

"What's going on here?" Robin asked. Linda almost moaned out loud, but Tony replied with the patience of a born diplomat.

"It is Sunday, *señorita*," he answered from behind the wheel. "They are going to pray."

"Oh," Robin replied.

"There is food in the cooler, and drink as well," Tony offered. "There is juice, and there is coffee in the thermos."

Linda was impressed with Tony's English. His accent was almost flawless.

Bottles of orange juice were passed around. Only Pete Hamilton refused.

"Come on, Pete," Linda teased. "Juice is good for a hangover." Pete's answer was to groan and slip on his sunglasses.

They drove out of the town and into some rugged hills thick with trees. So far, the narrow dirt road remained clear and easily passable. Within a mile, they came upon a wide clearing.

"Soon this area will be another resort hotel for tourists," Tony remarked. "Over there they are building a golf course…"

They drove farther and higher along the dusty road. Soon the gentle, rolling hills gave way to the rugged Sierra Madre mountains. The verdant vegetation gradually changed to rocky cliffs and jagged outcroppings.

"The village of Tehetepec is about five miles from here," Tony informed them. "It is an interesting place. The whole town is built around a man-made stone circle of pre-Columbian origin."

"Do they know *who* built it?" Mike asked.

"No," Tony replied, shaking his head. "No one knows who built it—or *why*. They do know it was built long before the coming of the Mayans and the Aztecs."

Robin grew excited. "Colonel Huerta told me all about that circle!" she exclaimed. "It sounds like a really cool place."

"Well…" Linda sighed. "At least this trip won't be a *total* waste."

"Varan's here!" Robin insisted. "You'll see. Colonel Huerta told me that his men were coming up here to patrol tomorrow! There have been reports of missing cattle and noise in the hills. Colonel Huerta told me that his superiors think that Varan came down around here."

Pete Hamilton adjusted his sunglasses. "It would be nice if the Mexican Air Force could actually track him on radar."

"They can't," said Mike, "according to the reports. On radar, Varan just looks like a cloud formation or a flock of birds."

Pete snorted. "What is it, Stealth Lizard?"

"That's what headquarters told me," Mike insisted. "But the U.S. military can track it by satellite, and their surveillance suggests that Varan has flown south—toward the border of Guatemala."

"Colonel Huerta says different," Robin argued.

Linda rolled her eyes again but didn't speak.

"Varan's taken to the air twice before," Mike stated. "Both times, the creature headed southwest."

"Varan is *not* in Guatemala," Robin argued stubbornly. "Why would Colonel Huerta be *here* if Varan was *there?*"

The kid's got a good point, Linda conceded. *And the so-called kaijuologists have been wrong more than they've been right...*

Suddenly, Linda's musings were interrupted by a thunderous rumbling. The Land Rover had driven onto a rickety wooden bridge that quaked and vibrated under its wheels. As she peered out the window at the worn, battered structure, Linda wasn't sure it could hold the weight of a mule, let alone a car.

Everyone suddenly grew very quiet. Even Robin shut up.

Tony Batista drove briskly along, humming tunelessly, not even bothering to slow down.

When the vehicle was in the very center of the hundred-foot span, the whole bridge actually began to sway. A board from the roadway broke loose and crashed to the forest far below as Linda watched in horror. Her keen eye spotted a few other pieces of the bridge lying down there, too.

When the Land Rover finally drove onto the dirt road again, the INN news team breathed a collective sigh of relief. Tony continued to drive along as if nothing had ever been wrong, but Linda swore she caught a hint of a smile on his face in the rearview mirror.

I'm gonna have to keep an eye on this bird, she thought slyly.

Suddenly, everyone was thrown forward as Tony slammed on the brakes. The Land Rover bounced off a huge stone in the road, then skidded to one side in the loose dirt. Finally, it came to a shuddering halt. As the cloud of dry dust settled around them, the stunned news team peered through the windshield.

At a bend in the road ahead, the stone and adobe remains of a crushed building blocked the road. On the opposite side, a wall remained standing—though it leaned precariously against a splintered tree.

Linda popped open the door and stepped out. She gazed past the ruins up the road to a huge stone wall in the distance.

No, not a wall, she remembered. *That's the stone circle.* Mike appeared at her side. "What do you think?" he whispered.

"I think—" But Linda was interrupted by a blast of cool, sweet air that swept down through the center of the ruined village.

"Do you smell that?" Tony hissed.

"Yeah," Mike nodded. "Pure oxygen…"

"It's up there," Pete whispered. "Varan is up there. I *know* it."

"What do we do?" Tony asked.

It was Robin who replied in a firm voice. "We're reporters, aren't we? What do you think we're going to do? We're going to go up there and film a report."

"Out of the mouths of babes," Linda muttered.

Together, the INN news team returned to the vehicle and collected their equipment. Linda glanced at the wall again and snatched up the lighter of the two cameras. She figured she'd be doing some climbing. When they were all ready, the group trudged up the road toward the ruined village. As they walked through the debris-laden streets, it was apparent that Tehetepec was deserted.

The people must have fled, Linda thought as she scanned the ruins. There was hardly a wall left standing in the tiny village. Even the stone well was broken and filled with debris.

Finally, they reached the stone circle. It rose almost thirty feet upward from the center of the town. The stones were uneven, and moss and vegetation grew between them.

"Over there," Mike said, pointing. Linda and Robin turned and saw a flight of high, irregular steps leading up to the top of the stone circle.

Just then, they were blasted by another gush of cool, oxygen-rich air. Linda shivered.

At the stairs, Mike took the lead. He climbed quickly, though sometimes he had to pull himself upward with his arms because the stairway was so uneven. He turned and helped Linda and Robin. Tony and Pete struggled on by themselves.

When Mike scrambled up the last step, he froze.

"What do you see, Mr. Timko?" Robin called.

"Shh, quiet," the director whispered.

On top of the huge stone ring, Varan lay sprawled out in the hot tropical sun. Like most reptiles, Varan, it seemed, liked sunning itself on a rock.

The sight was incredible. The creature's eyes were closed, and its breathing was slow and regular. The multicolored, pebbly hide of the giant reptile gleamed in the bright Mexican sun.

"Get your camera ready, Linda," Mike whispered. Then he turned to Robin. "Here's your chance, kid," he said.

Robin swallowed hard, but she was determined to do her job. Pete broke out his sound stuff, and the team was ready in minutes.

"Okay," Mike announced. "Let's get this on the first take—and then get the hell out of here!"

But just as Robin took up a position with the sleeping monster directly behind her, a Mexican military helicopter appeared overhead. Another chopper flew in behind the first.

The noise was incredible, and the downdraft almost blew the INN news team off the edge of the stone structure. Linda dropped to her belly and started to film. Pete dropped to the stone wall next to her, extending his boom mike.

Tony and Mike ducked, too, and huddled against the warm stone. Robin just stood there, paralyzed.

"Get down, kid!" Mike hissed. Linda and Pete were too busy doing their job to notice Robin. Just then, Varan's reptilian eyes opened, and the creature awoke with a threatening rumble. With a speed that belied its tremendous size, Varan rose up on its four legs as the helicopters hovered overhead.

The first chopper quickly sped out of range when its occupants saw the creature, but the other just hovered over it.

Robin stood, still clutching her microphone, frozen in place.

Suddenly, Varan turned to face the hovering helicopter. The creature scrambled sideways and whipped its long tail. Linda and Pete and Tony and Mike all ducked their heads as the tip of the tail swished over them.

But Robin did not move, and the tail brushed her off the stone circle. Robin squealed and disappeared over the edge.

"Robin!" Linda cried.

Varan roared and rose on its hind legs.

"Get off the wall!" Mike shouted, grabbing Linda by the scruff of her neck. The four of them tumbled down the stone steps as Varan spread out its forearms and inhaled. Gusts of wind roared around them as the creature filled its sacs with hydrogen. Then, with a final gust, Varan leaped into the sky.

Linda looked up in time to see the Mexican Army Huey helicopter explode as the monster swiped it out of the air with its forepaw. The main part of the burning wreckage tumbled into the jungle below the hilltop, though smaller debris rained down all around them.

Finally, Mike rose. "Is everyone all right?" he asked. Linda lifted the remains of her camera and nodded. Then she pulled out the tape cassette from the battered device and pocketed it. Pete was bruised and bleeding, but he was okay. So was Tony.

"Oh my god!" Linda cried. "Where's Robin?"

In the eerie silence that followed the skirmish, they heard the young woman calling for help. The four of them ran around the base of the stone structure, searching for the lost intern.

"There she is!" Tony shouted, pointing.

Robin was waist-deep in a pool of slime, trying vainly to drag herself out of the slippery, slimy slop.

She looked up when she saw the others approach. Linda held her nose, and Pete, still suffering from the effects of a hangover, gagged.

"I fell in a swamp!" Robin whined.

Linda got closer. "That's not a swamp," she announced. "That's Varan poop!"

Mike almost laughed. Then he took a closer look.

"Come out of there, Robin," he said ominously. "And whatever you do, don't turn around."

Of course, like Lot's wife, the stubborn intern did just that. Then she began to scream and scream. Robin didn't stop screaming until Mike and Tony dragged her out of the pool of dung.

Linda held her nose and stepped closer for a better look.

Well, she thought grimly, *at least we know what happened to the people of Tehetepec.* Linda turned away from the pile of half-digested human remains that floated in the slimy pool of lizard droppings just in time to watch Pete blow chunks.

MOTHRA™

14
DREAMS AND
PROPHECIES

"Yes, I hear you," Lori replied. Or maybe she didn't really speak. Maybe she just thought the words.

Out of the darkness, motes of brilliant light and color began to form all around her. Then she heard the music…a melody so beautiful it tugged at her soul. Uncontrollably, tears welled up, and she squeezed her eyes shut as she painfully relived every regret, every shameful moment she ever had in her young life.

"I'm so sorry," Lori whispered through tears.

She felt forgiveness wash over her like warm spring rain.

When she opened her eyes again, the motes of light had transformed themselves into a million butterflies. Each one floated in the air and gazed at her with jewel-like, multifaceted eyes of brilliant blue.

Then, in the center of the swarm of beautiful, delicate winged creatures, more vibrant colors swirled and collided, forming a blinding-bright mass that glowed with an inner fire.

Suddenly, the form of a woman wearing a

diaphanous gown of many colors stood before her. The woman was so close that Lori could touch her. But as she reached out, the glowing entity spread its gown wide to reveal its true self to her.

And Lori realized that it wasn't a woman at all. What she saw now was the being's true shape— the shape of a huge butterfly with gentle, intelligent eyes.

Mothra...the name sprang into Lori's mind.

"Mothra?" Lori asked. The creature stared at her but did not answer.

"What do you want?" Lori pleaded. "I want to understand."

"It comes..." The creature's thoughts filled Lori's mind. *"The destroyer with three heads...the king of terror, the devastator of a hundred worlds, and the enemy of all life..."*

"What?" Lori pleaded. "What comes? Who comes?"

"Gaze at me and I will show you the face of it..."

Lori's screams cut through the medical center and echoed off the antiseptic white walls. She violently thrashed about on the bed, tearing the sheets off her body and ripping the electronic monitors off her forehead.

Inside the lab's glass booth, Dr. Irene Markham hastily shut down the computers and hit the mike.

"Are you okay, Ms. Angelo?"

Lori heard the doctor's voice over the intercom. She blinked away tears and sat up in the bed. Her fingers closed on something, and she looked down.

The electronic monitoring sensors were clutched in her hand.

"Did I rip these off in my sleep?" Lori asked dazedly.

Dr. Markham, behind the soundproof glass wall, keyed the mike again. "It's okay," she said, trying not to sound concerned. "I think we've got what we need now, Lori. You can go back to your room, if you like."

Monday, May 31, 1999, 12:47 A.M.
Ninunak, Alaska

Craig Westerly was awakened by the sound of the old man moaning in his sleep. Hastily, he pulled the down comforter off and crawled to the other side of the tent.

The old shaman was dreaming again.

Westerly reached into his parka and pulled out his handheld tape recorder. He switched it on and held it above the shaman's face. As the old man mumbled in his sleep, Westerly recorded his words.

The shaman talked in his sleep almost every night now. Though the undergraduate didn't speak the shaman's language very well, he sometimes understood the Athabaskan words and phrases. By taping the sleep talk, Westerly was preserving it for translation at a later date by someone more fluent in the shaman's language than he.

Westerly had come to Alaska to record some of the native folktales, legends, tribal histories, and myths that had been overlooked by previous researchers. He'd done okay, but the work hadn't been as rewarding as he had hoped.

That is, until he met this shaman.

Though Westerly rejected the old man's warning about the coming of the Thunderbird, he realized that the ancient medicine man was a fount of knowledge about the myths of his people. So, with the shaman's grudging permission, Westerly had followed the old man from one native Alaskan village to another, each time taking part in the sweat bath rituals, listening to the stories and the prophecy about the coming of the Thunderbird.

In the last few days, Westerly had noticed a change in his attitude toward the shaman. He had once regarded the old mystic as a curiosity—a living anthropological exhibit. Lately, he'd come to respect the old man's wisdom more and more. Some of Westerly's anthropology professors had warned him away from that kind of thinking.

"Don't identify with your subjects," Professor Hendricks cautioned. "It ruined Margaret Mead, and it will ruin you!"

In truth, the old shaman reminded Westerly of his college professor. It was odd to compare a famous scholar with a tribal shaman, but there were more similarities than differences. Perhaps science and religion were just two equally valid ways of looking at life and searching for truth.

Suddenly, Westerly was jolted from his memories of college as the old man opened his eyes and looked up at him. Embarrassed, the student hid the tape recorder. The old man blinked with confusion, then looked right at him.

"Rodan is coming," he whispered.

At that moment, the wind abruptly kicked up. The blasts whistled across the tundra, and the canvas tents began to shake as the air battered them. In the hunting camp, others began to awaken and cry out in confusion and alarm.

Westerly heard a loud crash and watched the party's satellite dish and cellular phone system roll across the tundra, sparks flashing.

As the shaman rose from his sleeping bag, Westerly pulled on his boots and stumbled out of the tent. The Alaskans were running about the camp excitedly, trying to secure their kayaks—and their valuable pelts—before the freak windstorm carried everything off.

Westerly barely got to his feet before he was knocked backward by a tremendous gust of air. The tent collapsed behind him, the tent poles rattled as they were swept away. The icy water of the tundra began to blow too, filling the air with cold droplets of stinging ice.

"Look!" a frightened voice cried. *"Look at the moon!"*

Craig Westerly looked up into the night sky. Darkness had only fallen a little over an hour before, and daybreak was less than three hours away. But at the moment, the moon was big and bright.

Westerly gazed upward, squinting against the cold wind. The sky seemed empty, except for a few high, thin clouds. And then he saw it. A moan escaped his lips when he saw the huge, batlike silhouette cut across the bright face of the moon.

Suddenly, a wild, sustained, cackling roar echoed

across the tundra. The sky was filled with electric flashes, like heat lightning on a hot summer night.

Magically, the shaman appeared at Westerly's side. The old man gazed up into the sky with eyes filled with joy and awe.

"The Thunderbird," the shaman cried, his arms spread wide. "Rodan, the mighty Thunderbird, has awakened!"

Ninety minutes later, an object of tremendous size and speed was tracked on radar as it approached the air space over Fairbanks, Alaska. Air traffic controllers warned commercial aircraft away as the object rapidly approached Nenana Airport.

The object was moving through the sky from the northwest at nearly 400 miles per hour, at an altitude of 55,000 feet. When an air corridor was hastily cleared of all other aircraft, four F-16A Fighting Falcons were scrambled out of nearby Eielson Air Force Base to intercept the object and determine its nature.

The aircraft flew in a classic "finger four" pattern—two flights of two planes each. One aircraft, the aggressor, flew with eyes forward and down. His wingman, on defense, flew looking back and up. Each all-weather fighter was equipped with four AIM-9 Sidewinder air-to-air missiles and a fuselage-mounted Vulcan cannon with 500 rounds of ammunition.

If this bogey turned into a bandit, then the Falcons from Eielson were ready.

At 60,000 feet, the formation approached the unidentified object. The dawn was just breaking in the skies over Fairbanks when Captain Bill Wellman painted the bogey with his forward-looking infrared targeting system.

"This is Kodiak One," he radioed. "I got the bogey coming in dead ahead and below us, at 55,000 feet. Do you have a visual?"

"We got 'em," Captain Philip "Bud" Bundy radioed from Kodiak Three. He and Kodiak Four split from the formation and dived toward the target.

"You see him yet, Three?" Captain Ken Kelly asked from the cockpit of Kodiak Four.

"Negative," Captain Bundy replied. "Just a lot of clouds. But I got it on my scopes."

Captain Kelly and his wingman, "Bud" Bundy, were often paired for duty lately. A television station in Fairbanks had started airing old reruns of *Married...with Children,* and everyone got a good laugh when they saw "Kelly and Bud" on the duty roster.

"Coming out of some clouds here," Captain Bundy reported. "But—wait a minute!"

"What the hell is *that?*" Captain Kelly cried.

High above them and out of visual range, Captain Wellman was getting antsy. "What do you see, Kodiak Three...Kodiak Four? Reply immediately," he demanded.

"It's...it's a giant *bird,* Kodiak One!" Captain Bundy replied incredulously.

In his cockpit, Captain Wellman rolled his eyes. "Can you verify, Four?" he asked skeptically.

There was a pause before Captain Kelly replied. Then, in a calm, even, businesslike voice, he answered his flight leader. "That is an affirmative, Kodiak One," he said. "We are tracking a giant flying animal."

Captain Wellman keyed his mike. "Okay," he said. "Get a picture."

"Roger," Kelly replied. "I'm going to line up behind it and make like Spielberg. The intel boys are gonna love this footage!"

"Roger that, Kodiak Four," Captain Bundy radioed. "I'm going to move alongside of it for a visual."

Captain Kelly keyed his mike to order his wingman off, but Wellman spoke first and overruled him.

"Roger. But be careful, Kodiak Three," the flight leader commanded. "And keep your mikes open…"

Damn, Kelly thought. *I got a bad feeling about this…*

The other pilots could clearly hear Captain Kelly and Captain Bundy breathing into their face masks as they kicked in their afterburners to catch up with the creature, which had increased its speed in the last few moments.

Finally, Kelly maneuvered his fighter behind the *kaiju.* As he avoided the creature's slipstream, Kelly activated both the infrared and video cameras. Meanwhile, Bundy pushed his F-16 forward until he was flying alongside the tremendous airborne monstrosity. He whistled into his mask. The sky was getting brighter, and Captain Bundy could make out some of the details.

"This is not a bird," he announced. "There are no feathers. It's a reptile, I think. It looks like one of those dinosaurs you see in movies."

Bundy urged the stick ahead, and the Falcon cut through the air like a bullet.

"I don't see what is propelling the creature forward. It's not flapping its wings," Captain Bundy informed the others. "I'm moving up toward its head," he said, fighting the stick. "It's pretty choppy here…"

A moment passed before Bundy spoke again. "Okay, I see its head," he said. "There is a beak, and red eyes on either side of it. There are spikes, or horns of some kind, on the crest of the creature's head." There was another pause in the transmission. When Bundy spoke again, the other pilots could hear the apprehension in his voice. "I think it sees me, Kodiak One," he said. "Its head is turning in my direction…the pupil of its eye has just narrowed…"

Suddenly, his voice grew more excited. "I see some flashes, like electricity, along the spikes…it's turning—"

Then Kodiak Three went off the air.

"Kodiak Three!" Captain Wellman cried. "Kodiak Three…come in, Bundy!"

"Mayday, mayday…I see him," Captain Kelly radioed from his position behind the creature. "Kodiak Three is in a flat spin, heading for the deck. Repeat, Bundy's aircraft is out of control."

"Get out of there, Kelly," Kodiak One commanded. "Get away from that creature *now!*" Kodiak Four was about to cut his speed and drop back when the gigantic creature dived to one side and cut directly across his jet's path.

"The bird is changing direction!" Captain Kelly cried as he fought his joystick to avoid a midair collision. Just then, a warning beeped in his cockpit. "I'm caught in the slipstream," he cried. "I'm in a stall. Repeat, I'm in a stall…"

Captain Kelly didn't need the alarms going off in his cockpit to know that his engine was dead. He shut out the sound of the klaxons and the urgent questions over the radio and concentrated on regaining control of his aircraft.

"Kodiak Four! Come in, Kelly," Captain Wellman demanded over the radio. He still flew behind and above the other aircraft. The captain cursed. Ken Kelly was off the air, too.

Captain Wellman sent out a general SOS. Back at Eielson, emergency crews were already lifting off with rescue choppers.

Because their fuel was mostly depleted, the two remaining aircraft of the Kodiak flight were ordered back to base.

The bogey, whatever it was, was moving quickly toward Canadian air space, and a Canadian Air Force base across the border in British Columbia had been alerted. The air controller assured Captain Wellman that this mission was over.

As Kodiak One led his wingman back to base, he wondered just what the missing pilots really *had* seen…and what really had happened to them.

Once before in his Air Force career, Captain Kelly had stalled out. He was flying an F-16 that time, too, on a training mission over Arizona.

Another fighter cut across his path, and the slip-stream choked his engine. At that time, Kelly had only a few dozen hours in the F-16, and no matter what he did, he just couldn't regain control of his aircraft. To his shame, Kelly had to eject.

The multimillion-dollar fighter plane had been lost. The inquiry had cleared him of all wrong-doing, but Kelly always believed he failed both the Air Force and himself that day.

Now, as he spun toward the earth in the Alaska dawn, Kelly vowed he would not lose a second air-craft. He methodically followed all the procedures to restart his engine, and when they all failed, he improvised. He fought the controls, trying every-thing he knew, and suddenly, he had a successful restart.

With the engine back on-line, it was only a moment more before he regained control of his air-craft. With a whoop of triumph, Captain Kelly was back in business.

Suddenly weak from the tension of his near-fatal ordeal, Kelly took stock again: He was low on fuel and was now flying only a thousand feet above the Alaskan countryside. As he climbed to a safer alti-tude, he reestablished contact with Eielson AFB, and with Captain Wellman in Kodiak One.

They were glad to hear from him.

Then Wellman asked him about his missing wingman. "I saw him go down," Kelly answered. "No chute."

"Roger, Kodiak Four," Wellman replied.

"But, hey, sir," Kelly added hopefully, "Bundy had a long time to punch out…if he had to, that is…"

Still weak from his brush with death, Captain Ken Kelly guided his fighter—with the valuable video of the creature—back to base.

Captain Bundy wasn't so lucky.

When the single blast of Rodan's electric fire struck his Falcon, it shorted out every electronic system in the aircraft.

The Fighting Falcon, touted as the world's first electric airplane because of its wireless control surfaces, was rendered totally inoperative by the electronic disruption. Even systems that were supposedly shielded from a nuclear weapon's electromagnetic pulse were totally fried by Rodan's ray.

Everything froze, including the radio, the distress signal, and the ejection seat. Bundy tugged at the handle a dozen times, but the ACES II ejection seat failed to respond.

It took several minutes for Captain Bundy's aircraft to spin to the ground. Though the forces of gravity tore at him and threw him from side to side inside the cockpit, Captain Bundy never lost consciousness.

He fought the dead control stick the whole time, and watched with grim fatalism as the ground rushed up to meet him.

15
LOSSES

Monday, May 31, 1999, 3:23 P.M.
Project Valkyrie headquarters
Nellis Air Force Base, Nevada

General Taggart hung up the phone and rubbed his tired eyes.

Another kaiju, he thought grimly. *And this one can fly at incredible speeds....* The general promptly lifted the receiver again and dialed his second-in-command.

"Colonel Krupp," the voice on the other end answered crisply.

"We've got a Code One," Taggart announced.

"I understand sir," Krupp replied after a pause. Then the line went dead.

At that moment, there was a knock on the general's door.

Who in the hell is bothering me now? the general wondered sourly.

"It's Dr. Markham," the woman said from the other side of the door. "May I come in, General?"

She didn't wait for an answer. Instead, the strong-willed psychiatrist pushed the door open and stepped in, then closed the door behind her.

Dr. Markham, an attractive woman in her early forties, was wearing her white lab coat and clutching a bundle of papers under one arm. She wore little makeup, and her auburn hair was streaked with a hint of gray. She wore it tied back, rather haphazardly. Some errant strands had broken free and were dangling in front of her green eyes. As she pushed the hair away from her face with a casual gesture, the general looked up at her.

"I'm sorry, Doctor," Taggart said with undisguised irritation. "I don't have time to speak to you right now. We're about to go on alert."

"Then you'd *better* speak to me, General," Dr. Markham said, thrusting the printouts under Taggart's nose, "because this is about one of your recruits!"

The general blinked. "You have two minutes."

Dr. Markham met his gaze, then unfolded the printouts and placed them in front of him.

"These are the results of our tests on Ms. Lorelei Marie Angelo, Caucasian female, age seventeen," the psychiatrist announced. "I want you to take note of this brain scan."

The general skimmed the lines on the printout, but it was clear he didn't understand their importance.

"Angelo has exhibited sleep disorders in the last several weeks, correct?" Dr. Markham asked.

The general nodded.

"And this sleep disorder has impacted negatively on her performance in the program, correct?"

The general nodded again.

"We placed electrodes on her head to measure brain activity during her deep sleep cycle, when she was experiencing what we call Rapid Eye

Movement, or REM, sleep," Dr. Markham continued. "This is the result."

She pointed to a ragged line on the printout. "At this point in the REM cycle, Lori Angelo begins to dream." She traced the line with her finger. "Look at how agitated her brain activity becomes at this point. Now look at this. *This* is where the actual dream begins..."

She stared at the general, waiting for him to react.

"What's that second line underneath the first one?" the general asked. "I don't think that's normal."

Dr. Markham raised her eyebrow. "Precisely," she replied.

"So what do you think it means?" the general demanded.

"Let me put it this way," Dr. Markham replied. "If this were *The Exorcist*, I'd say Lori Angelo is possessed."

Half a world away, the Japanese Defense Force *Yubari*-class frigate *Yubetsu* arrived at the last known location of the research vessel *Kongo-Maru*.

The commander, Captain Kubo, approached the area cautiously, both with sonar and search radar active and pinging. The naval officer knew the reason the missing ship was in these waters in the first place, and he also understood that there could be only one possible reason for the *Kongo-Maru*'s disappearance.

The *Yubetsu* circled the area in a wide search

pattern for six hours. At 0800, they found debris—
life vests, a broken plastic chair, some plastic foam
packing material, some instant *ramen* packs.
Fifteen minutes later, they spotted the life raft. It
looked, from a distance, as if there were three people aboard the tiny inflatable craft.

Captain Kubo sounded general alert and notified
the medical staff that casualties were about to be
brought aboard. The *Yubetsu*'s horn blared continuously, but no one on the life raft responded to her
repeated calls.

Project Valkyrie's command center was fully activated when the G-Force team responded to the
Code One alert. But when they took their assigned
places at the control stations, one seat was still
empty. "Where's Lori?" Toby asked Tia Shimura.

The girl shrugged her shoulders. Then General
Taggart and Colonel Krupp entered the center.

"We've got a situation," the general announced.
"I want you all to pay attention to the large monitor..." But before the lights could dim, Toby spoke.

"Where's Lori?" he demanded. "Where's my co-
pilot?"

Krupp looked at General Taggart, but the officer's stony face was unreadable. The silence
stretched on.

"Ms. Angelo has been removed from active duty,"
Taggart announced finally. "We hope this situation
will be temporary."

"What's wrong with her?" Tia asked.

"No further questions!" Colonel Krupp barked.
"Eyes front."

The lights in the command center dimmed, and the general began to brief them.

"Sixteen hours ago, seismic instruments detected a mild earthquake near the North Pole. The epicenter was in such a remote area that there were no witnesses or casualties.

"Six hours later, radar tracking stations all over Alaska began to detect a large object in the sky, moving at about 400 miles per hour at an altitude of 55,000 feet. The object was moving from the polar region toward Fairbanks.

"Four F-16s were scrambled out of Eielson to intercept. This footage was shot by one of the pilots…"

The large center television screen came alive—first with static, then with a video image of a dawn sky. Suddenly, a tiny object appeared in the center of the monitor. The image quickly grew in size.

"Wow!" Toby exclaimed. Martin Wong whistled. Tia, Kip, and Pierce Dillard remained gravely silent.

"This creature has been identified by kaijuologists as a mutated *Pteranodon,* a kind of prehistoric flying reptile," General Taggart continued.

"Infrared and other analyses indicate that this creature, like Godzilla, is considerably radioactive. How it was exposed to radiation is still a mystery, though we have a theory…"

Colonel Krupp stepped up to the podium, and the video image of the gigantic flying *kaiju* was replaced with a map of the polar region. On the map, an area near the East Siberian Sea was highlighted.

"Military intelligence believes that the area near

the earthquake's center, here in Siberia, was used by the former Soviet Union as a nuclear waste dumping ground. The epicenter is less than two hundred miles from the radioactive site, and they probably share the same water table."

"So," General Taggart added, "if this flying *kaiju* is indeed radioactive, then it probably came from this remote area in Siberia and was released by the quake."

"Where is the *kaiju* now?" Pierce asked.

"In Canadian air space," Colonel Krupp answered. "Even as we speak, elements of the Canadian Air Force are set to intercept and shoot down the creature..."

In the skies over the central Canadian province of Saskatchewan, a battle was raging.

Sixteen Canadair CF-5 Freedom Fighters, armed with thirty-two AIM Sidewinder missiles, intercepted Rodan. From maximum range, the fighters fired all of their missiles in the hope of bringing the creature down.

With the exception of one Sidewinder, which malfunctioned and dropped to the earth, all of the missiles struck the creature. Though Rodan's flight speed diminished, it was not harmed, so the jets moved to attack with their 20mm M39 cannons.

When the creature spotted the jets, it shifted direction and came at the fighters head-on. The jets fired their cannons, then scattered to avoid a midair collision.

Two of the Freedom Fighters could not move in

time, and Rodan slammed into them. One aircraft disintegrated instantly. The other broke in two, and the pieces spun to earth.

Neither pilot ejected in time.

As Rodan blasted past the offending airplanes, the squadron quickly re-formed and went after the monster. Coming in from behind the *kaiju*, the fourteen remaining CF-5s opened up with the cannons once again. And once again, Rodan quickly changed direction in an incredible high-speed turn that rivaled the maneuverability of the top-of-the-line fighters in NATO's arsenal.

The fighters scattered again. This time, two of the Canadian jets collided with each other. Only one pilot was able to punch out. The other was killed in the collision.

Angered by the attack, Rodan did not seek to elude the Canadian pilots. Instead, it attacked the airplanes aggressively.

Blast after blast of electric rays issued from the mutant creature's beak. With each arc of lightning, a CF-5 exploded. At one point, Rodan actually took off after an individual fighter. Though the pilot jinked and turned, he could not avoid Rodan's crushing beak.

In the end, the lone jet was snapped up in Rodan's jaws like prey. The CF-5 exploded in the creature's beak, and the pilot died. But at least the pilot had led the creature away from the rest of the squadron—allowing his comrades to escape.

The seven CF-5s limped back to their base, their ammunition and fuel nearly exhausted.

After the attack, Rodan was tracked on Canadian

and U.S. military radar. The creature had resumed its original course, and was moving toward the border of the United States at over 400 miles an hour.

When it looked as if the briefing had ended, the G-Force team rose to leave the command center. They were halted by General Taggart.

"One more thing," the general announced ominously. Everyone took their seats again.

"I have just received word that the Japanese research vessel *Kongo-Maru* was destroyed in the South Pacific. Three survivors have been picked up in a raft. One of them was dead, a victim of radiation burns."

A grim hush fell over the assembled teenagers.

"The Japanese government has just informed us that Dr. Emiko Takado, the ship's kaijuologist, was pulled alive from that raft," the general added. "She has sustained injuries and is unconscious, so we don't know what happened yet…but I think you all know the probable cause of the ship's destruction."

The general studied their faces. Kip felt as if the Air Force officer could see right through him.

"Tonight," Taggart announced, "at 2000 hours, we will redouble our training efforts and practice night attack strategies utilizing a single aircraft—at least until our personnel problems are resolved."

"Dismissed!" Colonel Krupp cried, and the G-Force team—minus one—filed out of the command center.

For the first time since he had arrived at Project

Valkyrie, Kip felt he was in real danger. As he prepared for the night flight in Raptor-One, he recalled Lori Angelo's first words to him, on the day he arrived at Nellis.

"I know you think it's cool to be selected for this mission," she said. "But just remember one thing …in Norse mythology, the Valkyries were also called the Choosers of the Slain."

GODZILLA™

16
VICTORY AT SEA

It took the combined navies of the world six days to locate Godzilla. The delay was due to the fact that everyone was looking in the wrong place. The authorities assumed that Godzilla would return to Japanese waters, as he had the last two times he made landfall.

But Godzilla surprised everyone. This time, he headed east.

The USS *Altoona*, a *Los Angeles*-class submarine heading back to its southern port at Pearl Harbor, Hawaii, located Godzilla quite by accident. In fact, there almost *was* an accident.

The submarine narrowly avoided colliding with the monster in the ocean depths. The captain surfaced immediately after the close encounter. He reported the incident, as well as his location, to Pacific command headquarters. He also informed them of Godzilla's speed and direction.

The *Altoona*'s broadcast caused consternation in military circles, and the president was notified. After a hastily arranged conference in the Oval Office, it was decided that, for the moment, the government would keep the news a secret.

The president wasn't quite ready to inform the

American people that Godzilla was only 500 miles away—and heading for the coast of California. Because the chairman of the Joint Chiefs of Staff supplied the president with weekly reports on Project Valkyrie, the commander-in-chief knew about the staff crisis in G-Force.

The president decided, in the end, that General Taggart should be notified of Godzilla's approach. However, the general was not to pass on that information to the G-Force team at this time.

The commander-in-chief wanted to try conventional forces before he committed teenagers— albeit exceptionally well-trained and well-disciplined teenagers—to mortal combat with the most powerful and destructive *kaiju* of all.

So while General Taggart pushed his team in simulated and live-fire exercises in Raptor-One and Dr. Markham conducted more experiments on Lori Angelo, elements of the Pacific fleet were steaming toward a section of the Pacific Ocean where a confrontation between an ancient monster and modern, high-tech weapons was about to commence.

The presidential order put General Taggart between a rock and a hard place. More than anything else, the general wanted to get the team in shape for a confrontation with Godzilla in the near future. But he was not permitted to give them the knowledge that would spur them on and give them a sense of urgency.

Worse still, the general was facing a kind of mutiny over the situation with Lori Angelo. Her teammates remained loyal to her, and wanted to know why she'd been suspended from G-Force so unfairly. Even Colonel Krupp questioned his commander's decision.

General Taggart wanted to know why, too. So he kept Lori on the base—isolated from the others—instead of sending her to a psychiatric institution for more extensive study, as Dr. Markham had suggested. So far, Lori was cooperating, and she remained under the watchful eye of Dr. Markham.

On the morning of June 8, elements of the Pacific fleet, under the command of Rear Admiral John C. Shiller, prepared to face Godzilla as the creature arrived in the shallow waters off the coast of California.

On the bridge of the nuclear-powered aircraft carrier USS *Nimitz*, Admiral Shiller watched the tranquil waters of the Pacific. Because Godzilla was being escorted by two *Los Angeles*-class submarines, Shiller knew its location at all times.

On the bridge with the admiral, Dr. Max Birchwood scanned the electronic instruments. He watched the image of Godzilla on sonar as the creature moved into attack range.

"Has all commercial shipping been cleared out of the area?" Admiral Shiller asked.

Captain Niles Carnahan nodded. "The last ship was moved out of the area two hours ago," he informed his commander.

"Then you have my permission to alert the submarines," the admiral announced. Instantly, officers on the bridge sent the command out to a fleet of subs waiting in Godzilla's path.

Dr. Birchwood listened to the radio chatter with anticipation. He knew the plan. He had helped formulate it. But the kaijuologist wasn't confident that the scheme would succeed. He had studied Dr. Nobeyama's research on Godzilla, and was convinced that the creature was indestructible.

However, Dr. Birchwood had been ordered to formulate a plan, so he did. But now, as Phase One of his attack went into action, the nervous kaijuologist had grave misgivings.

"All submarines stand by," the First Officer spoke into the radio. Then, after a moment, the admiral gave the command.

"Launch torpedoes!"

A hundred miles away, the fleet of submarines fired a battery of torpedoes at the oncoming monster. The torpedoes were not intended to kill, but to drive Godzilla to the surface for the *real* attack—for even as the torpedoes were being fired deep beneath the blue waters of the Pacific, a squadron of F-14 Tomcats launched from the *Nimitz* circled in the sky like birds of prey.

Hovering less than fifty feet above the waves, three Sikorsky CH-53E Super Stallion helicopters waited for Godzilla to appear. Equipped with anti-submarine warfare gear, the choppers acted as forward air control for the fighters that circled above. The helicopter crews listened intently to their radios and the sonar operator as the torpedo attack was launched in the ocean below.

For what seemed like an eternity after the command to fire was given, nothing happened. The sea below the choppers remained calm.

Then, suddenly, the helos' ASW sonar picked up the sound of the torpedoes detonating underwater. Almost immediately, great spouts of water shot into the sky as the torpedoes struck.

On board SEACAP ONE, Ensign Dale Delany and her co-pilot, Bob Michaelson, exchanged meaningful glances. They were both well versed in naval warfare and, despite what they heard in the pre-mission briefing, neither thought that Godzilla would survive the initial undersea attack.

"I wonder if a carcass the size of Godzilla's will float?" Michaelson mused out loud. "Otherwise, we could be here all day…"

Ensign Delany chanced a quick glance at her co-pilot. "Stop exaggerating," she quipped. "We've only got five hours of fuel!"

More geysers shot into the air. One explosion was so close it rocked SEACAP ONE and sprayed seawater all over the windshield. "That was close," Michaelson noted calmly.

Another line of blasts tore up the otherwise tranquil waters. Finally, the torpedoes were spent, and the ocean grew calm once more. Ensign Delany turned to her sonarman.

"Got anything?" she asked.

The man shook his head. "I think the explosions fried our sonar buoys," he informed her.

Delany nodded. "Get ready to drop more remote sonar detectors," she commanded. But before her crew could comply, the ocean underneath SEACAP ONE's hull began to bubble, then boil.

"Look!" Michaelson cried, pointing to the water

below and in front of them. Ensign Delany stared as the ocean bubbled and began to steam.

"Uh-oh," Michaelson moaned.

As the crew of SEACAP ONE watched, Godzilla, the king of the monsters, rose out of the Pacific depths with a bawling roar. Seawater poured off its charcoal-black hide in torrents, and the water churned all around the enormous prehistoric leviathan. The stunned crew of the Super Stallion found themselves eye-to-eye with a beast that should have died sixty-five million years ago.

"It's Godzilla!" the sonarman cried, even as Ensign Delany tried to take the chopper up and away from the creature's grasp.

With astonishing speed, Godzilla lashed out. His feral head lunged toward the helicopter, even as his terrible jaws opened to swallow them whole.

The crews on SEACAP TWO and THREE fired flares at Godzilla and radioed the monster's position to the squadron above.

Ensign Delany pulled her chopper back, her eyes fixed on the twin rows of irregular teeth that lined Godzilla's blood-red mouth. The helicopter accelerated backward so fast that when Godzilla's jaws snapped shut, they closed on empty air.

"Go! Go! Go!" Michaelson cried as Godzilla's eyes narrowed and the pupils focused on them. Godzilla prepared to lunge again.

But the agile Sea Stallion had flown too high too fast, and the prehistoric monster lost its chance to destroy the helicopter. "We have incoming!" Michaelson announced. "Tomcats at three o'clock—"

"Let's get out of here before we're caught by friendly fire!" Ensign Delany cried as she pushed the throttle forward again. The Sea Stallion spun on its axis and darted away.

As SEACAP ONE raced out of the attack zone, the F-14s, directed by the flares, dived toward Godzilla. The Tomcats from the *Nimitz* carried a special payload.

After evaluating the attacks made against Godzilla on land and sea, the United States Navy, with the help of kaijuologists, had devised a new strategy to destroy Godzilla. Given that the creature was a radioactive mutant, possessing incredible powers of organic regeneration, it was decided that most conventional weapons would be useless.

Most...but not all.

The strategists in the Pentagon deduced that if enough damage could be inflicted on Godzilla in a short span of time, the monster's powers of regeneration would be overwhelmed. There would be no chance for the creature to regrow its cells and organs before mortal wounds could be inflicted.

But what conventional weapon could inflict such damage?

The answer was something called a fuel-air explosive.

The six Tomcats that dropped out of the sky toward Godzilla each carried a fuel-air explosive canister—basically, a container filled with a flammable mixture of petroleum and chemicals fitted with a timer and a parachute. A fuel-air explosive was designed to drop slowly over a target, then explode *above* it at a predetermined altitude.

The weapon provided what is known in military parlance as a "double whammy"—it smashed its target with the force of a gigantic hammer, and it covered the area around the target with a layer of burning chemicals that could not easily be extinguished.

It was not a compassionate weapon. Dr. Birchwood felt it was so cruel that he had reservations about using it. But he also understood that the lives of thousands were at stake, especially if Godzilla came ashore on the densely populated West Coast.

The final result was that now, in the sky over Godzilla, the Tomcat pilots dropped their lethal payload as they swooped over the creature.

Their mission completed, the jets climbed back into the clouds. It was time for them to "get out of Dodge City"!

Godzilla gazed up with catlike curiosity as six parachutes blossomed open directly above him. Slowly, the canisters drifted down until the lowest one was right above his wedge-shaped head.

Godzilla grunted. Then the electric discharge that preceded his radioactive blast danced along his dorsal spines.

At that moment, an electronic signal was sent from the lead SEACAP helicopter—a signal that detonated all six of the explosive devices at the same time.

Even though the helicopter crews were briefed on what to expect, the intensity of the fuel-air explosions took them by surprise. As they watched from two miles away, their choppers were buffeted by the hot blast. The blue Pacific sky turned bright yellow as it was lit up like a second sun.

A tremendous glowing ball of fiery force smashed down on Godzilla. The violence of the blast knocked the stunned creature onto his side. The surface of the Pacific began to boil as a flaming blanket of burning chemicals descended on the area. The burning cloud covered the monster completely.

Roaring with rage and pain, Godzilla thrashed about on the surface, churning the red waves with each agonized movement. Every exposed section of the creature's hide was burning in the aftermath of the explosion.

As the creature's cries of mortal agony echoed across the water, Ensign Delany felt her breakfast rising back up her throat. She had to look away, but she could not shut out the horrible cries of pain and confusion. Delany had been raised on a farm and loved animals, and she couldn't watch this magnificent creature as it writhed in its death throes.

Finally, Godzilla's suffering seemed to end. The creature stopped thrashing, and his burning body began to sink beneath the simmering waves. The last of the flaming cloud of burning liquid and gas settled over the ocean, turning the pale blue waves to a bright, bloody crimson. Godzilla was gone.

SEACAP ONE, TWO, and THREE hovered in place as the ocean burned for miles around. No one aboard the choppers spoke.

Ensign Delany ordered a new batch of sonar buoys to be dropped into the ocean. The tiny portable sonar devices pinged the depths as soon as they sank beneath the waves.

The submarines, too, began a sonar sweep of the area, searching for Godzilla or his remains. But even after an hour, there was no sign of the mighty *kaiju*.

It appeared, even to the skeptical Dr. Birchwood, that Godzilla might indeed be dead.

Lori Angelo thrashed about in her bed as the dream overtook her. This time the images were more vivid, more powerful, and more emotional than ever before. And this time, the truth was finally revealed to her.

The dream lasted only a few minutes, but when Lori awoke, she was at peace for the first time in weeks. Now she understood what was happening. Lori knew that Mothra was the Protector of the Earth, and that she had come down from space to save humanity from something worse than Varan, or Godzilla, or Rodan—or even a swarm of killer asteroids.

Most of all, Lori knew what she had to do.

Rising from her bed, she went to her personal computer and began to work. The clock was already ticking, and Lori didn't have much time to plan her escape from Project Valkyrie.

17
THE HIGH FRONTIER

Friday, June 11, 1999, 0703 mission time
The Mir space station
In orbit, 125 miles above the earth

Slowly, carefully, the space shuttle *Atlantis* docked with the primary module of the Russian Mir space station high above the blue Pacific Ocean. Through the viewports in the other modules on Mir, the station personnel watched the gleaming white shuttle slip smoothly into the docking collar.

The shuttle was a welcome sight, bringing much-needed supplies of food, water, oxygen, and scientific equipment to the overworked, aging space station. It also brought with it another guest for the already overcrowded Mir, Dr. Chandra Mishra.

Since the discovery of the Reyes-Mishra asteroids, Mir had become one of the focal points in a planet-wide effort to destroy the asteroids before they collided with Earth. The station, which was designed to function with a crew of five and perhaps three scientists or researchers, now had thirteen full-time residents and temporary crews coming and going on a monthly basis.

Now another crew member was being added to the roster. The crowded conditions put a strain on the Mir's scanty resources, and supplies were now being replenished from Earth weekly.

NASA was breaking all previous performance records toward that end. Each of the four American space shuttles was sent up in turn, alternating with Russian *Soyuz* resupply vehicles.

Mir had been designed and built to last only five or six years. At fifteen years, the station was not only still in service, it was starting to look like Grand Central Terminal.

The newest member of the Mir team, now disembarking from the *Atlantis,* Dr. Chandra Mishra pushed his way clumsily through the narrow hatch that connected *Atlantis* with the Mir module. He was not yet accustomed to weightlessness, and though he had experienced no nausea or motion sickness, he had had a lot of trouble maneuvering in zero-Gs.

His first impression of Mir was the smell. A distinctive odor of unwashed bodies assailed his nose, making him flash on the memory of the smelly locker rooms from his cricket-playing college days.

Dr. Mishra, forty, had actually been selected for the NASA astronaut training program over a decade before. Unfortunately, a previously undiagnosed thyroid condition washed him out of the program in his second year. The Indian-American scientist thought his dreams of space flight had ended then and there.

Now, to his delight and amazement, he was orbiting high over Earth in Mir, about to witness the destruction of the asteroid swarm from the telescopes in Mir's *Kristall* and *Kvant* science modules. Despite the discomfort and overcrowding, Dr.

Mishra was glad he was aboard, and he was greeted warmly by the international team of astronauts and cosmonauts on the Russian-designed space station.

The greeting was sincere and heartfelt, for Dr. Mishra was the primary architect of the plan to destroy the asteroids.

Today, the final steps in Dr. Mishra's plan were about to be implemented. The National Aeronautics and Space Administration was ready to launch the last of its three robotic smart bombs from a launching pad in Florida.

Mishra's plan had been simple, but infinitely difficult to set into motion. Since there were only three large asteroids in the swarm, they would be targeted individually—by as many remote-control nuclear bombs as the nations of the world could launch in the limited time they had left.

The plan was idiot-proof and included quadruple redundancy. The attacks would be coordinated, and each asteroid would have a total of four warheads coming at it after today's launch. If one or two missiles failed, there were more to take their place.

The United States, Russia, Japan, and France, with international technical and financial assistance, were launching the nuclear missiles. The Russians had already launched six *Energia* rockets carrying multiple nuclear warheads. Those guided missiles were heading for the asteroid swarm, and would intercept them at a point in space between the moon and Mars.

A second group of three nuclear missiles were

being launched by a French/Japanese consortium —the Japanese supplied the boosters, and the French supplied the warheads.

Now, a third and final group of three high-tech robotic bombs were about to be launched from the United States on three separate Air Force boosters. These super-smart warheads contained their own guidance systems and rocket motors. They were designed to seek out and destroy any smaller pieces of the asteroids that might continue on toward Earth after the initial detonations.

It was an ambitious plan, and not without risk— though, as it turned out, most of those risks were political.

Project EarthFirst had been hotly debated on the floor of the United Nations. Some of the smaller countries unfriendly to the West had actually tried to stop the project through political pressure, debate, and even an oil embargo.

The actions of these rogue nations came to a head when an Iranian-backed terrorist group tried to sabotage the joint Japanese/French space launch. The bomb the terrorists planted at the launching pad was discovered before it detonated, and French security teams captured the terrorists and interrogated them.

Three days later, French warplanes and cruise missiles struck Tehran, slaughtering many high government officials and doing a considerable amount of damage to Iran's infrastructure.

The punitive actions taken by the French military frightened the rogue nations, and no further terrorist action was taken against Project Earth-

First. Even the debates in the UN General Assembly became more civil—if not more civilized.

In the end, when faced with extinction, most nations put aside their petty squabbles and pledged full cooperation. It was the closest thing to a united world as humanity had come, though it was far from a utopia.

As Dr. Mishra moved through Mir, shaking hands and listening to words of support and encouragement from scientists and cosmonauts from a half-dozen nations, he still harbored secret doubts.

As the swarm approached Earth, Dr. Mishra's observations revealed that there was something strange about the largest asteroid. It behaved like no other space rock recorded in the annals of astronomy. The asteroid moved when it shouldn't have. It spun for no apparent reason. And lately it had seemed to have developed a mind of its own.

Other scientists had explanations for the weird behavior, but none of their answers satisfied Dr. Mishra. The problem vexed him so much that in the last several days he'd even experienced a series of colorful nightmares—featuring a golden dragon with three heads on long, snakelike necks.

Sigmund Freud would have a field day with that image, the astrophysicist thought wryly.

Dr. Mishra pushed aside his misgivings as a handsome young Russian cosmonaut floated toward him, his right hand outstretched in greeting. Dr. Mishra was introduced to Captain Yuri Sheglova, chief cosmonaut aboard the Mir station.

The two men shook hands warmly.

*   *   *

At his office at Nellis, Colonel Krupp reviewed the daily information brief supplied to him each morning by the Pentagon.

Surprisingly, the news was almost all good.

The swarm of Kamacuras had been totally destroyed. Though the seeds of new creatures still fell out of the sky inside the swarm's meteors, teams of scientists had discovered a way to detect them on the ground. Trained soldiers retrieved the rocks that contained the alien DNA.

There were reports of a new outbreak of Kamacuras in South America, but the Chilean government seemed to have the situation well in hand. Images of tiny Cessna A-57 Dragonfly fighters bombing swarms of Kamacuras in the jungles were broadcast daily.

Meanwhile, in Mexico, Varan had disappeared just as suddenly as it had appeared. The strange airborne creature had not been seen since destroying an isolated village in the Sierra Madre.

Most kaijuologists suspected that Varan might have gone into hibernation once again, in some remote freshwater lake, or even under the Gulf of Mexico or the Pacific Ocean.

Meanwhile, the flying creature that an Athabaskan shaman dubbed Rodan had taken refuge deep in the Canadian forests along the eastern shore of Lake Winnipeg. All commercial and private boats and aircraft had been banned from the area.

Though there were fears that the *kaiju* would destroy all life in the lake or devastate the forest, Rodan had, thankfully, not taken any more human lives. For the present, the Canadian government was taking a "wait and see" attitude toward dealing with the creature.

Another bit of good news concerned Dr. Emiko Takado, one of the survivors of Godzilla's destruction of the *Kongo-Maru*. The young kaijuologist was recovering in a Tokyo hospital, and would be released in a few days. Colonel Krupp recalled meeting Dr. Takado—and her fiancé, a famous Japanese photojournalist—at a scientific conference the previous year. He was happy that she was okay.

But the best news of all was that Godzilla had not been seen or heard from since the U.S. Navy's attack less than a week ago. While nobody was about to go out on a limb and say that Godzilla was dead, hopes were high.

So far, Godzilla's resurrection and possible destruction were still top-secret, pending confirmation of the *kaiju*'s ultimate fate. Colonel Krupp was impressed that the military had kept a lid on Godzilla's third coming for *this* long, not to mention hiding the sea battle from the general public. *That* secret would end just as soon as one of those ships reached a U.S. port!

The colonel sat back in his chair and sighed.

Yes, Krupp thought with a warm glow of satisfaction, *things are almost returning to normal...*

In times of trouble, the vast majority of human beings rise to the occasion and do their best for themselves, their neighbors, and their fellow man.

Then there are those who stumble and fall in the

face of adversity, not because they didn't try, but because they lacked the strength or tenacity to weather adversity.

Finally, there are those members of that tiny segment of humanity whose only concern is for themselves, who seek to profit from chaos and the suffering of their fellow humans through legal or illegal means.

Three such men were assembling on a tiny wooden pier in North Moose Lake—fifty nautical miles from Lake Winnipeg—just before daybreak on a foggy Saturday morning.

Mist still rose from the lake's surface as the men loaded a twin-engine seaplane with extra fuel, tools, guns and ammunition, and a few special provisions.

At the end of the pier, near a battered Jeep Cherokee, a short, stocky man with bushy eyebrows watched the others. He was a French-Canadian ex-convict named Claude, and he was the pilot and leader of the group.

Claude grimaced and took another gulp from a tiny flask while the others loaded the aircraft. The seaplane, stolen by Claude a week before and hidden under a tarp here on North Moose Lake, bobbed in the calm waters.

Last night, before he went to bed, Claude painted over the serial numbers on the airplane. He didn't want to leave the authorities any clues in case his airplane was spotted.

"What's with the fishing stuff?" the youngest member of the group, a youth with shoulder-length blond hair and a fine beard, asked. He pointed to a couple of rods and reels, and some fishing tackle, piled haphazardly on the wooden dock.

The third man in the group, a hard-faced rough-neck with bulging muscles and a tattoo of an anchor on each forearm, smiled. His grin revealed a gap from a missing front tooth.

"If we get caught by the Army, we tells them we were only hunting for a fishing spot, eh?" he explained.

The younger man grinned and nodded. "That's brilliant, man," he said, brushing his long hair from his face. The youth, a fugitive from the United States who had fled north after a failed bank rob-bery, looked at the muscular man in open admira-tion.

Unseen by the other two, Claude rolled his eyes.

Idiots, the French-Canadian thought. *And how do you explain the automatic weapons? Do you tell the military you were going to hunt bears?*

Claude was smart enough to know that if they were caught, no explanation they offered could possibly matter. The authorities weren't stupid. They would know just what Claude and his gang really were. Looters and pirates.

When the aircraft was loaded, Claude crossed the pier and closed the baggage compartment. Then he climbed into the cabin and checked the instruments one last time before starting the engines. As the propellers caught and began to spin, the other two men clambered aboard, arguing over who would get the front seat. The tattooed man won.

Just as the sun was breaking over a tall line of

pines, the twin-engine aircraft raced across North Moose Lake and struggled into the sky like a bloated seabird. As the airplane lifted off, the whine of its overworked engines dislodged another predator from its nest. A hawk rose from the forest and took to the air.

"Man," the youth whistled from the back seat. "We barely made if off the ground."

The muscular man was too busy finishing the contents of Claude's flask to hear his friend.

Claude smiled. *This aircraft is much too heavy, and it will be even heavier when we are done looting,* he thought. *Fortunately, I have a plan.*

Claude glanced at the muscular man sitting next to him, and gauged his weight at over two hundred pounds. *Dead weight,* he thought, chuckling.

"What's so funny?" the tattooed man said in a surly voice.

"I am thinking of the booze I can buy with the loot we are going to steal," Claude replied. The other two men laughed, too.

Claude banked the plane sharply and headed for Lake Winnipeg's western shore. The town of Grand Rapids and the brand-new luxury resort hotel at Long Point had both been hastily evacuated by Canadian authorities after Rodan arrived.

Ripe for the picking, Claude thought. *And good places to start. Later we can move down the coast and hit some of the smaller communities.*

Claude had heard that there were people living on the shores of Lake Winnipeg who refused to be moved. They had remained behind to protect their homes and property.

Well, he shrugged, *that is why I brought the guns and these two louts along*. Claude didn't like to dirty his hands with messy things like murder.

As the aircraft flew over the rugged landscape, the pontoons brushed against the tops of some tall pine trees. Inside the cockpit, the youth in the back seat yelped fearfully. "Can't you fly this hunk of junk any higher?" the young man cried.

Claude shook his head. "The Canadian Army has banned all flights in this area," he replied. "They are afraid that the giant bird will take to the air again. I am flying low to avoid their search radar…"

"Yeah," the tattooed man added. "Yesterday the government threw out of the country a British reporter who tried to get aerial photos of Rodan! We're livin' in a state of emergency, kid!"

Indeed we are, Claude thought as he deftly guided the aircraft through valleys and between trees. *But at least they aren't shooting looters…yet.*

Because he had to fly so low, and zigzag so much to avoid hitting trees, the flight to Lake Winnipeg took almost forty-five minutes. Finally the airplane broke from between two hills and swooped over Winnipeg's tranquil waters. Still, Claude kept the airplane flying at a low altitude and close to the coast. He didn't want to be spotted by the military.

"How's it feel to be a pirate, kid?" the tattooed man asked the youth. "Just like Long John Silver, eh?"

The American looked puzzled. "You mean that guy who sells fish and chips is a pirate?" he asked.

The tattooed man shook his head. "You're thinkin' of Arthur Treacher's," he replied.

"Shut up!" Claude cried. "I'm trying to fly the airplane." *These idiots are giving me a headache.*

The two men sank into a stony silence. They both feared the fiery French-Canadian man.

The aircraft flew on and dipped lower, until the pontoons were almost skimming the surface of the lake. In the distance, Claude could see the gray line of a deserted highway.

"Give me that map," he demanded. The tattooed man reached for the folded paper between them. But before he could retrieve the map, he was interrupted by a startled cry from the backseat. He turned and saw it too.

Struck dumb, the tattooed man reached out and grabbed Claude's shoulder. The French-Canadian man was taken by surprise and lost control of the aircraft for an instant.

"Don't *do* that when I'm flying!" Claude barked angrily. But the tattooed man's hand didn't leave his shoulder. Instead, his grip tightened.

Irritated, Claude turned and looked behind him. That's when he saw a gigantic prehistoric bird of prey with a reddish brown hide, a crest of horns on its head, and a wingspan of over 400 feet flying directly behind their seaplane, and gaining on them.

As Claude watched in numb horror, Rodan opened its massive, toothless beak and cackled.

"Dive!" the tattooed man cried.

"Turn around!" the young man in the back seat squealed.

"No!" Claude screamed.

Then Rodan's beak snapped shut on the twin-engine seaplane. The force of its jaws broke the aircraft into pieces. The three men, along with the cockpit, were swallowed up by the creature, but the better part of the wings and fuselage, including the fuel tanks and the engines, dropped into the forest. The debris struck the ground with a tremendous explosion.

The gallons of extra fuel that the looters carried spread fire over a wide radius. Within minutes, the flames stretched across the wooded area, sending wildlife scurrying for their lives.

A half an hour later, over a hundred acres of Manitoba's virgin forest were burning out of control.

Rodan, disturbed by the flames, and unsatisfied by its paltry meal, took to the air once more in search of new prey. And once again, Rodan headed south, toward the border of the United States.

VARAN™

18
DEATH FROM
THE SKY

Sunday, June 13, 1999, 2:23 A.M.
The Gulf of Mexico
355 miles southeast of Galveston, Texas

The *Texas Star* was riding high in the calm waters of the Gulf of Mexico. The massive supertanker, a "ULCC"—*ultra-large crude carrier*, in oil industry lingo—was empty. The two million barrels of crude oil it had carried from South America had been pumped into a tank farm on the Texas coast. Now the ship was returning to Venezuela for another load of South American crude.

The *Texas Star* had been busy lately. The short-lived embargo of Middle Eastern oil increased United States dependency on South American product, and the *Star,* along with her sister ships the *Texas Queen* and the *Texas Belle,* had been making continuous runs from North to South America, and back again, for the past six weeks.

The crew was overworked, but Captain Charles Dingle ran a tight ship, and things were still going smoothly.

At 0200, Captain Dingle had turned over his vessel to the night watch. First Mate Scott Howard, a ten-year veteran of the South American run, had taken the bridge.

Night on the Gulf was calm and peaceful, unlike

life on *shore* lately. *What with monsters appearing out of every corner of the globe and rocks from space threatening to destroy the earth, life on dry land was getting nuttier all the time*, First Mate Howard thought as he gazed into the darkness.

The bridge of the *Star* was antiseptic white, and all the surfaces gleamed. Over twelve hundred feet from stem to stern, and fifty feet across, the ULCC was one of the largest ships in the world. But despite her size, the crew and officer compartments were cramped, jammed inside the raised superstructure on the extreme end of the ship's stern. The other nine-tenths of the vessel was taken up by the ship's huge oil containers.

The flat deck of the supertanker was covered with cargo pipelines for pumping the oil ashore. At the very center of the deck was a heliport. Right now, a chopper from the corporate fleet was secured to the deck.

The supertanker traveled at a leisurely eight knots an hour. Because of her tremendous size, the *Texas Star* needed at least a mile to come to a complete stop, and the ship's turning radius was equally absurd. The supertanker needed computers to navigate and radar to avoid collision.

First Mate Howard came up behind the wheelman and glanced at the compass and the navigational computer's readouts. The ship, he duly noted in the log, was on schedule and on course, so he went to his command station on the bridge. He listened to the radio chatter from Coast Guard and civilian shipping, then switched over to AM radio.

Mariachi music blared out of the radio. Howard

quickly twisted the dial. He settled on a country-music station out of Galveston; he leaned back in his chair, and listened to Garth Brooks sing about standing outside the fire.

Suddenly, the peaceful night turned to chaos.

There was a tremendous crash that rocked the massive ship. Then the lights dimmed and the whole supertanker listed to port, throwing sleeping men out of their bunks onto the steel decks.

On the bridge, First Mate Howard was tossed to the floor. The sailor at the controls, who was standing in front of the huge glass windows, clung to the wheel. Suddenly, the thick windows shattered, and rushing winds and splinters of sharp glass filled the bridge. The blare of the collision alarm echoed throughout the craft.

"What happened?" the first mate cried, picking himself off the tilted deck. But the wheelman did not answer. He clung to the wheel with one limp hand, and the first mate saw a river of blood running across the spotless white floor.

Howard leaped to the wheelman's side and clutched the man by his shoulders. The first mate eased the stricken sailor to the deck as more blood washed over his shoes.

With mounting horror, Howard saw that the sailor had been hit by a shard of glass. The piece, bigger than a carving knife, had struck him in the throat, severing the carotid artery.

The wheelman's eyes slowly closed. He was already dead.

First Mate Howard remembered his duty to the ship. He reached up and pulled the throttle, cutting the power to the huge five-bladed screw propeller. The ship was still listing to port, so Howard grabbed the mike and demanded a damage report.

At that moment, Captain Dingle, in a robe and slippers, dashed onto the bridge. He halted and visibly paled when he saw the sailor lying in a pool of blood.

"Collision?" the captain asked.

First Mate Howard shook his head. "There's nothing on radar," he replied.

"Then what—"

But the captain did not finish the question. He was interrupted by a thunderous, shuddering roar of rage and confusion that echoed throughout the corridors of the ship.

The captain and the first mate exchanged nervous glances.

"Turn on the exterior floodlights," Captain Dingle commanded. The first mate complied.

A moment later, the floodlights snapped on and bathed the entire deck in brilliant light. The captain and the first mate peered through the shattered windows.

Two gigantic eyes, each one the size of a luxury car, stared back at them.

The captain grabbed the radio and contacted the Coast Guard. He informed the authorities that the monster Varan had landed on the deck of his supertanker.

At that moment, on the opposite side of the United States, F-15 and F-16 fighter planes were being scrambled out of Minot Air Force Base in North

Dakota. Rodan was being tracked by military radar stations in the United States and Canada. It was heading across the border at speeds in excess of 450 miles per hour and at an altitude of 20,000 feet.

Elements of the Canadian Air Force had already engaged the *kaiju*, with heavy losses. Now, as Rodan crossed the border, it was the United States Air Force's turn.

Lori Angelo tossed and turned in her bed inside Project Valkyrie's medical center. She was caught in the throes of another dream.

Lori! a voice screamed inside her head.

Yes, she replied.

Wake up, daughter. It is time.

Lori opened her eyes. For a moment, she was confused. *Where am I?* she wondered. Then her mind cleared. She sat up and gazed through the glass wall that separated her from the outside world. Lori could see Dr. Markham slumped over her desk. The psychiatrist was asleep, a pen still dangled from her fingers.

Lori crept out of bed and went to the closet. But instead of her everyday overalls, she drew out her flight suit, which she'd hid, days before, in a box on the closet floor.

She quickly stepped into it and loaded on her gear. When she was finished, she crept through the glass doors, across the medical center lab, and out the exit. Then she rushed through the corridors of Project Valkyrie headquarters until she reached the back exit.

Only when the cool desert air hit her did Lori sigh with relief. The she took off in a dead run toward the hangars.

The battle over North Dakota was short and decisive. Every missile fired at Rodan seemed to bounce right off. The creature was unharmed by the Sidewinders and by the cannon fire from pilots brave or foolhardy enough to get their aircraft close enough to use them.

As the flying monster streaked through the night sky, warplanes continued to press their attack. But in the end, most of the fighters limped back to Minot Air Force Base with little fuel and no ammunition. Five of them—two F-15s and three F-16s—didn't come back at all.

Each time Varan shifted its weight on the deck, the *Texas Star* shook and threatened to capsize. Captain Dingle ordered the sailors to fill up the hull with ballast to level the ship and keep her steady.

In the glow of the floodlights, Varan looked like a gigantic lizard sunning itself. Its scales gleamed in the harsh white light, and the creature closed its eyes against the glare. Its steady breathing and an occasional twitch of its tail were the only signs that Varan was alive and not a huge museum display.

The mayday call from the stricken tanker brought an instant response. Rescue choppers hovered in the air but kept their distance. A United States Navy destroyer was steaming toward the *Texas Star* and would probably arrive by daybreak.

The Coast Guard suggested that the tanker be abandoned, but Captain Dingle wouldn't hear of it. As long as the *Star* was afloat, he and his men would stay aboard her.

So far, the creature had done no more damage. It rested on the main deck, with crushed pipes and a smashed corporate helicopter beneath its belly, like a fat family dog lying on a child's paper models.

If the situation hadn't been so grave, it would have been funny.

Klaxons blared throughout Project Valkyrie headquarters. Kip rolled over in his bunk and checked the clock. It was after three in the morning. *This is no drill,* he thought grimly.

After jerking on his overalls, Kip rushed to the tactical command center. He was the second team member to arrive. Pierce Dillard was there before him, and the young pilot was speaking to General Taggart. Colonel Krupp was there, too, but Dr. Birchwood was nowhere to be seen.

He must be on yet another top-secret assignment, figured Kip.

Then Tobias Nelson, Martin Wong, and Tia Shimura arrived. Toby looked bright-eyed and ready, but Tia looked groggy. She yawned and rubbed the sleep from her eyes.

When everyone took their seats, the general rose. He was about to speak, but suddenly Dr. Markham rushed into the center and up to the project commander.

She spoke with Taggart for a moment, and the general seemed to explode. He threw a briefing file on the podium and whispered an angry command that sent Dr. Markham scurrying away with Colonel Krupp in tow.

To Kip's surprise, the general's usually calm demeanor was shattered. He was genuinely agitated as he spoke to them.

"Listen up," Taggart said. "We've got a problem… *two* of them, in fact."

Lori Angelo powered up the Osprey as the klaxons began to blare. For a moment, she thought that an Air Force security team would rush in at any moment and drag her butt out of the cockpit. Then she realized that the alarms were meant for G-Force, and a wave of regret rose up inside of her.

Am I crazy? she wondered. *Am I doing the right thing?*

Lori waited for the voice from her dreams to answer her desperate plea, but there was nothing.

I must be crazy, she decided.

But crazy or not, nothing was going to stop her now. Lori put the helmet on her head, keyed in the navigational coordinates, and taxied out of the hangar. When the aircraft was ready for take-off, she slid the infrared night-vision goggles over her eyes.

Moments later, the CV-22 Osprey tilt-rotor lifted off in a cloud of blowing sand.

Lori swung the aircraft in a low, tight circle through the desert night and then headed west. She continued flying nap-of-the-earth—and well below the range of search radar—until the Osprey flew across the state line and out over the Mojave Desert of California.

* * *

Ellsworth Air Force Base pilots scrambled near dawn. The base had already been on alert for five hours, so the pilots were ready.

Barely a week after Rodan first appeared, the squadron commander at Ellsworth got the Pentagon's permission to try something completely different.

Up to now, the Air Force had been sending up fighters armed with air-to-air missiles against Rodan.

Unfortunately, Sidewinders and Mavericks were fine for shooting down other aircraft, but their tiny warheads were worthless against a flying *kaiju*. Something bigger was needed, and the base commander thought he had a better mousetrap.

There were several AGM-109 MRASM cruise missiles on the base—each with enough high explosives to sink a warship. Why not configure them to hit a moving, aerial target, mount them on a couple of F-111s, and fire them directly into Rodan's path?

As Rodan flew across North Dakota, the airmen at Ellsworth were loading three F-111 fighter/bombers with six reconfigured missiles.

Minutes later, the F-111s were airborne and heading for a showdown with Rodan.

Despite the weight of two cruise missiles attached to their wing pylons, the F-111s ambushed Rodan on schedule over the town of Eagle Butte in the Cheyenne River Indian Reservation.

The widely scattered residents of the area were

awakened near dawn by the sound of jet fighters screaming overhead. Rodan had descended to an altitude of less than 15,000 feet, and the F-111s dropped down to meet the *kaiju* head-on.

From a distance of five miles, the F-111s released their payload. Five of the six cruise missiles streaked toward the flying monster. The sixth suffered an engine malfunction and crashed in the Little Moreau State Recreational Area.

Seconds later, four of the cruise missiles struck Rodan, one after the other. The fifth did not lock on to the target and flew on until it self-destructed, according to its programming.

Radar trackers whooped with excitement. Because the F-111s had lost the *kaiju* on their scopes, they were given the good news by the base commander at Ellsworth.

Rodan, stunned, had flown on for a few minutes after impact. Then the creature dropped out of the sky like a rock. The carcass landed in Lake Oahe, near the city of Pierre, South Dakota. The force of the creature's impact in the water battered nearby Oahe Dam, but the concrete structure held firm against the pressure.

While several witnesses watched, Rodan's still form slowly sank beneath the lake. The lead F-111 did a victory roll over Ellsworth as the squadron landed.

"We did it!" the jubilant squadron leader cried as the rest of the aircraft taxied down the runway and onto the flight line. "We took out Big Bird!"

19
GODZILLA RISING

Sunday, June 13, 1999, 6:10 A.M.
Fort Baker Military Reservation
Sausalito, California

Lori Angelo tossed the infrared goggles onto the empty co-pilot seat. The sun had just risen, and she wouldn't be needing them anymore. She double-checked the GPS navigational monitor, which constantly tracked and verified her location with an orbiting geopositioning satellite.

Then she glanced at her fuel gauge.

She was running on empty. Even with the auxiliary drop tanks on her wings, which nearly doubled the Osprey's 500-mile range, Lori's aircraft had just barely covered the distance from Nevada to San Francisco with the fuel aboard.

Now if I only knew why I was here, she thought.

Lori shifted in her seat. She'd been flying for three-plus hours without a break. The grueling flight time had taken a toll on her sore, tired muscles. So had her misgivings.

Now where do I go? she wondered.

Suddenly, the joystick moved in her hand. *Or did my hand move the joystick?* she wondered. *The classic Ouija board dilemma!*

The Osprey dipped and banked to the right.

Then the aircraft began to descend. Ahead of her was a foggy expanse that, according to the computer, should be San Francisco Bay. Occasionally, the clouds seemed to part and she caught a glimpse of garish orange towers—the very top of the Golden Gate Bridge.

Then the tiny hairs on the back of Lori's neck began to tingle. She shivered uncontrollably. Suddenly, mystically, the clouds parted. Below and ahead of her, Lori spied a rugged, windblown cliff that overlooked the fog-shrouded bay.

After another glance at the fuel gauge, Lori reduced speed, and the airplane became a twin-engine helicopter.

She landed on top of the hill with a gentle bump. Then she idled the engines and shut them down. When she was through deactivating all the systems, Lori stared through the windscreen at the bridge, which was still partially obscured by thick fog.

Unstrapping herself from the ejection seat, Lori pulled off her helmet and dropped it on the other seat, next to the night-vision goggles. Then she rose and stretched.

As soon as she cracked the hatch, the cool ocean air revived her. She took a deep breath, smelling the salt-tinged ocean breeze. Lori had been living in the middle of the desert for so long that she'd forgotten what it was like to be near water. The moist air felt good, but it made her shiver again.

The aircraft ticked and cracked as engine parts cooled in the brisk morning air. Lori jumped down from the hatch, turned her back on the Osprey, and walked away. She headed directly to the edge of the cliff, stepping over windblown tree branches. When she reached the abyss, she peered into the fog.

Then Lori sat down on a huge boulder that jutted out of the ground. She fumbled in the pocket of her flight suit until she found a Snickers bar. As Lori began to feast on her favorite treat, she faced the fog-shrouded bay and waited.

Far below the cliffs, on the opposite side of the bay, a young off-duty San Francisco police patrolman jogged along the shore at the Golden Gate National Recreation Area.

It was a Sunday ritual for Dennis Flynn. Up at five, a quick drive to the shore, then a five-mile run. Followed by a thermos of coffee, a corn muffin, and maybe the Sunday paper.

But today was not like any other Sunday. Dennis Flynn had high hopes for this particular morning.

For the past three weeks, he'd noticed a young woman who also came to the beach, ran a couple of miles, and then sat and sketched in a notebook for a few hours. The woman always came alone, and left alone, too.

A few weeks before, Flynn had casually run by to check her out up close. He was delighted to see she wasn't wearing a wedding ring.

A week later, Flynn spotted her again. This time she was getting out of her car, a late-model Infiniti. He memorized the license number, then tapped a friend in the traffic division to run her plates. It was unethical and an abuse of his authority.

But sometimes you've got to bend the rules if you want something... And Flynn had never wanted anything more in his life. It was love at first sight.

Her name was Annabel Maguire. No prior convictions, not even a parking ticket. She lived in Pacific Heights and worked at an advertising firm. Best of all, she was recently divorced.

Flynn realized that dating her would be a stretch on his paltry patrolman's salary, but he didn't let that deter him. Last Sunday, while still unsure of how to use the information he had on the attractive woman, a lucky accident occurred.

Or maybe it was fate, Flynn reckoned.

As he jogged past her, a stiff wind kicked up and blew some of her notebook pages across the beach.

Like a perfect gentleman, Flynn had helped her retrieve the errant papers. Then he struck up a conversation. Though things were awkward at first, the chat soon became more relaxed. But just when things were getting good, she had claimed an early lunch date with a friend and left—without giving him her name or phone number.

Divorced and gun-shy, Flynn concluded.

But he was not without hope. Flynn *did* notice that the young woman liked croissants from Andre's, a bakery on the edge of the Embarcadero. He had spotted a half-eaten pastry on the bench next to her, and the bag sticking out of her purse.

Now, armed with an extra thermos of coffee, another of tea, and a bag of Andre's French pastries, Flynn was prepared to lure the lovely Annabel

Maguire into conversation once again.

As he jogged past the parking area, he noticed her cherry-red Infiniti in the lot. It was parked only a few cars down from his Honda.

How convenient, he thought gratefully.

But when Flynn scanned the beach, he didn't see her anywhere.

She must still be running, he thought. *But sooner or later, she has to come back for her car.*

Flynn planned to wait all day, if necessary.

His run completed, Flynn grabbed a towel and a clean sweatshirt from the trunk of his car. Then he went over to a public shower and ran some water on his face to freshen up. It was icy cold on the shore, and the water coming from the pipes was even colder.

As he shook the water off his hands, Flynn noticed that the ground seemed to quiver beneath his feet.

He froze. The earth shook again.

Then he heard a rumbling sound like distant thunder, and the earth shook for a third time. Another jogger, a middle-aged bald man in an expensive running suit, slowed to a stop. When the earth quaked for the fourth time, he bolted off the sand toward the concrete sidewalk.

"Get off the beach," the bald man yelled at Flynn. "The sand turns to quicksand in an earthquake. You'll be swallowed up!"

But Flynn, who'd survived the quake of 1989, instinctively knew that this was no earthquake. Another rumble came, and a flight of seabirds bolted into the misty sky.

It sounds like the footsteps of a giant, Flynn realized. The young policeman turned and faced the water, searching for the cause of the quaking.

At that moment, the fog began to clear in the middle of the bay. What it revealed made Flynn's mouth drop open and the man cry out behind him.

"I can't believe it…" Flynn murmured.

"It's…it's *Godzilla!*" screamed the bald man.

Flynn watched, too stunned to move, as Godzilla waded, hip-deep, in the waters of San Francisco Bay. After a few more rumbling, lurching steps, the gigantic monster looked up into the overcast morning sky and opened his jaws. A second later, the creature's bellowing roar echoed across the water and bounced off the San Francisco skyline.

The creature strode past Alcatraz Island and moved ponderously toward the shore of Oakland on the opposite side of the bay. Earthquake sirens began to wail in the distance. Soon the whole city would be alerted to the danger.

Without hesitation, Flynn pulled on his sweatshirt, grabbed his towel, and raced for the parking lot.

In a city emergency, all San Francisco cops had to report for duty as soon as possible. Flynn guessed that Godzilla's arrival qualified as an emergency.

As he rushed toward his Honda, Flynn passed Annabel's red Infiniti. In the distance, he thought he saw her heading toward her car, but he couldn't stop now. A wave of frustration and regret washed over him. Now he'd have to wait yet another Sunday!

Damn that monster! he cursed bitterly, mourning his lost opportunity.

From her vantage point on top of the cliff, Lori watched as Godzilla lurched toward the distant shore. The *kaiju*'s mighty legs churned up waves, and his long tail sent great fountains of water high into the morning sky.

In the distance, Godzilla looked like a black shadow, a shadow with bone-white spikes running down his back and glowing, malevolent eyes. The creature moved through the bay, pushing back the water with each massive stride.

You're a magnificent creature, Lori had to admit.

Like everyone who ever saw Godzilla in the flesh, she felt awe and respect—as well as fear. And as she watched Godzilla lumber ashore, Lori understood why Mothra had led her here.

But what can I possibly do to help? she wondered.

At that moment, as if in reply, the air around her seemed to come to life. Motes of brilliant hues and sparkling lights like a thousand fireflies twinkled around her. The brilliant particles brushed her skin and caused her whole body to tingle.

Then the overcast sky seemed to open up directly over the Sausalito cliffs. Thick clouds parted over Lori's head, and a column of radiant energy streaked down from the heavens and bathed her in its mystical glow.

Lori slowly raised her eyes and squinted into the radiance. In the center of the sky, where the clouds had parted, Lori saw the most beautiful creature in the universe.

"Mothra…" she whispered, awestruck.

On multicolored wings of gossamer, the gigantic butterfly-like creature Mothra floated in the sky.

Tell them, daughter, Mothra's voice spoke inside Lori's head. *Tell them that Mothra is not their enemy. Tell them that the great creature who strides ashore below is not their enemy, either…*

"But…but Godzilla will kill hundreds," Lori blurted.

In order to save billions… Mothra whispered into her mind.

"I don't understand," Lori said.

You are my herald, Mothra sang. *You have heard my song as no other, understood it as none before you. Tell the world that the Destroyer of All Life is coming down from the stars. Tell humanity that their true enemy is the Three-Headed Monster with Wings of Gold.*

Then the colors faded, and the column of light disappeared. The clouds high in the sky closed around the gigantic winged creature, and Lori suddenly felt abandoned and alone.

Mothra was gone as abruptly as she had come.

Lori dropped to her knees at the edge of the cliff and began to sob. *How can I convince them?* she raged, pounding the earth.

Who will believe me now?

At this early hour on a Sunday morning, only sanitation crews and a few shopkeepers were in Jack London Square, a section of Oakland's docks named to honor the city's most famous citizen and the author of *The Call of the Wild*.

London Square ran along the bay and was Oakland's version of San Francisco's more renowned Fisherman's Wharf.

The restaurants and T-shirt shops in the square and in Jack London Village nearby weren't due to open for hours yet. The only vehicle near the water was a sanitation truck.

The garbage men were lazily loading overflowing bins of garbage into the truck's noisy compactor. Suddenly, one of them looked toward the bay. What he saw nearly turned his hair white.

He slapped his comrade on the shoulder, cried out, and pointed. Then the three men bolted, leaving their truck behind. They ran into the middle of Jack London Village, where a group of pickup trucks and vans filled with fresh produce were unloading and setting up for the Sunday morning farmers' market.

When the vendors spotted Godzilla looming over them, his terrible roar vibrating every object around them, they fled in panic.

Slowly, ponderously, Godzilla's foot rose out of San Francisco Bay and crashed down next to the sanitation truck. The force of the creature's tread was so powerful that the truck bounced on its wheels and tipped over.

Godzilla's gigantic leg looked like the bole of a huge redwood tree. The monster's hide was charcoal black, with brown and gray streaks, and grooved with deep lines. Seawater washed down the deep, pitted grooves in rivulets. The water soaked the pavement, which cracked under the monster's tremendous weight.

As Godzilla thundered past the sanitation truck, his long tail slammed against the vehicle, sending it flying through the air like a toy. Garbage spilled everywhere as the tail pounded against the facade of a pricey restaurant.

Again, Godzilla's tail lashed out, and utterly demolished the brick building that housed a famous Oakland landmark, the First and Last Chance Saloon. The century-old structure collapsed in a cloud of dust and smoke.

Meanwhile, flames leaped from the shattered restaurant. The smell of natural gas filled the air. Suddenly, the gas flowing out of a broken main ignited. An orange fireball rolled into the sky, and flames spread along the seaside district. Sirens began wailing, and two Oakland Fire Department trucks sped around the corner. Godzilla suddenly shifted on his feet, and his tail swiped the first emergency vehicle as it tried to rush by.

The fire truck flipped over, spilling men onto the pavement. Before the emergency crews could flee, Godzilla brushed past another building, raining tons of debris down on the helpless firefighters. Oblivious to his victims, Godzilla moved inland, toward the expensive homes that crowded the Oakland hills.

Thinking it was just another Sunday morning, Northern Californians awakened and tuned in their radios and televisions, hoping to hear the weather report.

Instead, they found that the local channels were off the air and that the Emergency Broadcast Network had taken over.

Less than five minutes after Godzilla appeared, news of his return was being spread by the wire services. First Reuters, then AP, then the rest. The cable news networks followed quickly.

On INN, Nick Gordon, the host of *Science Sunday,* went on the air with constant updates. An Independent News Network chopper broadcast the first live pictures to a stunned and frightened nation.

Panic spread as the grim reality sunk in. Godzilla had come to America.

GODZILLA™

20
AMERICA
INVADED

Dr. Markham answered the phone on the first ring.

"Dr. Markham?" a tearful yet defiant voice pleaded from the receiver.

"Lori?" the doctor replied, surprised.

"I want to come home…"

The psychiatrist sighed. "That's not my decision, Lori. *Or* yours," Dr. Markham said after a pause. "It's up to the general."

"I know."

"Where are you now?" Markham asked.

"In San Francisco," Lori said.

Dr. Markham gasped. *How did she know?* she wondered. Yet the psychiatrist should not have been surprised. Not after what she learned in the past few hours.

"I saw it all!" Lori cried. "I knew when and where to be when Godzilla showed up—"

Dr. Markham interrupted her. She wanted to hear what Lori had to say, but not over the phone. She wanted Lori back here, in the base hospital.

"Is the aircraft you took still intact?" Markham demanded.

"Of course! Not a scratch," Lori said defensively.

"All I need is some fuel and I can come home."

"All right, Lori," Markham said. "I'll see what I can do. Now, I want you to follow my instructions to the letter…"

Five minutes later, Dr. Markham hung up. Then she gathered up the handwritten notes spread across her desk and headed down the hall to General Taggart's office.

I'm convinced that Lori's not insane, and I've convinced her of that, the doctor reflected. *Now all I have to do is convince the general.*

Somehow, Dr. Markham thought, fighting *kaiju* would be easier.

Helicopters hovered in the air around the *Texas Star.* Some were Coast Guard, some United States Navy, some belonged to the press. The latter were being turned away by the military authorities.

The supertanker still listed to one side, and the creature called Varan still lay across her deck, unmoving except for an occasional twitch of its reptilian tail.

Throughout the night, Navy warships had cautiously approached the tanker—quietly and without running lights. The Navy wanted to get their ships close to Varan without frightening the creature back into the sky. Two frigates and a destroyer warily circled the stricken tanker, waiting.

General Taggart now had two monsters within the continental United States to contend with—and a third in territorial waters.

He'd also lost a member of the G-Force team,

and a multimillion-dollar aircraft. Worst of all, the president was still keeping G-Force out of the fight. The last thing General Taggart needed was a visit from the project's headshrinker.

"General," Dr. Markham said as she pushed open his office door, "we need to talk."

"Don't you doctors believe in knocking?" the general barked. Then he dropped his pen on the desk and stared at the woman. "Come in…" he said, relenting.

Dr. Markham sat down across the desk from him.

"I just heard from Lori," she announced. The general raised his eyebrows but said nothing.

"She's in San Francisco," the doctor continued. "She watched Godzilla arrive this morning. Now she wants to come back."

The general shook his head. "Out of the question," he stated flatly.

"Listen to me before you make up your mind, General Taggart," Markham insisted. "I think you should hear this…" As she spoke, she spread out handwritten notes on Taggart's desk.

"I was puzzled by Lori's apparent delusion—that some entity was trying to communicate with her through dreams," the woman said. "I conferred with a colleague at Brown University this morning. He told me that he had two cases in the last few weeks…cases very similar to Lori's."

The general's face remained stony, but he was listening.

"Two cases of normal, healthy young women with no prior history of mental distress suddenly having dreams about a winged angel or a giant butterfly," the doctor stated, almost tripping over her words in her haste to get them out.

"Each of these women was convinced that the being in her dream was trying to communicate with her."

The general sat up in his chair, still attentive.

"Then I called other psychiatrists that I know," Markham continued. "In Pittsburgh, Denver, Detroit …Every single one of my colleagues reported at least one patient who had developed a similar delusion. All of these patients are young women, and all showed their first symptoms in the past month!"

The general looked impressed. But Dr. Markham knew she had to hit him with something that he could understand, something concrete.

"Do you know what the statistical probabilities of such similar conditions existing within the same time span are? It's out of the ballpark, General…a billion to one, at the least!"

The doctor looked hard at Taggart. "I'm not always impressed with statistics or probabilities, General," she declared. "In this case, it was the brain scan that convinced me."

Dr. Markham pulled a copy of the brainwave pattern from the pile of papers spread out on the desk.

"Not even multiple personalities can have *two distinct brainwave patterns*. Yet that is exactly what Lori exhibited.

"Something else is going on here," she concluded.

"Just what are you suggesting, Dr. Markham?" Taggart asked.

The psychiatrist took a deep breath. *Here goes my reputation.*

"I'm suggesting that Lori wasn't suffering from a delusion," Dr. Markham said finally. "I'm suggesting that an entity of some kind *was* communicating with her...and that this entity has something to tell every man, woman, and child on this planet. But so far, at least, it can only speak effectively through Lori Angelo."

Despite the fact that the U.S. Navy was warning away unauthorized aircraft, an INN helicopter out of Mexico sneaked under the radar cordon and flew toward the *Texas Star,* so low that it literally skimmed the waves.

The other media helicopters had been chased out of the combat area an hour before, but the crew of this particular INN chopper was determined to broadcast pictures of Varan on live television. The team, which consisted of news director Mike Timko, Robin Halliday, the young on-camera intern, and their cameraperson, Linda Carlisle, were hot on the trail of a story they'd been chasing for weeks.

At the controls of the chopper was the young Mexican liaison officer Tony Batista. He'd stayed with the team since Jamiltepec, and Mike had learned to appreciate the man's talents.

They were so hot to get the story that Mike ordered the pilot to turn off the radio. That way, they didn't have to acknowledge the Navy's commands to clear the area.

But without the radio, the INN crew didn't hear

the Coast Guard and Navy broadcasts warning that any unauthorized aircraft would be fired upon. As the chopper streaked past the bow of a Navy destroyer, the captain of the warship ordered warning shots to be fired at the intruder.

A Vulcan anti-aircraft gun opened fire, and bullets streaked toward the helicopter. As tracers whizzed past the cockpit, Tony Batista panicked and pushed the throttle forward. The helicopter raced past another warship, which also opened fire.

Soon, a Coast Guard patrol boat opened up, too. But this time, they weren't warning shots. Several rounds ripped through the helicopter's engine, shattering an oil pump. Black smoke began to pour out of the fuselage, and the helicopter stalled.

As the INN chopper plunged into the Gulf of Mexico, the noise of the gunfire startled Varan.

Awakened, the creature began to move...

As Godzilla's shadow loomed over the shattered ruins of Piedmont, the monster's booming roar of triumph echoed through the hills of Northern California. Even miles away, fleeing citizens on the Warren Freeway could hear the creature's ear-shattering howl over the sound of the bumper-to-bumper traffic.

Godzilla's devastating march through Oakland, and now Piedmont, went unopposed by the military. The Pentagon had decided that using weapons in populated areas would do more harm than good. Instead, they tried to predict Godzilla's path and evacuate the population ahead of it.

Three National Guard units were on the scene in Piedmont, carrying out the high command's decision to evacuate. They had their hands full dealing with the panicked, fleeing population.

Local emergency services had their resources taxed to the limit, too. They were busy evacuating the wounded and freeing those who were trapped in collapsed buildings left by Godzilla's passing. Fortunately, they had extensive training and experience in earthquake relief, and that knowledge served them well.

In Godzilla's wake, hospitals and clinics were jammed—except for those few that were in ruins. The fire departments and ambulance crews could not keep up with the spread of fire and destruction. Shattered gas mains fed the blazes, and emergency trucks could not get past the traffic that jammed every thoroughfare out of the cities. Humanity had been all but routed.

As the dreadful day progressed, Godzilla smashed his way across Skyline Boulevard and crossed the upper tip of Redwood Regional Park. Finally, he took to the high ground, climbing toward the tiny town of Canyon in the Berkeley Hills.

In the early afternoon, over a strip mall outside Moraga, a fleet of AH-64A Apache helicopters appeared on the horizon. Slowly, cautiously, they approached Godzilla. Each attack copter was equipped with two "quads" of Hellfire missiles—one on each tiny wing—and twin rocket pods with nineteen rockets each.

Sensing the oncoming threat, Godzilla swung his

head toward the sound of the engines. The reptile's eyes narrowed and his lip curled, baring long, irregular teeth in a savage snarl.

Throwing its forearms into the air and bellowing a challenge, Godzilla faced his attackers.

As Varan began thrashing about, the *Texas Star* rocked like a rowboat filled with wrestlers. The crew huddled in the stern were dashed to the steel deck as the ship tossed on the waves.

On the bridge, emergency lights went on. Captain Dingle read the control screens, and the news was not good. The *Texas Star* was taking on water.

Because of the unique construction of ULCC tankers, it was very difficult to sink one. But Varan was doing its best to try. Captain Dingle ordered his first mate and wheelman off the bridge. When they were gone, he peered through the shattered window at the creature that was tearing his ship apart.

As he did, a sudden wind kicked up. Its violent gusts seemed to come from everywhere and nowhere. It became more and more intense, and it felt much different than a normal wind.

The air felt cool...and it smelled sweet.

Then Captain Dingle realized what was happening. He'd been briefed over the radio on what to expect from the creature. Varan was about to take to the sky again. The effort caused the creature to produce great winds—gusts of pure oxygen.

As Dingle watched, Varan raised itself up on its hind legs, tilting the ship even more. While the gyrostabilizer fought to keep the *Star* level and afloat, Varan launched itself into the sky.

As the team of Apache attack helicopters approached Godzilla, they spread out in an irregular offensive line. The fighting machines closed in on the monster, and as they drew near, the sound of their propellers thrummed and beat against the creature's ears.

Godzilla grunted and blinked in an almost human gesture of surprise, as if he understood the massive amount of firepower that was arrayed against him. Acting as a team, the helicopters simultaneously opened fire.

The Apaches led the attack with their rocket pods. In a blast of smoke, the rockets left the pods in a sustained rapid spin to ensure stability. The accuracy of individual rockets was poor, but due to their sheer numbers, the attack was devastating.

The projectiles slammed into Godzilla's body, stunning and confounding the gigantic creature. It took almost a minute of sustained fire to empty the pods of their rockets, and when the four hundred projectiles were finally spent, the Apaches launched their ninety-six Hellfire missiles.

As Varan lifted off, the U.S. Navy warships aimed their anti-aircraft guns at the flying creature.

The military experts assumed that the creature would ascend slowly into the sky, and move equally slowly once there. The experts also assumed that Varan traveled on the winds of the upper atmosphere, and was not truly in control of its flight.

So everyone was taken by surprise when Varan shot into the sky as quickly as a helicopter. They were even more surprised when it stretched out its arms and legs and—with a sound not unlike a supersonic jet aircraft—streaked away.

Even as the ships opened fire, the monster was moving out of range. The Navy guns failed to inflict any damage.

The captain of the lead warship radioed a warning to his high command. He reported that Varan was heading due north, toward the nearest land. If it continued its present course and speed, it would be over the Texas coast in an hour...

Just seconds after Varan disappeared into the blue sky over the Gulf of Mexico, a rescue helicopter from one of the Navy ships moved toward the wrecked INN helicopter. The shattered fuselage was still afloat, though it was sinking fast.

Linda Carlisle kicked the door on her side of the helicopter. When it didn't budge, she kicked it again—this time with both legs. Water was already gushing around her feet from the broken windows in the front cockpit. She knew they didn't have much time before the wreckage sank.

Linda braced herself against the seat and kicked out for the third time. The door popped open, and a torrent of seawater rushed in, threatening to drown her then and there.

At least Mike made us all wear life vests, she thought as she grabbed Robin Halliday, who was unconscious. Keeping Robin's head above water,

Linda dragged the unconscious girl out of the wreckage.

Briefly, she saw Mike Timko trying to rouse Tony, the pilot.

"Get out!" Mike screamed at her.

Linda obeyed. She swam away from the sinking helicopter, dragging the limp intern with her. The rescue helicopter dropped out of the sky overhead, buffeting the two women with the wind from its blades. Two Navy divers in wet suits dropped out of the chopper door and splashed into the water beside her.

One took Robin out of Linda's tired arms, while the other grasped her about the waist. Exhausted, she surrendered to the sailor's strong grip.

A few moments later, Linda found herself being pushed into an orange rubber raft, next to the still-unconscious Robin. Then Mike tumbled in right next to her, followed by a man in a wet suit.

Linda sat up and looked around. A second man in a wet suit was clambering aboard. She didn't see anyone else.

Linda turned and looked at her producer.

"Where's Tony?" she demanded.

Mike, still coughing out seawater, looked away. Then he cleared his throat.

"Tony...Tony didn't make it," he whispered hoarsely. "He was killed when we hit the water..."

GODZILLA™

21
A PLAGUE OF
MONSTERS,
A MONSTROUS PLAGUE

Sunday, June 13, 1999, 3:45 P.M.
Dan's Computer Store, Moraga Road Mall
Moraga, California

From the vantage point of his computer store, less than a mile away, Dan Burgleman watched as U.S. Army helicopters attacked Godzilla.

With rapt attention, the portly, bearded man witnessed this titanic struggle between mankind and mutant monster and concluded that he'd made the right decision to stay.

When the National Guardsmen had come through the area an hour before, everyone in the strip mall who had not already abandoned their businesses fled with the soldiers. Everyone, that is, except Burgleman.

He'd worked too long and too hard on his computer store. He wasn't going to abandon it now. After all, Godzilla was just an animal. A *big* animal, sure…but just an animal.

When Burgleman had woken up that morning in his apartment in nearby Canyon, he had turned on the radio. That was when he first heard that Godzilla was in California.

Instead of panicking, Burgleman drove to work

and opened his shop, just as he would on any other Sunday. He wasn't about to leave all he'd ever worked for to the mercy of looters or worse, just because some big dumb dinosaur was running loose in Northern California.

Burgleman almost changed his mind when he saw Godzilla in the flesh. First, he felt the earth tremble at the monster's approach. Next, the electrical power winked out, but came back on.

That was when he looked out of his shop's plate-glass window and saw the gargantuan thing called Godzilla lumbering past on the main highway. The creature's tail thrashed, leaving a trail of smoke, fire, and destruction in its wake. Burgleman couldn't believe that anything that big could be alive!

To Burgleman's relief, the creature seemed to be passing the mall right by. Then the helicopters arrived. Now Burgleman watched in awe as the rockets struck Godzilla again and again in a seemingly endless stream. The explosions looked tiny against Godzilla's bulk, but there were so many of them that they soon obscured the monster in smoke and fire.

Though there was a considerable risk of shrapnel—Burgleman had seen and heard chunks of metal and debris striking the pavement of the almost-empty parking lot since the attack began—the shopkeeper ventured outside to get a better view. The sound of the battle was deafening.

He almost went back inside when one rocket actually bounced off Godzilla's tough hide and spun away. Burgleman watched as the spinning projectile arced into the air. When it finally came to earth, it struck the mall's huge sign on the other side of the immense parking lot. The electric billboard exploded in a shower of sparks and shattered glass.

Despite the risks, Burgleman was too amazed by the titanic struggle taking place right there in front of him to move.

When a second wave of much more powerful missiles struck Godzilla, the creature let loose with a bellow of rage and pain that shook the windows of Burgleman's store.

Godzilla's bony spines danced with electric fire as powerful explosions racked his tortured mass.

Suddenly, the yowling monster threw up his claws in a defensive posture and tumbled down. When he struck the earth, the ground trembled. Then a wave of tectonic force moved under the parking lot, rippling the pavement. The wave continued forward until it buckled the sidewalk where Craig Burgleman stood.

Behind him, the plate-glass windows of his computer shop cracked. Two stores down, the front windows of a dress shop shattered, spilling a shower of glass and several mannequins onto the sidewalk.

To Burgleman's surprise, gouts of melted green plastic and chunks of rubber began raining down on the mall's parking lot. He jumped backward, trying to get under the awning of his store before he, too, was hit.

He didn't move fast enough. Before he took a step, his face, neck, and shirt were splattered by the green slime. Startled and sickened, Burgleman hastily wiped the sticky stuff off his face with his hands.

The liquid was thick, and had a peculiar metallic smell—not unlike the electronic smell of his storeroom. As Burgleman looked at the stuff on his hands, another chunk of black rubber dropped to the ground at his feet. Despite a feeling of mounting horror, Burgleman bent down to examine the debris.

He discovered that it wasn't rubber at all. Nor was the stuff on his shirt melted plastic. The black rubber was really chunks of Godzilla's flesh, blasted away from the creature's body. And the green goo was…Godzilla's blood.

Burgleman gagged and rushed to the bathroom at the back of the store, but when he turned on the water, nothing came out. In desperation, he ran to the tiny refrigerator and used some cold bottled water to rinse off. He tore off his shirt, balled it up, and threw it into the trash bin.

When the Hellfire missiles were spent, the Apaches aimed their chin-mounted machine guns at the monster. The helicopters did not back away. Instead, they circled the fallen beast like a swarm of impatient vultures. Godzilla was almost completely obscured in billowing clouds of black smoke and orange fire.

The creature's roars of rage and pain had subsided, and though his long tail still thrashed through the maelstrom of smoke and fire, it looked as if Godzilla had been stopped, at least temporarily.

Thirty seconds passed. Then the flight leader

inched his helicopter closer to the billowing smoke. The commander was about to don his infrared goggles in an attempt to see through the conflagration when he noticed flashes of blue lightning rippling in the smoke.

"*Pull back! Pull back!*" the commander cried into his microphone. But even as the Apaches began to disperse, a bolt of blue fire blasted out of the smoke and struck the commander's Apache. The helicopter—and its two occupants—evaporated in a bright yellow ball of fire.

Then, out of the blazing turmoil, Godzilla struggled to his feet with a mighty bellow that drowned out the thrumming beat of the helicopter blades.

As the choppers scattered like angry wasps, Godzilla spat fire at them. Two more Apaches and their crews were blasted to atoms before the rest of the helicopters fled into the afternoon sky.

Grunting, Godzilla flailed his tail in anger, demolishing a used-car dealership and knocking the vehicles into the surrounding buildings. The creature's massive bulk had left a huge hole in the pavement where he had fallen. Godzilla had left chunks of his own flesh and blood behind as well.

With single-minded determination, the creature resumed its trek eastward, moving toward the city of Stockton, and perhaps beyond—to the very heartland of America...

Dan Burgleman couldn't walk. He couldn't even stand anymore. The sickness came on him fast, before he knew what hit him.

And it hit him hard.

Gagging, he rushed back to the restroom and began to vomit. Since he was totally unnerved by what had happened to him, the vomiting and nausea that hit him in waves didn't surprise him at first—even though he never thought he would hurl just because of a little gore.

But when the symptoms got much more violent, Burgleman began to worry. He decided he'd better leave the store and find help. In the distance, he could hear sirens wailing.

But try as he might, Burgleman just couldn't control the spasms in his gut. Long after everything was out of his stomach, Burgleman still felt the convulsions rip through his abdomen.

He was so sick he couldn't move, couldn't walk. He just gagged and writhed on the tile floor of his store's restroom.

Maybe if I rest here for a while, the sickness will pass and I can get out of here, he thought hopefully.

Daniel Burgleman *was* found, seven hours later, by National Guard troops wearing protective biological warfare suits. The soldiers had been searching for survivors in and around Moraga.

When the soldiers found Burgleman, he was lying in the middle of the computer store, unconscious. He had managed to crawl that far before finally collapsing.

Immediately, the soldiers rushed the still-living Burgleman to the hospital. While his computer store remained virtually unharmed, Burgleman was anything but.

Like thousands of others, he had only feared being crushed by Godzilla. He had never thought about the dangerous side effects from Godzilla's radioactive flesh and blood.

General Taggart and Dr. Irene Markham waited on the tarmac as Lori Angelo came in for a landing.

The rest of the G-Force team was busy in the command center, getting up-to-the-minute situation reports on Godzilla's activity, on Varan's airborne approach toward the Texas coast, and the continuing search for Rodan in Lake Oahe.

The desert afternoon was hot and dry, and the Osprey's twin-rotor blades kicked up dust as the aircraft touched down and taxied toward the main hangar.

When the engines stopped, the hatch on the fuselage opened and Lori stepped out, blinking against the sun and the dust.

Or maybe she's fighting back tears, Dr. Markham thought with compassion for the confused young woman.

The psychiatrist watched as Lori and General Taggart silently stared at each other from across the runway. The girl's face was torn with emotion. General Taggart's eyes, hidden behind sunglasses, were unreadable.

Lori approached the general with a brisk, military step. Taggart stood stock-still, waiting.

Finally, Lori stood toe-to-toe with the general, and she saluted. "Reporting for duty, sir," she announced, suddenly calm and in control.

"Do you think you're ready for active duty?"

General Taggart barked at the girl.

Lori nodded, then smiled. "I just need a little sleep, sir," she replied.

"We'll just have to see about that," the general retorted. Then he pointed at Dr. Markham.

"I want you to go back to the medical facility with the doctor here," he declared. "When Dr. Markham examines you, and clears you for active duty, you are to report to the command center."

Lori couldn't hide her delight. "Yessss, *sir!*" she cried, saluting again.

General Taggart returned the salute briskly. Then, without another word, he turned on his heels and strode back to headquarters.

The beautiful city of Galveston, Texas, built on the long, narrow stretch of land between the Gulf of Mexico and Galveston Bay, was no stranger to natural disasters.

In the past, the city had suffered more than its share of deadly hurricanes. In September 1900, the city was hit by one, which was followed by a devastating tidal wave that left the entire city in ruins and six thousand people dead.

After that disaster, Galveston was rebuilt. This time, however, the city planners raised the city at least six feet above its original level. They also built a seventeen-foot-high concrete seawall all along the coast to protect their city from the ravages of the Gulf of Mexico.

When another, even more powerful, hurricane hit in 1915, the seawall held firm, and the city was spared from destruction.

Now, as the late spring sun set over the peaceful, unsuspecting scene, a disaster of a different kind descended upon the island city of Galveston.

And no mere seawall could hold it off.

As spring crowds strolled along the sandy beaches near Seawall Boulevard and folks moved in and out of Galveston's Convention and Visitors' Bureau, death dropped out of the sky.

At first, it was the beachgoers who noticed it. They saw a black silhouette framed against the golden dusk. Some folks pointed toward the phenomenon and called to their friends.

The black figure got larger and larger, until it looked as if a huge blimp was moving from the sky above the gulf toward the shore. Then, at the last possible moment, the black form seemed to speed up. As the crowd watched in horror, the object swooped down and dived toward the populated beach below.

People began to flee the waterfront in panic as Varan approached. Seawall Boulevard became a mass of running, frightened people.

The monster swooped over the beach, and a rushing wind in its wake blew white sand across the city, carried off beach umbrellas and furniture, and even overturned cars.

Varan slammed against the steel and glass Marriott Hotel with an earsplitting crash. The building literally imploded under the force and weight of the creature's assault. The luxury hotel collapsed, floor upon floor, until nothing stood.

In the center of the rubble, Varan roared and thrashed about angrily, scattering debris and uncovering victims trapped in the building's collapse.

When Varan dug enough of the ruins away, dozens of bodies, and a few survivors, were lying in a heap in the center of the ruined hotel. Some cried out, but most were dead and silent. Varan opened its yawning, slavering mouth and began to feed on its victims.

Everyone looked up in total surprise as Lori Angelo reported for duty in the G-Force command center.

Tia, who was monitoring communications from a dozen military commands in California, South Dakota, and Texas, yelped with surprise and delight. Kip looked up from a printout and nudged Martin Wong. "Look...Lori's back!" he declared.

"Looks like you're not the only screw-up around here anymore," the Chinese-American flight engineer replied.

Toby Nelson practically ran to his co-pilot and embraced her in a bear hug.

Unnoticed by anyone except Tia Shimura, Pierce Dillard's iron facade broke. He actually smiled, with much more emotion than Tia thought the head pilot was capable of.

Tia's intuition kicked in, and she wondered if there wasn't something more going on in Pierce's mind than just military strategy.

Colonel Krupp, from his position in front of the command monitor, also looked surprised to see Lori. He was even more startled when General Taggart stepped into the command center right behind the young woman.

The general stepped up to the podium in the center of the room. That was the signal for the G-Force team to take their briefing positions.

The big television monitors were shut off, except for the one in the center, which showed Godzilla towering over the suburban sprawl of an unnamed town in Northern California.

"I'd like your attention," the general said after everyone had taken a seat.

"First, I'd like you all to welcome back Ms. Angelo," he said. "She's been returned to active duty after being on...special assignment."

There was an enthusiastic round of applause in the command center. At her briefing station, Lori blushed. Silently, she thanked the general for not disclosing the *real* reason for her absence. When the applause died down, the general's face suddenly turned solemn.

"As you all know," he continued. "In the last twenty-four hours, no fewer than three *kaiju* have arrived on our nation's shores..."

The general withdrew a printout from his uniform pocket.

"I just received orders from the President of the United States," he announced grimly. "G-Force has just been activated. The commander-in-chief has ordered us to fly Raptor-One and Raptor-Two to Texas tomorrow morning."

This was definitely *not* what they expected. The general stopped reading and looked up at his team.

"I know you want to fight Godzilla," he told them. "But there has been a complication.

"During the helicopter attack in Moraga, some of Godzilla's blood was spilled over the town. A mysterious radioactive blood-borne toxin was also released. It has resulted in the hospitalization of hundreds."

The general turned to Colonel Krupp. The other officer stepped up to a microphone.

"The Centers for Disease Control in Atlanta have sent out a team of experts," the colonel informed them. "But until the doctors have come to some conclusions, no further attacks will be launched against Godzilla. Instead, the military will continue to try to evacuate the population in Godzilla's path."

Pierce struck his fist into his hand. Toby shook his head in frustration. Kip felt a wave of relief...which was almost immediately replaced by shame. *Am I that afraid?* he wondered.

General Taggart spoke again.

"We're going to fight Varan," he said simply. "We leave at 0500—five o'clock tomorrow morning."

His cold eyes scanned the room one last time.

"Get a good night's sleep," he commanded them. "You'll need it."

22
BAPTISM OF FIRE

VARAN™

Sunday, June 13, 1999, 4:55 P.M.
G-Force mobile command headquarters
Houston Intercontinental Airport
Houston, Texas

Things began to fall apart all across the United
States the moment Godzilla stepped out of San
Francisco Bay. It was one of the blackest days in the
nation's history.

Twenty-six hours after Godzilla arrived, the
stock market took its first step toward a historic
plunge. At the same time, gold and precious met-
als shot up in value as investors began to fear the
worst.

Fortunes were made and lost—but mostly lost.
And not even financial giants or Fortune 500 companies were immune to the precipitous plunge in
stock prices. In the end, the Securities and
Exchange Commission stepped in and shut down
the stock market early. They did not say when it
would open again. After all, the nation was in a
state of emergency, and the whole nation's infrastructure was now threatened.

The president went on television for the fourth
time in three weeks. After the military's failure

against Varan and Godzilla, he was no longer taken seriously. His calls for calm were greeted with derision and accusations of incompetence.

Riots broke out in several cities. A militia group took to the Montana mountains with a ton of weapons in tow.

Meanwhile, the environmental group Greenpeace hailed Godzilla's return, calling the monster an "eco-avenger" who would return the world to a "more natural state."

In Nashville, Tennessee, a popular and much respected televangelist began around-the-clock live broadcasts. The preacher—formerly the spiritual counselor of presidents, governors, and captains of industry—called his broadcast "live coverage of Armageddon." He claimed, in a calm, reasonable tone, that his show would soon be the only program on the air.

Godzilla, the evangelist declared, was the Beast of Revelations. Judgment Day was at hand.

In Los Angeles, a New Age guru also announced that the Second Coming was near. Using her own system of numerology—a means of divination that assigns "mystical numbers" to each letter of the alphabet—the guru calculated that the names Rodan and *Gojira,* the Japanese name for Godzilla, both added up to in the demonic number, six.

The self-styled "Prophetess of Doom"—and former editor of a Marilyn Manson fanzine—predicted that a *fourth* creature, also numerologically a six, was yet to come, forming the "Number of the Beast," 666. This final monster, called "King Ghidorah," would come from the depths of space, the prophetess announced, and would end all life on Earth.

Her followers moved into their spiritual leader's recently purchased San Diego mansion to await the end. An MTV film crew joined them, and soon weekly sessions were aired on the music channel in which the prophetess—in full Goth regalia—spoke at length about "King Ghidorah."

By sunset on that grim Monday, as live footage of Godzilla striding across California—and Varan sleeping off its meal of several hundred citizens on Galveston's seawall—was constantly broadcast on every network, the country was in a panic.

Not widely reported in the media were much more disturbing developments.

There was widespread looting, riots, and general social chaos in the wake of Godzilla's coming. Hundreds, perhaps thousands, were dead—not only from Godzilla's actions, but also at the hands of their fellow men.

There were reports of heroism and common decency, too. Everyday people from all walks of life risked their own safety to help others. Many of those who still had food, clothing, and shelter shared their good fortune with those who had lost everything.

Especially inspiring was the story of a San Francisco cop named Dennis Flynn, who saved three children from a blazing inferno in the ruins of Oakland, only to die trying to pull a fourth victim to safety.

So far, casualties among the various armed services, including the National Guard, were light. Military experts felt that this situation would not last—especially if conventional forces were once again pitted against Godzilla or Varan.

General Taggart finished reading the Pentagon report, snorted in disgust, and tossed it on the desk. It was not much help. General Taggart knew most of this stuff already. He had learned it from watching network news coverage of the continuing crisis.

And anyone as old—and presumably wise— as General Taggart, could have predicted the rest. *People never change,* the general thought sadly. He realized that it was up to his highly trained, but as yet untested, teenagers to save the world.

In Hangar B, where Raptor-One and Raptor-Two were hidden from prying eyes, Kip Daniels sat in his command seat inside the cathedral-like cockpit of Raptor-One. His fingers flew across the keys of the weapon control panel, but his mind was far away.

Kip was just finishing the last of his systems checks. Everything was working at peak efficiency, thanks to some last-minute tinkering by Martin Wong. The Raptor was ready for combat.

But am I ready? Kip wondered, his mind whirling with doubts.

Can I really pull the trigger on Godzilla when it comes right down to the moment of truth? And is destroying him the right thing to do? Godzilla must be here for a reason. Why can't we figure it out what that reason is?

Pierce Dillard sat alone in his tiny bedroom, inside the belly of a C-130 transport that served as the G-Force mobile command center and headquarters.

Two compartments away, Martin Wong, Tia Shimura, and Toby Nelson sat in the command station, watching the color monitors that displayed vast amounts of information—everything from weather reports to military data, navigational programs, network news feeds, live satellite imagery, and aerial surveillance of Godzilla and Varan. It even carried pictures of the continuing search for Rodan—on, above, and below the waters of Lake Oahe.

While all this was going on, Pierce sat alone. He wanted nothing more than to join them. To talk about the coming battle. To share his doubts and hopes with them.

But he was their leader. He had to stay aloof. Separate. That was part of being a commander. *The lonely part*.

Pierce suspected that a *real* commander wasn't supposed to feel doubt, or fear, or even a simple case of pre-combat nerves. Yet he felt all of those emotions, and more.

He was ready for the fight. He *knew* he was. But there was always an element of combat that was outside of his iron control. And that bothered him.

Since the project began, there had always been

problems. First it was Lori. Pierce took her in hand and solved that problem. Then Kip became the chaotic element.

How can I control the mission when everyone else seems to fall apart? Pierce wondered. *Am I the only one in complete control?*

Pierce Dillard closed his eyes and sighed. *Am I really in control after all?* he wondered grimly. *I've been trying to control the mission, the team, and every element of strategy and tactics all along.*

But maybe the thing I can't control isn't out there…Maybe it's in here. Inside of me.

Lori looked away from the computer screen and out the cockpit window. On the other side of Hangar B, she could see Raptor-One. Its cockpit lights were on, too. Someone else found comfort in work, she noted.

Lori had been downloading street and topographical maps of the Houston-Galveston area into Raptor-Two's computer. Once the battle began, she would have accurate, up-to-date maps of the region at her fingertips.

When another file finished downloading, Lori shut the system down. Again, her eyes drifted toward the floor of the hangar. *Still no sign of Pierce,* she thought.

Lori suspected that the pilot of Raptor-One was in his quarters—alone. She wondered why he stayed so aloof from the rest of them. Lori knew that everyone thought Pierce Dillard was a cold, ruthless leader, but she suspected that he was as vulnerable, as *human,* as any of them. Pierce just chose to bury that side of himself for the good of the project.

Lori wished that Pierce would let his guard down—with someone, anyone—for his *own* good. She decided it was time she had a talk with their fearless, solitary leader.

But just as she rose from her chair, alarms sounded.

Varan was on the move.

There was no time for a briefing. Varan had awakened, and as the tanks and fighting vehicles that surrounded it opened fire, the monster took to the sky.

Right now, Varan was heading directly toward Houston. The creature was drifting over the outer suburbs of that city at 100 miles per hour, at an altitude of 10,000 feet.

Raptor-One and Raptor-Two lifted off from Houston Intercontinental Airport just minutes after the alarm was given. The two aircraft flew toward the monster in a sandwich formation. Raptor-One, with its payload of weapons, flew low and forward, with Pierce at the controls.

Raptor-Two, under the command of Toby, with its forward-looking search radars and navigational systems, flew high and behind. Sitting beside Toby in Two, Lori scanned the sky with radar, searching for the floating *kaiju*.

Although both aircraft possessed advanced search radar, Raptor-Two's system was much more sophisticated. With it, Lori quickly located Varan in the darkening sky.

"I've got him," she reported. Then she radioed Varan's position to Pierce.

His face a mask of concentration, Pierce banked the huge twin-bladed aircraft and positioned it in the sky so that the Raptor was hovering between downtown Houston and the oncoming monster. If Varan wanted to destroy the city, it would have to get by Raptor-One first.

Pierce pointed the nose of his aircraft toward the oncoming monster, and as Varan drifted into sight, he turned over control to Kip.

"Go get him, Kip," Pierce said as he transferred command. Martin sat at the engineering console, waiting for Kip's first move. Behind Martin, at her command station, Tia monitored the navigational computer. With Lori's help, Tia knew their location at all times, and her computer was fed constant updates from geopositional satellites.

Kip, at the very front of the huge Raptor cockpit, gripped the control stick with sweating hands.

Varan had spotted them, though it seemed undaunted by the Raptor's presence. The creature floated toward them slowly, its eyes locked on the approaching aircraft.

Focusing his concentration on the target ahead, Kip peered through the heads-up display. The HUD showed the monster was still out of range of most of his weapons. Slowly, he pushed the joystick forward, edging the Raptor closer to the target.

Far below, thousands of people came out onto their lawns and looked up into the sky as news bulletins informed them of the battle about to be waged above their heads.

Suddenly, without warning, Varan shot forward, its claws outstretched. Kip twisted the stick. The Raptor dropped in a stomach-clenching plunge that brought a yelp from Martin.

Varan rushed over the Raptor, its tail slamming against the fuselage as it passed. The aircraft shuddered, and some warning lights on Martin's control panel lit up, but it could have been much worse. If Kip had been even a half a second slower, Varan would have collided with them.

As the monster shot past, Kip could actually see the pupils of its reptilian eyes staring back at him.

"He's behind you, Kip!" Lori cried over his headphones.

Quickly, Kip turned the Raptor completely around on its axis and pointed the nose at the retreating monster. Pushing the joystick, Kip propelled the aircraft forward, right on Varan's tail.

Kip chose to lead the attack with the eight GAU-8/A Avenger cannons mounted on the fuselage of Raptor-One, four to each side. He keyed in the selection on his weapons menu.

Inside the bowels of the Raptor, hundreds of thousands of rounds of 30mm armor-piercing shells were fed into the guns automatically. When the cannons were armed, the HUD turned green.

Kip aimed the cross hairs of the targeting computer at the retreating monster and opened fire. Over 4,000 rounds per second blasted toward Varan from each of the eight cannons. Kip used a three-second burst—any more would slow down the Raptor's forward momentum and put them out of range.

The shells bounced off Varan's thickly armored flanks, but the attack got the creature's attention. With surprising maneuverability, Varan turned in midair and rushed back toward them.

This time, Kip opened up with the cannons right before he dived. In the darkening sky, the bullets glowed brightly. Kip, busy fighting the controls, could not tell if he inflicted any damage with his second attack. But at least Varan was heading away from the heavily populated Houston area.

"He's coming around, Kip!" Lori warned.

Again, Kip spun the Raptor like a top and pointed its nose at the monster. As Varan rushed toward the aircraft, Kip opened up with the cannons for a third time.

Varan bellowed as the shells pounded its neck, face, and head. The mighty roar was so loud it shook the Raptor. But instead of retreating, Kip faced down the creature and continued to pump shells into its body at a murderous rate.

Still, Varan came at them. Finally, like a game of chicken played by titans, Kip flinched. He dived the Raptor in another gut-wrenching descent as Varan again passed over their heads.

And once again, Kip turned the Raptor around and charged.

Martin whooped, and Tia's eyes never left her monitors. She noticed that they had lost altitude each time Varan attacked.

Kip was successfully leading Varan away from Houston, but they were getting dangerously low over the suburbs.

Because the 30mm shells had been ineffective,

Kip quickly called up the menu and switched over to the rockets. The Raptor carried a soupçon of various missiles, all of them armor-piercing. Under the Raptor's wings, four rocket pods containing fifty projectiles each dropped out of their protective bays.

Kip aimed at Varan through his HUD and, when the targeting computer signaled that he had a lock, he depressed the trigger.

Dozens of rockets lanced out of their pods and streaked toward Varan, trailing fire. One by one, the rockets struck the creature, detonating upon impact. Clusters of tiny explosions riddled Varan's tortured body. Finally, as the last few projectiles were fired, the creature began to lose altitude.

Though there was no way to be sure, Kip believed that Varan had finally been hurt. It was time to press the attack. As he guided the Raptor into position, Kip calculated their altitude. Man and monster were less than a thousand feet from the ground.

"What's that ahead of us?" Kip demanded over the radio.

Aboard Raptor-Two, Lori checked her navigational maps. They were over Galveston once again. Pier 22 and the Galveston Ship Channel were right below them. Lori could see the *Elissa*, a tall wooden ship that dated from 1877, moored to the pier.

She tried to discern what Kip was referring to. Then she saw a line of huge fuel tanks on the far shore and a small tanker moored near them.

"It's a tank farm," Lori replied a few seconds later. "Diesel fuel for ships…and it's been evacuated."

"Good," Kip grunted, fighting the control. "I'm going to force Varan down right there."

"What the hell—" Pierce snapped. But Martin grasped Kip's plan immediately.

"The scientists think Varan has sacs filled with flammable hydrogen!" Martin cried. "Kip's going to try to ignite Varan's internal gases."

As Martin spoke, Kip maneuvered the Raptor so that he was behind and above Varan. He switched to the cannons again and opened fire.

The shells ripped into the creature's hide. Kip concentrated the stream of armor-piercing projectiles on just one small section of Varan's torso. The creature suddenly lost altitude, until its soft, unarmored belly was directly over the largest of the fuel tanks in the depot.

Quickly, Kip switched menus and called up the Raptor's Hellfire missiles.

He aimed, not at Varan, but at the fuel tank underneath it. Six missiles leaped from their wing pylons and streaked toward the metal tank.

The fiery explosion lit up the dusk and rocked Raptor-One. A column of fire shot into the sky, completely engulfing Varan. A huge secondary blast followed the first, and more fire leaped into the air. The tremendous explosion could be seen from miles around. The blast shattered windows in downtown Galveston, and knocked down power lines, toppled a radio tower, and capsized the tanker moored to the pier.

In the middle of the conflagration, Varan bellowed in agony. As the fires spread, another tank blew up, sending more smoke into the air.

Hovering over Galveston, the occupants of Raptor-One watched in amazement as Varan rose, phoenix-like, from the destruction. But as it limped into the air, Kip could see that the monster was wounded, perhaps mortally.

Turning, Varan floated toward the waters of the Gulf of Mexico. The creature was burning in the sky as its shattered gas pockets leaked hydrogen, which continuously fed the flames.

Cautiously, Kip followed the monster, but he did not attack again. When Varan was miles from the Texas coast, another explosion rocked its body. As the crews of Raptor-One and Raptor-Two watched, Varan dropped out of the sky and into the Gulf, where it vanished beneath the waves.

Dead or alive, Varan was no longer a threat.

G-Force had fought its first battle—and *won*.

TM
RODAN™

23
TRAIN WRECK

Wednesday, June 30, 1999, 1:39 P.M.
Lake Oahe, South Dakota

Slowly, life around Lake Oahe returned to normal.

Though the military still searched the lake for the remains of the monster Rodan, their zeal had ebbed. Two U.S. Marine sonar ships cruised the length of the lake, sounding the bottom, searching for signs of the vanished *kaiju.* Another ship, from the Institute for Undersea Exploration, used remote-control robots to search through the sediment, so far without success.

Even the reporters who covered the Rodan story soon moved on to more pressing duties. After all, it was Godzilla's continuing trek across the heart of America that was capturing the attention of the world.

Godzilla, currently marching through Nevada, was only ninety miles north of Las Vegas. The casinos were taking bets on whether or not the creature would show up on the Vegas Strip, and there was talk of another Air Force strike against the monster while he was still in a relatively remote region.

Searching for a carcass of a dead *Pteranodon* was an uninteresting sideshow for the back pages.

But at dawn on Thursday, July 1, that sideshow took center stage once again.

As one of the Marine detachments was getting ready to launch their sonar vessel, the waters of Lake Oahe began to churn and bubble. One of the Marines pointed, and soon everyone was watching. The first lieutenant grabbed his video camera and pointed it at the frothing, churning turmoil.

Cackling wildly, Rodan burst from the lake. With each 175-foot wing flapping wildly, the bird monster took to the air. The force of the winds generated by Rodan struck the Marine detachment, blowing the men off the dock and nearly capsizing their vessel.

As they watched helplessly, most of them from the cold waters of the lake, Rodan circled once overhead. Then, with a burst of speed, the creature flew off in the direction of Rapid City.

As a precaution against Rodan's unlikely resurrection, a battery of Patriot missile installations had been placed around Lake Oahe. The moment the creature took to the air, sophisticated targeting radar began tracking it.

Inside the Patriot missile control vehicles, U.S. Army technicians watched the approach of the monster. The order was sent out to all missile batteries to fire at will.

In seconds, the boxlike missile launchers aimed at the sky, and twenty Patriot anti-aircraft missiles arced upward. Inside the mobile command center, the technicians watched the missiles streak toward their target. First one, then another struck home against Rodan's belly. They were followed by four more, which exploded on, or near, the still-moving target.

The radar screens were lit up with repeated detonations, which should have obliterated Rodan. But, unknown to the military, Rodan's underbelly was protected by a thick, bony armor that withstood the first few blasts. Rodan dispatched the rest of the missiles with its beam of destructive fire.

Now, confused and enraged, the creature dived toward the earth once again. It was searching the ground for prey—for something to lash out against. Suddenly, Rodan spotted a huge, snakelike object moving through the hills of South Dakota.

With an echoing cackle, Rodan dived headfirst toward its target.

Slowly, the train carrying a thousand head of cattle to the Chicago stockyards wound its way through the South Dakota hills. Near a town called Cherry Creek, the freight train slowed down as it moved onto a high bridge that was suspended over a deep gorge. At the bottom of the gorge flowed the Cheyenne River. The bridge consisted of a steel framework with a single track running along the top.

When fourteen of the twenty-two railroad cars had moved onto the steel bridge, Rodan struck.

With a wild, cackling screech, the gigantic mutant *Pteranodon* twisted in the sky and struck with its hind legs.

Clutching the stock cars packed with live cattle in its mammoth claws, Rodan literally carried away nine freight cars—along with a huge section of the steel bridge. The front three cars, including two locomotives, were thrown into the gorge. Their crews died screaming as the engines crashed into the shallow Cheyenne River.

Some of the remaining freight cars continued on through sheer momentum until they reached the shattered section of the bridge. Then they, too, plunged into the gorge, pulling the rest of the train down with them. Cattle howled in fear and panic as the cars carried them to an early grave.

In the caboose, two railroad workers witnessed Rodan's attack. When they saw the remains of the train being dragged to certain doom, they rushed out the back door.

The first man leaped immediately, jumping onto the tracks. He landed hard on the wooden ties, shattering his collarbone.

The second man hesitated—and was lost.

As the man on the tracks looked on helplessly, the caboose tumbled over the edge of the demolished bridge and disappeared into the gorge.

The second man still gripped the railing on the back of the caboose, too afraid to jump. He plunged with the train to his death.

Rodan, still clutching the stock cars packed with pathetic, bleating cattle, circled the sky until it found a suitable landing place. Finally, it spotted a line of low hills rising in the distance.

Wheeling in the air, Rodan turned and headed for the mountains. As it banked, a single stock car broke loose and plunged thousands of feet to the earth below.

*   *   *

Four hours after the attack on the cattle train, klaxons blared once again at G-Force headquarters at Nellis.

The team assembled in the command center to find Colonel Krupp filling in for General Taggart, who had gone to Washington.

Most of the G-Force team were already frustrated. So far, despite their success against Varan, they had been denied the chance to go up against Godzilla.

There would never be a better time to fight the monster, either. Godzilla was entering a remote area of Utah, where lives and property would not be endangered by an attack.

Still, as he had done for weeks, the president held them back. Kip, Toby, and Pierce all thought General Taggart had traveled to D.C. to convince the timid president to turn G-Force loose. So far, they had heard no news.

As the colonel briefed them, the G-Force team understood that they would never be sent to fight Rodan. The *kaiju* simply flew too fast, and too high, for the Raptors.

Raptor-One and Raptor-Two were built to fight land-bound *kaiju*—no one had suspected such a creature as Rodan could exist.

When Colonel Krupp completed his briefing, Dr. Max Birchwood took the podium.

"It looks as if the creature has evolved since it first appeared," Dr. Birchwood announced.

On the center monitor, footage of the creature taken by U.S. Marines was projected. The image froze, and the kaijuologist pointed to the creature's chest.

"This bony armor plating has proved to be impervious to Patriot missiles," he informed them.

"This indicates to us that the previous attack may not have harmed Rodan at all. Perhaps what drove the creature into Lake Oahe was pure instinct, a course of action made during, or because of, a particular biological event."

"A biological *event?*" Lori asked. "A hibernation period, maybe?"

Dr. Birchwood shook his head. "No. That's what we thought, until an hour ago, when we got this footage…"

The image on the central monitor changed. It now showed a familiar landmark—Mount Rushmore, with the faces of America's four most revered leaders carved into its cliff face: George Washington, Thomas Jefferson, Abraham Lincoln, and Theodore Roosevelt.

The G-Force team all noticed a black silhouette on top of Washington's head.

"Magnify the image," Dr. Birchwood instructed the projectionist. The image expanded until it was plainly visible.

It was Rodan. And the creature seemed to be sitting in a tremendously large nest, made out of twisted railroad track, parts from a shattered bridge, a tour bus, and tons of unidentifiable debris.

"The creature constructed this nest in under twelve hours," Dr. Birchwood said. He paused before he delivered his bombshell.

"I've just examined satellite photographs and real-time images transmitted to us," he said grimly.

"That nest contains an egg."

Late that same night, General Taggart returned to Nellis in an Air Force jet. Under his arm, he carried orders from the President of the United States. The orders activated G-Force, instructing them to attack Godzilla as soon as possible—preferably while the creature was in a remote region of the country.

As General Taggart climbed down from the cockpit of the F-4 Phantom he'd flown back from Washington, he planned his next move. He decided he would alert Colonel Krupp, Dr. Birchwood, and even Dr. Markham—whose counsel he had come to trust and respect—that the attack had been given the green light.

He would wait until morning to tell the G-Force team that all that they trained for was about to take place.

And may God protect them, he thought as he crossed the dark airfield.

GODZILLA™

24
G-FORCE VS.
GODZILLA!

In the end, the attack against Godzilla was delayed for many weeks, mostly because of the actions of the governor of Utah. In a political and constitutional battle, the governor forbade military action within the borders of his state. Editorial writers and television journalists all over the country sided with Governor Constable, and the attack was finally postponed until Godzilla left Utah.

G-Force used the time to hone their skills. But there was dissension within their ranks as well. Lori Angelo did not want to fight Godzilla at all. She told General Taggart that Mothra told her, in her vision, that Godzilla was an ally, not an enemy.

Though Dr. Markham and General Taggart were both inclined to believe her now, the general felt that G-Force should make an attempt to stop Godzilla's trek through America's heartland. It was what they had trained, and sworn, to do.

For the good of the team, Lori was convinced to keep her visions to herself and go along with the attack. She relented. In her heart of hearts, Lori believed that Godzilla was unstoppable, anyway. Nothing that G-Force could do would harm him.

On July 10, the day before the first wave of nuclear missiles was to strike the asteroid swarm in deep space, Godzilla passed through the suburbs of Grand Junction, Colorado, causing massive property damage. Fortunately, few lives were lost, since the military had previously evacuated the area.

As spy aircraft filmed the creature's movements from high in the stratosphere, Godzilla surprised the experts. Instead of traveling in a straight line, which would lead him to the highest peaks of the Rocky Mountain range, Godzilla turned.

As if guided by some higher power, Godzilla avoided the most rugged terrain and moved instead toward the Gunnison National Forest.

After Godzilla's turn southeast was confirmed, G-Force departed Nellis for Gunnison County Airport in Colorado.

On a beautiful Sunday morning, when the eyes of the whole planet were turned toward the heavens, G-Force prepared to make war on Earth's most dangerous monster.

As the team assembled in the mobile command center, they each watched the drama that was unfolding in the depths of space.

In two hours, at 12:21 P.M., local time, the first wave of nuclear missiles would strike the Reyes-Mishra asteroids. It was hoped that the nukes would obliterate the space rocks, but if they failed, there was still a second wave of missiles that would strike in another week. The G-Force team would learn the results of Project EarthFirst only after their mission was over.

If everything went as scheduled, they would be attacking Godzilla just as the missiles struck the asteroid cloud.

As he crossed the hot tarmac toward Raptor-One, Kip used the meditation techniques he had been taught to empty his mind of chaos and concentrate on the battle ahead. Pierce Dillard walked silently at his side, concentrating on his own doubts and fears.

Only Tobias Nelson and Martin Wong seemed unperturbed by the coming battle. Pierce wondered if they'd let their easy victory against Varan cloud their judgment.

He worried that they were too overconfident.

As Tia Shimura approached the aircraft, she was troubled by doubts of her own. Late the night before, Lori had knocked on the door of her tiny cabin inside the C-130 Hercules. The older girl had looked distraught, and Tia admitted her.

She wished now that she hadn't.

In violation of a direct order from General Taggart, and the wishes of Dr. Markham, Lori told Tia about her disturbing dreams and about the vision of Mothra she saw over San Francisco Bay.

"I wanted someone to know," Lori told her. "In case something happens to me…"

Tia wished she *didn't* know, for now she was racked by the same doubts as Lori. Now she wondered if the monster they were about to attack was mankind's deadliest foe—or greatest friend.

The forests of Colorado were green with the full-ness of summer. As Pierce flew Raptor-One toward Gunnison National Forest, he couldn't help but admire the forest's natural beauty.

Behind and above them, the Raptor-Two broadcast rock music to her sister ship. Martin had slipped Toby the tape before they lifted off. The music of Blue Oyster Cult blared into their ears. The tape began with "Don't Fear the Reaper," and now had moved on to the Cult classic "Godzilla."

"Is this Toby's idea of a joke?" Kip asked Pierce. The pilot turned and noticed Martin snickering beside him.

"I don't think so..." Pierce replied, staring hard at his giggling co-pilot.

Despite the weak attempt at humor, tension was thick inside the cockpit. Kip felt it too. But he also felt an adrenaline high, along with the rest of his teammates. After their first battle, and the weeks of inaction, the G-Force team was more than ready. They were pumped.

But Kip noticed that Tia and Lori were strangely silent, which was odd. Especially for Lori. He was about to remark on it when the music vanished, and the headphones in his helmet crackled to life.

"Target ahead," Lori announced.

Sunday, July 11, 1999, 1:55 P.M.
Johnson Space Center
Houston, Texas

At NASA's Deep Space Observation Station, Dr. Carl Strickler and Dr. Ramon Reyes watched the computer-enhanced images of the Reyes-Mishra asteroids as they appeared on a huge monitor in the front of the room.

Above the screen, a digital clock ticked down the minutes before the first wave of nuclear missiles reached its targets. In less than two minutes, the cloud would meet Earth's first line of defense.

The two men exchanged meaningful glances as a hush fell over the technicians and scientists who were there to witness humanity's salvation—or its most perilous failure.

At the back of the room, a group of journalists selected from a pool of all the networks stood, watching the monitors. By their sides, each journalist had a cameraman poised to capture the dramatic scenes. Pictures of this most momentous event were being broadcast live, all over the world. It was the most-watched television event in the history of the planet.

Carl turned and glanced up at the digital clock. One minute, forty-three seconds, and counting...

Godzilla loomed like a black shadow over the pine forests of Colorado. The creature moved with surprising grace, Kip thought, and not with the lumbering, clumsy stride of the computer-generated virtual monster they'd fought for months on end.

The difference served to remind Kip that *this* was the real thing. It was a sobering revelation.

As Kip waited for Pierce's final approach, when the pilot would turn over command of the Raptor to him, he studied the monster below.

To his surprise, Godzilla raised his head and stared right at the oncoming aircraft. Kip's heart seemed to stop beating. Suddenly, he had a flash-back to that day in the video arcade when Godzilla's roaring face appeared on the BATTLE-GROUND 2000 machine and he froze. And again, doubts about his mission assailed Kip. *Is it right to attack Godzilla?* he wondered.

A moment after the monster's mouth yawned open, the sound of a faraway roar battered their ship. Again, Lori's voice crackled in his head-phones.

"Okay," she said. "Attack low and from the rear. Let's avoid Godzilla's rays for as long as we can…"

"Roger," Pierce replied as he dipped Raptor-One and swung around and behind the *kaiju*.

"Ready, Daniels?" Pierce asked.

Kip swallowed hard. Then he gripped the joy-stick with both hands. "Roger," he said calmly.

The temptation was just too great. Every tabloid news show had sent the word out to their free-lance photographers, photojournalists, and camera-men. Pictures of the top-secret G-Force team battling Godzilla in Colorado would be worth *big* money. *Really* big money.

Dozens of them set out in cars, on horseback, even on foot, to the area around Gunnison. Of course, it was a restricted area, and the military was there, too.

By the morning of the battle, almost all of the freelance photographers had been caught and removed from the area. Two of them, however, had so far eluded capture, despite the fact that they were amateurs. Their names were Billy and Zelly Whitman, fifteen-year-old twins, who hailed from nearby Grand Junction. They'd "borrowed" their dad's video camera and two of their grandma's horses. They had sneaked away from home and entered the restricted area two days before.

They had waited, listening to reports on their radio and eating army rations rather than risk a fire that could be spotted by patrols. Billy was an Eagle Scout, so he knew how to live in the wilderness. Zelly wasn't happy living in the woods, but it had been her idea to try this stunt. She got it while watching *America's Funniest Home Videos.*

Now their wait was almost over. As she and her brother climbed a peak to find a good place to watch the action, they heard the monster's roar echoing through the hills.

"Wow!" Zelly cried. "Godzilla sounds *so* cool!"

In the valley below, Godzilla crashed through the trees and stomped through a small stream. Deer scampered among the trees at his feet. His thunderous tread shook the forest.

"There he is!" Billy cried, focusing the camera.

As Billy and Zelly watched, the roar of a strange engine rumbled toward them until the sound battered their ears. Suddenly, a huge flying machine popped up from behind a hill and rushed toward Godzilla.

"Wow!" Zelly screamed over the sound. "This is *amazing!*"

Billy pointed the camera at the aircraft.

The machine was drab gray and blended with

the sky. It had two huge horizontal rotors that looked half the size of football fields. The thrumming of the blades beat the ground and shook the trees.

Kip popped the Raptor over the low hill. The forest and verdant hills rushed past their cockpit with dizzying speed. Godzilla's spines filled Kip's HUD, and he nudged the aircraft to one side and targeted a point under the monster's right ear.

That should get his attention, Kip thought.

He keyed up the weapons menu, and chose the eight Avenger cannons. He ignored the treetops, which nearly brushed the Raptor's belly, and concentrated on the target.

He pressed the trigger, and the whole aircraft shook with the force of the guns. In the first *second,* over 42,000 armor-piercing explosive shells tore into Godzilla's neck.

That got his attention.

Godzilla whirled his head around, searching for his attacker. Even as he spun, blue flashes of electricity rippled through the tangle of bony plates on his back. His mouth opened, and Godzilla spat a burst of radioactive fire.

The blast was undirected, but it forced Kip to pull up, and he lost valuable seconds. As he flashed past Godzilla's left shoulder, Kip spun the aircraft, vainly attempting to reacquire the target in his HUD.

Smoke still poured from the wound on Godzilla's neck as Kip guided the Raptor to a frontal assault position.

Let's get this over with, he thought. He flicked a button on his control stick. The heat-resistant panels closed over the Raptor's transparencies. The cockpit got dark for a second, just enough time for the windows to convert to their second function—digital television screens. Hundreds of cameras on the fuselage and wings transmitted real-time images of the exterior of the aircraft.

The images were so realistic that there was virtually no difference between the television screen and the actual view outside of the cockpit.

Kip circled Godzilla as he slowed the Raptor to a hover position. Now the Raptor was face-to-face with the mammoth *kaiju*. The cross hairs on his HUD met in the middle of Godzilla's charcoal-black chest.

Kip's eyes narrowed ruthlessly as he depressed the trigger.

Once again, the Raptor was knocked backward by the recoil from its own multiple cannons. And again, over 40,000 rounds of explosive ammunition struck a single point on Godzilla's tough hide. The burst lasted a second and a half. Kip could not risk a longer burst because it affected the stability of the Raptor.

As the shells slammed into Godzilla, a bell-like yowl of pain burst from his throat.

It was followed by a blast of blue fire that struck the nose of the Raptor. The heat-resistant space-age tiles did their job. Instantly, they both reflected and dispersed the heat. Godzilla's radioactive burst was completely ineffective.

Kip steadied the Raptor and reacquired the target. Then he fired the cannons in another second-and-a-half burst.

"Get down!" Zelly cried, grabbing her brother's coat and pulling him to the ground. Despite the unexpected move, Billy was able to keep the camera focused on the action. Though the noise of the battle was deafening, he was about to ask what she thought she was doing when a rain of shrapnel came down all around them.

The expended chunks of depleted uranium tore leaves and branches off the trees. Billy could hear bits of metal striking the rocks and tree trunks, too.

Behind them, far down at the bottom of the hill, one of their grandparents' horses whinnied in fear or pain. Billy hoped that the animal had not been hurt by the shrapnel.

His heart was racing, and his adrenaline pumping, but Billy continued to aim the camera at the action.

"Twenty seconds and counting," Nick Gordon, INN's science reporter, said from the NASA observation station. Near the huge screen in the center of the room, Carl Strickler watched real-time images of the Reyes-Mishra Swarm. Everyone was waiting as the digital clock ticked down the last four seconds.

Three. Two. One...zero.

For a split second, nothing happened. Then multiple blasts engulfed the asteroid swarm. Everyone in the room exploded in wild applause.

At least the rockets made it to their targets, Carl

thought. *Now we have to wait and see if they did the job...*

A red emergency light lit up on Martin's engineering board. "Number five cannon failure," he announced. "I think it's jammed."

"Roger," Kip said, releasing the trigger and ending his third burst. Kip flicked a switch and took number five off-line. Inside the bowels of the Raptor, the cannon unloaded itself and the ammunition was automatically transferred to a working cannon.

But suddenly Tia cried a warning. She'd seen something on her radar screen.

"We have an unidentified aircraft inbound," she informed them. One of the monitors inside the cockpit showed a light single-engine airplane approaching the combat zone.

"Damn!" Pierce cried. "This area was supposed to be cleared of unauthorized aircraft."

"I'll take care of it," Toby announced from Two.

"No," Pierce replied. "Don't bring Two in that low. It's too dangerous!"

"Don't worry," Toby declared over the radio. Pierce was about to protest again, when another blast of Godzilla's rays rocked the aircraft. A secondary explosion caused Raptor-One to shudder.

"What's the problem?" Pierce barked.

"The heat shield over missile bay two has failed," Martin said after scanning his engineering panel. "One of the Hellfire missiles detonated inside the pod."

"We have a fire," Tia announced. She, Martin,

and Pierce began firefighting procedures as Kip battled on against Godzilla.

The unauthorized aircraft that flew across the battlefield was flown by a journalist from a local Colorado newspaper. Next to him, a freelance photographer, who sometimes worked for the news show *Total Focus,* was filming the battle.

"Get in closer!" the cameraman shouted. But the pilot was worried. The Cessna was already in range of Godzilla's radioactive ray. He didn't want to think about what would happen if they were hit.

Suddenly, the pilot saw a CV-22 Osprey with gray-and-purple-mottled camouflage drop out of the sky right in front of the Cessna. It was Raptor-Two.

The pilot of the Cessna immediately dropped the small plane's flaps and swerved to avoid a collision, but Raptor-Two stayed in front of him.

"Attention, unidentified aircraft," a woman's voice said over their radio. "You are in restricted airspace, interfering with a United States military operation. I strongly advise you to leave immediately."

The Cessna pilot banked his small plane once again. And again, Raptor-Two got in front of him.

"Dodge them!" the cameraman cried. Though the pilot had second thoughts, he remembered his flagging career and dived the aircraft. But they had gotten very close to the much larger aircraft that was doing battle with the enraged mutant saurian. As Godzilla let out a blast of radioactive fire, it missed Raptor-One and streaked toward the helpless Cessna.

"Get out of the way!" Lori cried over the radio.

"I'm on it," Toby cried. As he spoke, he maneuvered Raptor-Two until it hovered between the Cessna and Godzilla's burst of radioactive fire. The full force of the monster's blast struck Raptor-Two.

Inside the cockpit, systems began shorting out and sparks flew from the consoles. Though Raptor-Two was armored, it was in no way as heat-resistant as Raptor-One.

One by one, Raptor-Two's systems shorted out. Worse than that, the rotor blades on the starboard propeller began to melt. Suddenly, the aircraft was crashing.

"Mayday! Mayday!" Lori cried. "We are hit and are going down—" At that moment, her radio went dead.

"Eject! Eject! Eject!" Toby cried. Then he reached behind him, grabbed the yellow-and-black-striped ejection control, and pulled.

The ACES II "zero-zero" ejection seat—so named because it can save the pilot from certain death even if his aircraft is at zero speed and zero altitude—blasted the pilot of Raptor-Two through the cockpit escape hatch.

In the Cessna, the pilot and cameraman watched in horror as Raptor-Two seemed to disintegrate before their eyes. Suddenly, the cockpit hatch blew open and one of the pilots was blasted free. He tumbled through the air and disappeared from sight.

As the reporter banked the Cessna away, the

cameraman noticed something strange. He grabbed the pilot's shoulder. *"Look!"* he cried, pointing.

The Cessna pilot struggled to control his plane, but he peeked out of the corner of his eyes in the direction his partner was pointing. Despite his fear, and his struggle to keep the aircraft in the sky, the pilot's jaw dropped in amazement.

As the two men watched, a huge swirl of whirling colors seemed to envelop Raptor-Two. For a second, the aircraft was entirely engulfed in a bright, throbbing glow. Then, abruptly as it appeared, the mass of light just vanished.

Raptor-Two struggled to stay in the air for another moment. Then, as the two reporters fled from the scene, Raptor-Two turned belly-up and plunged into the valley below.

For a second, Toby was totally disoriented. Then he felt a jolt that told him that his parachute had opened. Because Raptor-Two was so low, Toby tumbled through tree branches just seconds after his chute billowed open above him.

He broke through a thick bundle of branches and leaves and landed hard. He rolled over once, then struck the trunk of a tree.

Tia scanned her radar screen in horror. Raptor-Two was gone. "Is Two down?" Pierce asked calmly.

"Yes," Tia replied, fighting her emotions.

"I'm taking command," Pierce declared, just as Kip maneuvered for another attack on Godzilla.

"I'm ready to fire!" Kip protested, his focus still on the target. But Pierce was the commander, and he overruled Kip's objection and took control of the warplane.

"I was ready to hit him hard!" Kip argued angrily.

"The rules of engagement are clear," Martin reminded him. "If an aircraft is lost, the survivor is to break off the attack and return to base. Immediately."

Kip seethed, but said nothing. The excitement of the battle was starting to wear off. It was replaced by worry for his teammates in the other aircraft.

"Did anyone see a parachute?" Pierce asked as he flew out of the valley, away from Godzilla. The monster bellowed a challenge as the Raptor disappeared into the sky.

"I saw one," Martin replied. "Just one…"

Tia nodded. "That's affirmative," she said. "I only saw one chute."

The rest of the flight to Gunnison County Airport was conducted in silence. Everybody wondered who punched out…and who didn't.

25
CELESTIAL
PHENOMENON

Thursday, July 15, 1999, 2:15 P.M.
Project Valkyrie headquarters
Nellis Air Force Base, Nevada

Tobias Nelson was found by Billy and Zelly Whitman, the two teenagers who sneaked into Gunnison National Forest on a quest for video footage of Godzilla. They brought the unconscious G-Force member out by horseback on the evening after the battle—and then they sold the footage and exclusive rights to their story to a tabloid television show for $1.2 million.

Toby had a broken arm and a concussion, but the prognosis was good. He was isolated in the base hospital until the military could debrief him about the crash.

There was no sign of Lori Angelo. The Air Force investigative team that combed the wreckage of Raptor-Two found that the escape hatch and ejection seat on Lori's side of the aircraft were both missing—which indicated that she had ejected from the aircraft. The investigators concluded that her parachute had failed to open.

Military patrols were still in the area, searching for her remains. Hopes were dimming, however. It was a big forest, and there were many scavengers.

The unidentified small plane that had caused the crash of Raptor-Two had vanished. No doubt the occupants feared punishment. The Air Force sent the word out that any witnesses to the event would merely be questioned, but still, no one came forward.

Dr. Irene Markham was handling the debriefing of Raptor-One's crew. G-Force had suffered their first defeat—and their first casualty. Morale was low, and their mood wasn't helped by the executive order to pull G-Force out of combat. The team felt it was a signal that the president had lost faith in them.

General Taggart knew better. He understood that if they went into battle now, they would be short of both aircraft and personnel. He thought that it was best for G-Force to stand down.

Meanwhile, Godzilla continued his trek across the heart of the United States. The creature had completely crossed Colorado and was now just outside Garden City, Kansas.

The blinding flash against the black depths of starless space startled and temporarily blinded Dr. Chandra Mishra, and he pulled away from the space telescope's eyepiece. He blinked the stars out of his eyes and peered through the eyepiece again.

The bright after-blast corona from the mysterious event was still spreading outward. He checked the ultraviolet telescope GLAZAR. It, too, had recorded the phenomenon.

It was four days *after* the EarthFirst nuclear explosions. The Reyes-Mishra Asteroid Swarm appeared to have been successfully obliterated as a threat to the earth.

Could one of the nuclear missiles have detonated late? he wondered. Then he dismissed the notion as unlikely.

Yet *something* had exploded inside the small scattered remnants of the Reyes-Mishra Swarm. Dr. Mishra watched as the halo around the flash continued to expand.

Suddenly, a beep went off on the console beside the puzzled professor. He grabbed the radio headphones, which were floating in the gravity-free environment, and put them on.

"Dr. Mishra," he announced into the mike.

The voice on the other end of the radio came from NASA's Deep Space Observation Station. Because of the great distance, there was a split-second gap between the signal and its reception.

"Did you see it, Dr. Mishra?" the man on the radio demanded. Even distorted by time and distance, Dr. Mishra recognized his co-discoverer's voice.

"Yes, Dr. Reyes," Dr. Mishra replied. "I *did* see it…but how is this possible?"

The split-second delay seemed like an eternity. "We have accounted for all of the nuclear rockets," Dr. Reyes answered finally. "That flash was not caused by our weapons."

Dr. Mishra peered through the eyepiece of the space telescope. The event in deep space was still expanding. *Something is terribly wrong,* he thought ominously.

What have I done?

* * *

Dr. Max Birchwood watched the nest on Mount Rushmore from a hill several miles away. It was as close as anyone was permitted to get to Rodan, who had remained in its lair, minding its single egg, for days now, atop the magnificent sculptures carved over decades by the artist Gutzon Borglum.

The kaijuologist had a feeling that this might be the day when the egg finally hatched. There was no scientific reason for his optimism. It was just a hunch.

He looked away from his telescope and down at the Air Force radio that the military had given to him. In the event that Rodan took to the air, he was ordered to notify headquarters. Fighters would be scrambled, and the war against Rodan would begin again.

Sighing, Dr. Birchwood wondered if attacking Rodan was the right thing to do. He had a theory that the creature had only flown to warmer climes to lay an egg. He was convinced that once the egg hatched, Rodan would return to the North Pole, and would not trouble mankind again.

But it was just a theory, and the Air Force wasn't buying it. So Dr. Birchwood knew that he would have to make a decision soon. Should he trust his instinct, or obey his commanders?

Dr. Chandra Mishra and two Russian astronomers had waited for hours for the after-blast corona to fade so that they could get their first clear look at the event.

The aftereffects of the celestial explosion were still too bright for observation by the human eye, but the ultraviolet telescopes aboard Mir were beginning to make headway.

Finally, the ultraviolet and radio telescopes began getting decipherable photographs. The three scientists pored over them.

Then they looked up from the images and at one another as they realized the ominous implications of their discovery. When the scientists were sure of their conclusions, they contacted their various governments.

Something, they said, was twisting and writhing in the very heart of that celestial flash, in the exact spot where the EarthFirst rockets had exploded four days before.

Although they did not agree on what the object was, they all knew that the threat of the asteroid collision had suddenly been replaced by a totally unknown phenomenon.

Only Dr. Mishra seemed certain about the object. He maintained not only that it was an alien presence but that it also had somehow been released from the asteroid swarm by the EarthFirst blast.

The other scientists rejected his notion as bizarre conjecture, of course. But everyone could agree on one fact: Whatever it was, the object was still moving toward Earth, and it would still arrive in a few weeks.

On Friday, July 16, a press conference was held at the Johnson Space Center outside Houston, Texas. It was a follow-up to the announcement made four days before, which stated that the Reyes-Mishra asteroids had been successfully targeted in the initial nuclear blasts. Now, as the members of the international press converged on the center, Dr. Ramon Reyes opened with a brief statement.

"It has been confirmed by tracking stations all over the globe," he announced. "The asteroids that threatened Earth have been obliterated."

There was riotous applause, then the scientist continued.

"There is, however, a single small piece that is still on a trajectory toward Earth," he informed them. "This fragment is too small to be tracked by the second wave of nuclear missiles, and if it does enter the earth's gravity, it will almost certainly be burned up in the atmosphere.

"In short," Dr. Reyes concluded, "the earth has been spared from destruction by the combined technological advances of the human race. Let us use this second chance wisely."

Reporter Nick Gordon pushed to the front of the crowd of journalists and shot a question at the scientist on the podium.

"Is it true," Gordon demanded, "that Dr. Chandra Mishra believes that this object coming toward us is a space *alien?*"

Looking uncomfortable, Dr. Reyes tried to answer. "It is true that Dr. Mishra does not concur with the theories of the rest of the scientific community. Why, exactly, I cannot say…"

Still aboard the Mir space station, Dr. Mishra observed the object that approached the earth. The more he learned about it, the more he believed that the thing was no asteroid.

Though his theories about what it might be were dismissed as nonsense by his colleagues, Dr. Mishra continued to file daily reports to NASA, and continued his research aboard the space station well beyond the time when he was scheduled to return home.

To Dr. Mishra's eyes, the object was behaving too oddly to be natural. Was it a spaceship? An aberration? Or something else?

His gut feelings told him that it was far from harmless, and he watched its movements with increasing trepidation.

Of course, Dr. Mishra knew that gut feelings would never convince a community of scientists of anything. But, in truth, as he continued his observations, he hoped sincerely that his colleagues would turn out to be right, and that he would be proved dead wrong.

On Tuesday, July 20, at around two on a hot South Dakota afternoon, Dr. Birchwood wiped the sweat from his brow, swallowed hard, and grabbed the radio.

Rodan had begun moving around in its nest of debris and broken railroad cars. Something was happening.

Putting his eye to the lens of the telescope, Dr. Birchwood depressed the button that activated the video camera. Now he was shooting telescopic footage of the creature's activities even as he watched.

Dr. Birchwood jumped as Rodan suddenly raised its head. The creature cackled, and the sound echoed across the hills. Rodan reached down and knocked something around inside the nest with its beak. The kaijuologist saw it was a huge piece of the off-white eggshell.

Suddenly, a second, much smaller, head peeked over the edge of the nest. The baby was brown in color, but lacked the crown of spikes its parent possessed.

Yes! Dr. Birchwood thought excitedly. *Rodan's egg has hatched!*

As the excited scientist watched, Rodan lifted the baby *Pteranodon* gently with its beak. Dr. Birchwood noted that the chick's wings were still stubby and unformed. The infant seemed relaxed in its parent's beak, instinctively sensing it was safe. Then Rodan spread its wings wide and leaped into the air.

Dr. Birchwood scrambled for his radio. He snatched up the device and keyed it. Then he took his hand away from the button again. As he watched, following the beast with his telescope, Rodan circled the nest three times.

Then, without a second glance, the *kaiju* flew off in a straight line. It was heading due north, toward Canada and beyond, to the north polar region.

Dr. Birchwood watched the vanishing creature. Then he looked down at the radio in his hand. He opened his fingers and let the communications device drop. It crashed to the rocks at the bottom of the hill, where it exploded into a dozen tiny pieces.

I guess I've got communications problems, he

thought slyly. *Too bad I couldn't alert the authorities.*

Squinting into the afternoon sky, Dr. Birchwood watched as Rodan headed toward its solitary home with its hatchling.

"You're either the last of your breed…or the first," he whispered as the creatures vanished over the horizon. "Good luck to the both of you…"

Aboard the Mir space station, Dr. Mishra blinked in shock and surprise. The mysterious object that he had been observing for days seemed to have moved forward in a flash of blinding light. The scientist quickly increased the magnification of his telescope.

He paled when the outline of the object finally became clear. He could plainly make out two gigantic solar sails or wings and what looked like three long, snakelike projections.

At his side, the radio beeped. Dr. Mishra keyed the mike and spoke into his headset.

"Dr. Mishra here," he said. There was a pause, then Dr. Carl Strickler's voice came on the line. He was excited.

"I see it!" cried Carl. "It *is* an alien of some kind…a living thing, *flying* through space!"

Dr. Mishra nodded, but did not reply. Then Dr. Reyes came on the line. "I think the speed of that object is decreasing," he announced. "Can you confirm, Dr. Mishra?"

The scientist aboard Mir scanned his instruments. "Yes," he replied after a moment. "It is slowing."

The delay between transmissions seemed very long. Finally, Dr. Reyes came on the line again. "We will have to tell the authorities," the scientist announced. "I hope to God that this...*thing*...plans to bypass our planet."

Dr. Mishra remained silent. He had known, in his gut, that Earth had been this creature's final destination all along.

And it was my plan that freed it, Dr. Mishra thought grimly.

By July 25, it was apparent to all that the creature in space had slowed down significantly. The scientists agreed that it must be moving under its own power...but they did not know what that power was.

They did know that if the creature kept to its present speed, it would arrive above the earth in the last week of December—on or around the first day of the new century.

The ominous news was kept from the public because the governments of the world hoped that the creature, whatever it was, would simply fly past Earth and back out into deep space. They also spoke of launching a new series of nuclear missiles—this time in secret.

At NASA's Deep Space Observation Station in Houston, some of the younger technicians, who had been enjoying the antics of the "Prophetess of Doom'" on MTV, started calling the strange phenomenon in space "King Ghidorah."

The name stuck.

As "King Ghidorah" approached, constant communication was maintained between Mir and the celestial tracking stations on Earth.

Dr. Mishra, who had already been in space for thirty days, decided to remain aboard Mir, monitoring the creature's advance, until the end of the year.

Though Godzilla was cutting a swath of destruction across the center of Kansas, kaijuologists weren't the only scientists chasing across the plains in search of knowledge.

At about noon on Friday, August 13—a hard-luck day—the National Weather Service storm-monitoring center in Topeka issued severe storm warnings for five counties in northeast Kansas. By two o'clock, the storm brewing looked severe enough to produce a Category Five tornado, with wind gusts at up to 150 miles per hour.

Following the storm's path, a convoy of five vans crammed with meteorological equipment streaked along the highway near the town of Cummings.

When chief meteorologist Dr. Henry Dubois glanced out of his window of the lead van, he saw a funnel cloud forming about a mile ahead. He nudged his driver, a graduate student in climatology named Dexter Runsel. The youth stepped on the gas.

"We got one!" Dubois cried into his CB radio. The other members of the storm-chasing team whooped and put the pedal to the metal, too.

Suddenly, Dubois saw a service road that might get them closer to the point where the storm would touch the earth. He pointed, and Runsel put on the turn signal and took the bend without slowing down. Dust trailed out behind the lead van, and the other vehicles had no trouble following.

In the second truck, another graduate student, named Jim Paulis, noticed a military detachment on the main highway. The soldiers cried out and pointed at the passing storm chasers. Some of them waved their hands above their heads.

"What's that about?" Paulis cried over the noise of the road. Professor Kelly Ridgeway, the driver, glanced at the soldiers as the van streaked by them.

"They're probably trying to warn us that there's a tornado brewing ahead!" she replied. "They don't know that we're *looking* for one!"

Jim nodded. "Yeah," he said as the van increased speed to catch up with the lead truck. Unfortunately, nobody on the team was paying much attention to the news. They knew that Godzilla was somewhere in Kansas, but they thought they were far from the scene of his rampage.

But the storm chasers were wrong.

"Is that another funnel?" Dr. Dubois cried, pointing ahead where a black shape moved against the overcast sky. The doctor turned toward the radar operator in the back of the van.

"*Something's* out there," the technician cried. "And it's big and solid."

"It's coming down," the driver shouted, staring at the funnel cloud. Dr. Dubois turned around as the van screeched to a halt in a cloud of dust. As the van settled, huge drops of rain began to pelt it, and the winds kicked up.

Dr. Dubois jumped out of the van. His assistants were scrambling out behind him, dragging their monitoring equipment. But when they saw the shocked look on their professor's startled face, the group turned as one and stared out toward the descending tornado.

Standing, legs spread and tail flailing in the middle of a Kansas cornfield, Godzilla roared defiantly at the funnel cloud that came to earth fifty feet away from him.

The winds were so powerful that they almost knocked the storm chasers down. The technician looked at his instruments.

"It's a *four!*" he cried. "At least—" The rest of his words were lost in the storm.

The team of storm chasers set up their video equipment and watched as an epic struggle unfolded—in essence, an unstoppable force was about to meet an immovable object.

Less than a mile away, the crops were sucked up into the dark twisting mass of the storm's funnel cloud. The great beast Godzilla squinted his reptilian eyes against the buffeting winds that tore at his flesh.

Angrily, Godzilla bellowed again. Blue flashes ran along the creature's back. He blasted the funnel cloud with his flaming breath. The blast of radiation was sucked up into the funnel along with everything else. Blue flashes seemed to mix into the cloud like cream in a swirling cup of coffee.

Then the funnel spun forward and struck Godzilla full on. Debris battered and blinded the monster.

Suddenly, his trunklike legs were swept out from under him. The earth shook for miles around as

Godzilla tumbled to the ground. The wind continued to batter him, rolling him over a huge barn and silo that was nevertheless dwarfed by the *kaiju*'s sheer magnitude.

Godzilla roared again and belched more fire. The blue streak disappeared into the funnel. Flashes of fire could be seen as debris in the funnel cloud caught fire from Godzilla's rays.

The twister snaked sideways and struck Godzilla a second time. Still struggling on the ground, the enraged dinosaur tried to grapple with the storm. His tail flailed wildly as the full force of the tornado battered itself out against the incredible, near-immovable bulk of the giant mutant.

In the next few seconds, the funnel actually broke itself apart against Godzilla, scattering debris all around the area.

Grunting, Godzilla lumbered to his feet.

Then, as the storm chasers watched in disbelief, Godzilla's roar of victory and defiance echoed across the plains of Kansas.

That evening on every news channel across the country, America viewed the startling footage of Godzilla brawling with a Category Four tornado.

The sight had an unexpected impact on the country.

Many Americans were beginning to see Godzilla not so much as a monster, but as a force of nature. Suddenly, it didn't seem so terrible that the creature's trek across the nation could not be stopped.

After all, neither could a tornado.

26

THE BATTLE
OF GARY

GODZILLA™

Monday, September 13, 1999, 3:44 P.M.
Joint Command headquarters
Gary, Indiana

Godzilla moved east into much more densely populated areas of the United States. When he crossed the Missouri River, he was only twenty-five miles south of Omaha. Many suburban areas were destroyed, and once again, the president's decision not to interfere with Godzilla was questioned.

Despite the radioactive plague that had ravaged parts of California after the unsuccessful helicopter attack, and the fact that parts of the Gunnison National Forest had suffered ecological damage after the failed G-Force assault, some still pressed for another attack on Godzilla. There was economic as well as political pressure.

The government's disaster relief funds were exhausted, and hundreds of thousands of people were still homeless. Mining and agricultural interests suffered in Godzilla's wake, and in some regions the crops were never planted or harvested. The United States was having to import basic foodstuffs from its neighbors.

The stock market continued to plummet, and matters only got worse as Godzilla neared America's industrial heartland. The "Big Three" auto companies talked about moving their manufacturing facilities south of the border until the Speaker of the House of Representatives slyly reminded them that a dangerous and destructive *kaiju* had ravaged Mexico, too.

Research continued on re-creating the sound lure invented by Japanese scientist Dr. Nobeyama, which had been used once to successfully draw Godzilla away from Japan. But even though the scientists duplicated the frequency of the sound, Godzilla wasn't responding to it anymore. One kaijuologist suggested that the lure might only work at certain times—like a mating call, which only worked if the creature was "interested."

Finally, as Godzilla neared the Great Lakes region, a plan was developed to force him away from Chicago. After long consultation with civilian and military authorities, the site of a third attack on Godzilla was selected.

The "line in the sand" was drawn at Gary, Indiana.

General Leroy Cranford was put in charge of joint military operations. A veteran of the Gulf War and Bosnia, he possessed a level head and an organized mind. The president asked General Cranford for a strategy, and the general went to work.

First, a double wall of high-tension electrical towers was built to form a corridor through Illinois and Indiana. The electric "fence" was meant to herd Godzilla away from Chicago and toward Gary. The real attack wouldn't occur until Godzilla reached a huge, abandoned industrial park located outside the city, on the shore of Lake Michigan.

Construction began on the trap. A former steel-processing plant outside Gary was transformed into a deadly gauntlet. High-explosive chemicals were brought in. Mines filled with poisons and flammable chemicals were planted.

On the last day of September, as cold autumn descended on the Midwest, the combined forces under Cranford's command waited for Godzilla to approach.

Though Godzilla was obscured by a misty rainfall that soaked the battlefield, his approach was announced by the rumble of his monstrous footsteps.

Inside the cramped quarters of the M1A1 Abrams main battle tank, the soldiers waiting to spring their trap felt the earth move under the tank treads.

Sitting in the commander's station of the sixty-three-ton main battle tank, Lieutenant Chick Patterson wiped away the sweat that beaded on his oil-stained face. Then he used a rag to wipe off the eyepiece on his periscope before peering through the lens again.

Another rumble rocked the tank.

Patterson scanned the area through the GPS sight—an extension of the gunner's own targeting system.

All he could see was a wall of swirling fog. But Godzilla was close now—he could feel it. The lieutenant cursed the weather yet again. The mist was so thick it obscured even the walls of the ruined industrial facility a scant seventy feet away. It was the worst day of weather the battle group had endured in their three months in Indiana.

The big fear during preparation was that Godzilla would arrive in the dead of night, or in the middle of a snowstorm. But this rain and wet fog was much, much worse. It even confounded their computer-enhanced targeting systems.

It was a bad omen that Godzilla had picked today of all days to arrive.

Suddenly, the radio speaker crackled. "Lock and load," an emotionless voice announced. Finally, the code releasing the attack had been given.

Lieutenant Patterson looked down at Private Greene, the fastest loader in the battalion. It was his job to feed the cannon round after round of ammunition. Above Private Greene sat Sergeant George Hammond, in the gunner's station. Private Willy Hernandez sat in the driver's seat, gunning the diesel engines, ready to move at a second's notice.

The job of the 72nd Tank Battalion was not to stop Godzilla. They were there to force the monster into the box, where the traps that the scientists designed would be triggered.

With luck, they might never have to fire a shot. If Godzilla kept on walking in a straight line, between the two lines of high-tension electrical towers, then everything would be fine.

But it wasn't going to be that way, and Patterson knew it.

"I see something!" Sergeant Hammond announced, automatically reaching for the handle of his gun.

"Load!" Lieutenant Patterson commanded, peering through his viewer. In a battle against a *human* enemy, the tank commander would usually specify the type of ammunition to be used. But a new type of ammunition—a Teflon-coated depleted-uranium shell—was about to be tested against Godzilla. To the soldiers' dismay, the experimental shells were the only type they carried.

"Up!" Private Greene announced as he slammed the shell home.

Suddenly, the curtain of fog parted, and a black wall of rutted flesh appeared in front of the line of tanks. The gunner swiftly elevated the main gun twenty degrees. He centered the cross hairs on a section of Godzilla's neck. His finger closed around the trigger.

"Wait…wait…" Lieutenant Patterson and the other tank commanders' eyes were locked on two bright yellow lines painted on either side of the abandoned factory's parking lot. As long as the monster kept between those lines, they were to hold their fire. But if Godzilla moved to either side, then the tanks there were to open up—driving him back to the center of the park.

It sounded fine—in *theory*. But when Patterson saw Godzilla emerge from the fog, he wasn't prepared for the size of the monster. Somehow, the lieutenant was expecting something along the lines of the *T. rex* in *Jurassic Park*.

Godzilla was much more impressive than that!

Patterson kept elevating his periscope up and up, until—finally—he focused on Godzilla's reptilian head. The eyes seemed to gleam with feral intelligence.

The earth shook again as Godzilla took another step closer. As the gunner traversed the turret, keeping the sight on the creature's throat, Godzilla abruptly shifted his weight and turned, his tail lashing out and slamming against the factory.

The brick structure collapsed in on itself with a thunderous clamor. Godzilla bellowed a reverberating roar.

"Fire!" Lieutenant Patterson cried as Godzilla lurched across the yellow line and toward his tank—and the high-tension wires behind it.

"Awaaaaay!" the gunner cried as he depressed the trigger. The Abrams rocked from the cannon's recoil. The tank filled with the smell of cordite. A second later, their shell—and a dozen others—slammed into Godzilla.

Even as the shell struck home, the driver threw the tank into reverse and tried to back out of Godzilla's path. But for an agonizing second or two, the treads skidded in the mud and the tank would not budge.

Finally, the treads caught, and Patterson's M1A1 began to move. The gunner traversed the turret in a futile attempt to reacquire the target, but Godzilla was faster.

As they backed up, Godzilla's enormous foot slammed down right in front of their tank. Filthy water and oily mud washed up over the Abrams, splashing the periscope's exterior lens and coating it with muck.

Then Godzilla roared. The sound echoed through the tank. As Lieutenant Patterson peered through his scope, he spotted another Abrams floundering in the oily muck. Godzilla's mammoth foot came crashing down on top of it.

The tank was crushed. The ammunition inside detonated, and the explosion blasted another shower of mud and debris over them.

"Go! Go! Go!" Patterson cried, urging Hernandez to get them out of there. But even as the tank skidded from side to side trying to dodge the monster's feet, Godzilla swept over and past them.

As the creature slammed into the high-tension electrical towers, his tail casually brushed their tank, knocking it to the side. The tank slid through the mud and into a concrete foundation, where construction blocks caught the treads and slipped them off the wheel. As the tank skidded to a jolting halt, Patterson knew they were hopelessly stuck.

Without thinking, he popped the hatch on the turret. Cold, wet, fresh air washed down onto the gunner. He looked up as his commander stuck his head out of the hatch.

"No, sir!" Hammond cried. *"Don't go out there—"*

But it was too late.

As the gunner and the loader watched in horror, high-tension electrical wires, alive and crackling with thousands of volts of electricity, dropped down on top of their tank.

Patterson screamed. There was a terrible flash of blue lightning. Then the gunner covered his face as the tank filled with the smell of ozone and the stench of burning flesh.

Finally, what was left of Patterson dropped back down through the hatch as tons of steel from the shattered electrical towers rained down on the crippled tank and its occupants.

When Godzilla stepped across the yellow line and outside the killing box, he triggered a second line of defense.

Miles away from the industrial park, mobile artillery was preparing to unleash its fury. In dozens of mall parking lots, high school football fields, vacant lots and any wide, expansive space in the otherwise crowded urban landscape surrounding the killing zone, clusters of special mobile artillery vehicles awaited the signal to attack.

The angular, boxlike, treaded vehicles—called Vought Multiple-Launch Rocket Systems—each carried twelve 227mm rockets in a dozen launch tubes on their backs. These anti-armor rocket launchers, scattered all over Gary and the surrounding area, were ready to pour destruction down on Godzilla's head.

Alarms blared as the men ran to their vehicles. Suddenly, their radios crackled to life, and the final coordinates of the monster were sent to them.

As the launchers elevated and pointed into the rainy, overcast sky, General Cranford, at command headquarters, hoped that none of the lead tanks had gotten hung up. The whole area was about to be lit up by tons upon tons of high explosives.

At the command radio, Colonel Milford looked expectantly at his commander. Grimly, General Cranford nodded.

"Fire!" the colonel barked into the microphone.

From all over the city, rockets streaked into the sky, trailing bright yellow plumes of fire and white, misty smoke. First dozens, then hundreds of rockets poured into the sky, disappearing in the low cloud cover.

Miles away, in the middle of the ruins of a shattered factory, Godzilla bellowed out a challenge as the rockets mingled with the raindrops that fell out of the low clouds.

As night fell in Gary, Godzilla slowly lumbered past the industrial park and slipped below the waves of Lake Michigan.

The monster had avoided all of the traps set for it, as if it had been warned. As rockets rained down around him, Godzilla stoically made his way toward the fresh waters of the lake, where he disappeared beneath the cold, dark waters with barely a ripple.

27

THE KING OF TERROR COMES!

Saturday, December 25, 1999, 1905 hours
Kristall *docking module, Mir space station*
125 miles above the earth

The crew of Mir greeted the arrival of the space shuttle *Atlantis* with Christmas cake and cookies, along with a fine Russian tea brewed in portable packets.

The *Atlantis* docked on one try with the *Kristall* module of Mir, and the shuttle's main bay door opened to link with the docking ring as the earth revolved blue and serene far below.

The American astronauts who floated through the narrow docking collar looked fresh and clean next to the tired and haggard scientists and technicians aboard the Mir, some of whom had been in Earth orbit for many months.

The *Atlantis* was a welcome diversion. It brought necessary supplies, and would provide a ride back home for several Russian and American technicians. Mir would be a lot less crowded when *Atlantis* headed back to Earth the following morning—and not a moment too soon. The resources of the space station had been severely taxed by the demands of the previous few months.

Through oxygen generator failure, battery failure, a complete breakdown of one of the docking arms, and, most troubling, a catastrophic failure of the shipboard sanitation and waste facilities, those aboard Mir endured without complaint. For some, at least, the ordeal was almost over.

As the final airlock door swung open, the crew of the shuttle called out greetings to their Russian hosts. The American astronauts brought vitally needed replacement parts, fresh food and water, and a new scientist—Dr. Moshe Lipinski—to replace the departing Dr. Chandra Mishra.

All in the nick of time, Cosmonaut S. A. Romanenko thought, sighing. Though the Iron Curtain had vanished over a decade before, he still couldn't get used to the "new" order. Romanenko had been trained as a MIG-29 fighter pilot, and indoctrinated with the notion that America was the enemy.

Now the Americans are the victors, in a Cold War that was never declared, Romanenko thought bitterly. *And they won without firing a shot.*

But as the commander of the shuttle astronauts shook the Russian Mir commander's hand, Romanenko thought he detected a change in the once-invincible Americans. Something behind their eyes was different…something new was there, something that Romanenko understood all too well.

Defeat, he thought. *I see defeat in their eyes. Godzilla has humbled them.* For the first time in weeks, Romanenko smiled. *I wish there were gravity here, just to see if the American cowboys still know how to swagger.*

Romanenko remembered the international news

broadcast he'd watched earlier that day. He recalled that, just a week ago, Godzilla had emerged from Lake Ontario at a place called Rochester, New York. This time, the authorities had been caught off-guard.

The destruction was almost as great as when Godzilla first struck Tokyo. There were thousands of American casualties in New York State, and thousands more were homeless and destitute.

Even Romanenko, who'd seen the destruction in Afghanistan and Chechnya, was appalled by the footage he'd seen. Worse still, Godzilla had finally collided with a nuclear power plant, just outside Syracuse. Even though the creature had absorbed much of the radiation, there was still environmental damage.

An INN news commentator said the ecological damage was worse than at a place called Love Canal, but Romanenko didn't understand the reference. He knew all about Chernobyl, however.

As several other cosmonauts began passing the fresh supplies through the modules, Romanenko forgot about Godzilla and the new visitors, and joined his comrades in helping with the work.

Dr. Mishra was at the other end of the space station, in the cramped, instrument-laden *Kvant* module. The doctor was finishing up the last of his experiments and making final notes.

He hated to leave Mir with the job unfinished. But the mysterious creature that had appeared in the Reyes-Mishra Swarm continued to drift in space 780,000 kilometers from Earth, and it hadn't moved in weeks. Perhaps it would remain there forever...

For now, like it or not, it was time for Dr. Mishra to go home. After a significant time without gravity, human bones begin to lose mass and human muscles atrophy. Dr. Mishra already suspected that, when he arrived back on Earth, he would have to be carried from the shuttle like a helpless child, because he would be too weak to walk on his own.

In the last few weeks, he had even neglected his mandatory exercises and spent long hours in the lab. There was just too much to learn and too little time.

Dr. Mishra grabbed an overhead handle and pulled himself toward the optical telescope, situated right next to the GLAZER ultraviolet telescope. He wanted one last look at the phenomenon, unobstructed by miles of polluted atmosphere.

Squinting, Dr. Mishra peered through the telescope eyepiece. He found himself gazing at an empty section of space. Instantly, the scientist checked the instrument. The telescope was calibrated correctly.

It felt as if someone had dribbled icy cold water down Dr. Mishra's spine. *The creature had moved!*

The scientist jumped when the buzzer went off on the communications console next to him. An incoming transmission. Dr. Mishra snatched the microphone, which floated next to him.

"Dr. Mishra here," he said. There was the usual time lag due to the great distance between Earth control and Mir. Finally, Dr. Strickler answered.

"Did you see it, Dr. Mishra?" the young scientist asked from the NASA Deep Space Observation

Station back in Houston, Texas. "The creature is moving—at an amazing speed…"

"How fast?" Dr. Mishra demanded. A moment stretched into eternity as the scientist waited for an answer.

"Hard to tell," Dr. Strickler finally replied. "It is still accelerating. But it will reach the orbit of Earth in mere minutes…"

Minutes! Dr. Mishra pressed the emergency alarm. Klaxons sounded in every single module of Mir. He got on the intercom and informed the crew that the object was moving toward Earth—and *them*—at very high speed.

He recommended that Mir be evacuated immediately.

Seven minutes later, as the American astronauts were still scrambling to free the crowded *Atlantis* from Mir's docking ring, the mysterious object from the depths of space came rushing toward the space station.

But it was more than just an object—it was a living creature, and it was riding the winds of space on golden wings.

Dr. Mishra made no move to evacuate. Instead, he downloaded the shocking real-time images of the golden creature to the NASA monitoring station. It was the least he could do.

After all, it had been *his* plan to destroy the asteroid threat with nuclear missiles.

How could he have known that the blast would destroy one threat, but release another? How could he have known a terrible creature had been trapped within those cold, dark rocks that had been circling the galaxy for eons?

He could not have known. Yet, like so many scientists before him, who never anticipated the horrible ends their discoveries and inventions could create, Dr. Mishra felt somehow responsible.

As the golden-scaled being loomed larger through the viewport, Dr. Mishra activated Mir's exterior cameras and sent the signals with the rest of the data.

He no longer cared about his own life…only what he could do to help save the billions of lives back home.

At the NASA Deep Space Observation Station in Houston, the scientists and technicians watched the huge monitor as the first images of the space creature Dr. Mishra had discovered came into view.

Brilliantly lit by the sun's rays reflected off the earth's atmosphere, the immense, golden-hued creature with three heads filled the central monitor. The being was completely covered with golden scales. Its three snakelike necks were crowned by three independently functioning heads that looked almost exactly like traditional Asian sculptures of dragons.

On the smaller monitors surrounding the central screen, real-time images were downloaded from a surveillance satellite in orbit. These monitors showed Mir, with the *Atlantis* still hooked to the docking ring, floating helplessly in space.

"Hurry up, damn you…hurry up!" the usually calm Dr. Strickler shouted to the flickering, silent television screens.

On the satellite pictures, Mir appeared tranquil and serene. Yet Dr. Strickler knew in his gut that death was approaching it on huge golden wings.

Aboard Mir, Dr. Mishra felt the whole space station shake. He peered out the thick window and saw a *Soyuz TM* emergency evacuation capsule blast free of the station and drop toward the blue-and-green planet far below.

Mir shook again as a second *Soyuz* capsule followed the first.

Meanwhile, the American astronauts were rushing through the undocking and start-up procedures, even though the shuttle would never be able to launch in time.

In the pilot's seat, the commander of the *Atlantis* ran through the launch procedures faster than he'd even done before. Suddenly, he heard a gasp from the co-pilot. The commander looked up from his control panel through the shuttle's thick windows.

The three-headed horror was diving out of the star field toward them, the long necks twisting sinuously. As the commander and his co-pilot watched helplessly, the monster spat out powerful rays from each mouth.

A single jagged bolt of power struck Mir's central module, and Mir exploded instantly. The outer modules, which were connected to the central section by flimsy docking tunnels, broke into pieces, spilling their contents into the vacuum of space. As the astronauts watched, humans were dumped without protection into the airless void.

The occupants of the demolished space station didn't have time to suffocate to death—explosive decompression mercifully ended their lives in seconds.

As secondary explosions ripped through Mir, the docking ring broke loose. Debris and one of the solar panels pelted the fuselage of the *Atlantis* as the shuttle, still without power, spun free and tumbled uncontrollably down into the earth's gravity well, where the atmosphere waited to burn it up.

A third explosion tore the *Kvant* module apart. A huge portion of the cylindrical hull dashed itself against the floundering *Atlantis*. The shuttle's still-open bay door ripped free with the force of the impact. The hull of the *Atlantis* was ruptured in three places, and white-hot shrapnel ripped through the engine and into the fuel tank.

The orange ball of fire that was once the *Atlantis* expanded, engulfing the shattered remains of Mir.

The three-headed monster streaked past the explosion, toward the blue-green waters of the Atlantic Ocean below. As the creature encountered the earth's atmosphere, its golden scales began to glow bright red from the friction of reentry. The brilliant glare was visible all across the Northern Hemisphere.

The NASA Deep Space Observation facility immediately alerted the NORAD defense system that an unidentified creature was entering the atmosphere from outer space. NORAD instantly passed on the warning to other nuclear powers, just in case someone got the wrong idea and launched a nuclear strike.

As the monster plunged through the atmosphere, it left a bright trail of superheated gases that turned night into artificial day. The massive creature was easily observed on radar as well. American, Canadian, Russian, and European tracking stations followed the creature as it slowed its descent.

As it approached sea level, the monster leveled off and flew over the North Sea, between the coasts of Norway and Great Britain. Instantly, the British Royal Air Force scrambled interceptors from their northern air bases. In minutes, the night sky over the frigid North Sea was filled with warplanes.

The Gullfaks oilfield lies in the middle of the North Sea between Britain and mainland Europe. The nearest land is the Norwegian coast, over 110 miles away. In the middle of that oilfield, rising from the black waters, a cluster of a thousand floodlights and an intermittent blast of fire marked the location of the largest seagoing gas and oil production platform in the world.

The Gullfaks D oil pumping station, just completed in 1998, consisted of a steel platform resting on top of four massive concrete pillars and a base, which rested on the bottom of the sea almost 800 feet below the waves.

The highest point of Gullfaks D—the flare stack, where excess gas is burned off in spectacular bursts of rolling fire—rose almost 500 feet from the ocean's surface.

The framework was covered with many decks and structures and housed working and living quarters for 400 petroleum workers, a power station that generated enough electricity to run a whole town, production equipment, derricks for loading and unloading material, and a circular helicopter pad.

There was even a small hospital and a leisure center with a movie theater, a gym, and a coffee bar.

On this night, as the skies over the North Sea were lit up like day, many of the workers crowded on the upper decks, trying to get a closer look at the celestial phenomenon.

A few hundred yards away, clearly visible in the unnatural brightness, an oil tanker bobbed on the waves, waiting for the signal to dock and take on some of the 275,000 barrels of oil that the rig pumped up from wells under the ocean floor each and every day.

As the petroleum workers stared into the night sky, a ball of fire appeared on the horizon. The huge glowing object seemed to get closer and closer every second. Suddenly, a sonic boom washed over the men, shaking the platform as it echoed across the waves.

That sound was swiftly followed by the distinctive noise of jet engines. As the men of Gullfaks D watched the skies, three fighters flying in formation raced over their heads, toward the ball of fire in the sky.

"Has a bloody war broken out?" one of the British petroleum workers asked from an upper deck. The others shook their heads, wondering what crisis the world was facing now.

As they watched, the jets raced away, disappearing into the bright night. But before they completely vanished in the distance, the workers saw the aircraft fire their wing-mounted missiles at the brilliant ball of yellow fire on the horizon.

The booming sounds of the missiles detonating sent repercussions skimming over the North Sea. Then they saw an eerie bolt of lightning in the otherwise clear sky. The bolt struck something in the air and a small explosion, like a distant firecracker, flared up and vanished.

"The fighters are shooting at something," one petroleum worker cried.

"Yeah," an American replied. "And something is shooting *back*."

As the men watched, the brilliant ball of fire finally faded. But far away, a small object still glowed in the sky. The American peered through a pair of binoculars, then gasped.

"What is it, mate?" the Brit asked. The American said nothing, but he handed the other man his binoculars. The Brit raised them to his eyes and gazed through the lenses.

"Bloody hell!" he cried.

With a terrible fascination, the men on the platform watched as the glowing object came closer and closer. Soon, they could make out details... gigantic wings, three long necks, twin tails. And then, before it seemed possible, the thing was upon them.

The night sky was filled with a mad cackling sound. The necks writhed angrily as the tremendous golden thing flapped its massive wings. The central head seemed to focus on the brightly lit platform in the middle of the dark water. As the cold, alien eyes looked down at them, the workers began to panic. As one, the men rushed below-decks to the evacuation stations.

But it was too late.

The three-headed monster opened the gaping maw of its central head and spat a bolt of electricity at the Gullfaks D. The powerful ray skimmed along the North Sea, boiling the water where it touched. Then the jagged bolt of power reached out and struck the Gullfaks D's central section.

Metal seared and melted, and secondary explosions ripped through the Gullfaks living quarters and power station. Then a second bolt of jagged energy lanced out and struck the oil storage facility.

The result was the largest non-nuclear explosion ever to occur on the face of the earth. The Gullfaks D literally vanished in a dazzling, glaring, burning mass of fire. The blast reached into the sky in a fiery mushroom cloud.

The noise would have been deafening, if there had been anyone still alive to hear it.

The force of the explosion capsized the nearby tanker, trapping its helpless crew inside the hull as it sank beneath the tossing waves. On the ocean floor, pipes that led from the drilling stations on the seabed ruptured, spilling hundreds of thousands of barrels of crude oil into the North Sea.

Over a hundred miles away, windows were shattered in buildings along Norway's coast. The bright blast was visible in Norway, Scotland, and from ships at sea in the North Atlantic.

At dawn, a press conference was held at the United Nations headquarters in New York City, announcing the arrival of a new, unknown *kaiju*, more powerful than even Godzilla.

The monster, called King Ghidorah, after the monster predicted by the "Prophetess of Doom," was now circling over Europe. The UN delegates assured the citizens of Earth that everything was being done to protect them from King Ghidorah, and that they should remain calm.

28
THE COMING
OF MOTHRA

MOTHRA™

Friday, December 31, 1999, 3:45 P.M.
G-Force mobile command station
La Guardia Airport, Queens, New York

Outside the gigantic C-130 Hercules transport plane, the last afternoon of the twentieth century was windy, brisk, and clear. Miles away from the airport, across the East River, the jagged skyscrapers of Manhattan glittered under a bright blue sky. Even as far away as the airport, hundreds of helicopters were visible above the city.

The air over Manhattan was filled with military, commercial, and privately owned helicopters of every shape and size. Their crews were frantically evacuating the city, not of its citizens, but of its valuable government and corporate records, art objects, and anything else deemed irreplaceable.

The millions of New Yorkers who inhabited the mighty metropolis were already gone. They were camped in cold tents in the outer boroughs, upstate, in New Jersey, Connecticut, and even Pennsylvania. Manhattan was empty, except for the criminals, the homeless, and the insane who still roamed the streets, where they fought one another for the remaining spoils.

On this day, the traditional New Year's Eve celebration in Times Square was usually held. But, for the first time in almost a century, the event was canceled. In its place, Dick Clark was planning a live broadcast from Atlanta to celebrate the holiday.

As Kip Daniels crossed the concrete tarmac toward the aircraft that served as their mobile command center, he pulled his flight jacket close around his neck for protection against the buffeting winds. His mood was as bleak as the nation's.

In the next twenty-four hours, it was likely that he would once again go head-to-head with what he feared most—Godzilla. The monster was moving in a straight line toward Manhattan. At last report, Godzilla had entered the Hudson River near the U.S. Military Academy at West Point. Currently, he was moving at a steady pace downriver.

Some bridges had been destroyed, and some river barges overturned, but generally Godzilla caused less damage when he moved through the nation's waterways than when he traveled across land.

On the other side of the Atlantic Ocean, in the skies over France, NATO air forces were about to engage King Ghidorah. The City of Lights had drawn the space monster like a magnet. Hours ago, the monster descended on Paris without warning.

The death toll was staggering. The French government appealed for help.

Their appeal was granted, and the combined forces of the North Atlantic Treaty Organization were mounting a counterattack.

Kip climbed the ramp and entered the aircraft. Inside the mobile command center, the air was hot, dry, and tense. On a raised platform, General

Taggart sat in consultation with Colonel Krupp, Dr. Birchwood, and Dr. Markham. Kip saw Tia and Martin watching live images of King Ghidorah squatting in the rubble of the Eiffel Tower.

Another monitor displayed digital images of King Ghidorah. The statistics that flashed across the bottom of that screen were staggering.

At over 500 feet tall, King Ghidorah towered over even Godzilla. Its wingspread was wider than Rodan's, and its mysterious bolts of pure energy measured three times more powerful than the mutated *Pteranodon*'s and nearly as strong as Godzilla's own. King Ghidorah was, far and away, the largest and most powerful living creature in the known universe. *And we may have to go up against it next*, Kip thought grimly.

As he was watching the data scroll across the monitor, Pierce and Toby entered the command center. Pierce was wearing his flight suit, but Toby, still recovering from his ejection over Colorado, was wearing Levis and a sweater.

The three men exchanged ominous glances.

Soon, Kip knew, the attack on King Ghidorah would begin.

Over the English Channel, a squadron of Dessault Super Etendard tactical strike fighters lifted off from the deck of the French aircraft carrier *Foch*. Each aircraft carried two Exocet anti-ship cruise missiles.

Another flight of six Super Etendards lifted off from a land base in Brittany. Of these, only one jet was carrying a cruise missile—an Aerospatiale

ASMP stand-off missile with a tactical nuclear war-head. Despite a verbal agreement not to use nuclear weapons against King Ghidorah, the French government had decided—unilaterally and in secret—to use it if they got the chance.

It was an act of vengeance for the destruction of Paris.

A third flight of French Rafale fighters was launched from a base near Le Havre, while, off the coast of France, a squadron of British Royal Air Force Panavia Tornado fighter-bombers circled around their aerial refueling aircraft. The British would strike only if King Ghidorah left French air-space.

Off the British coast, the American aircraft carri-er *Theodore Roosevelt* waited in reserve. If the French and British failed to stop the monster, then the F-14 Tomcats and F-18 Hornets of the *Roosevelt* would launch and intercept the *kaiju* over the Atlantic.

It took only minutes for the first flight of French aircraft to reach the outskirts of Paris. The pilots were horrified to see the destruction that had been done to their beloved city. Not only the Eiffel Tower but also the Cathedral of Notre Dame, the Arc de Triomphe, and the Louvre had all been reduced to rubble.

The work of centuries lay shattered around the massive legs of the marauding monster from space. But even the vision of destruction below their air-craft didn't prepare the French pilots for their first look at the monster King Ghidorah.

Even the most battle-hardened French pilot was

struck with a kind of supernatural dread when he saw King Ghidorah in the flesh.

Streaking over the demolished city, the Super Etendards released their Exocets. The cruise missiles dropped from the belly pylons and deployed their tiny navigational wings. Then, as one, the ten missiles sped toward their target.

Meanwhile, the single nuclear-armed fighter circled the city, waiting for a chance to deploy the ultimate weapon.

Nine out of ten of the Exocets struck their target. The explosions rocked King Ghidorah as the missiles detonated against its golden flanks. The monster cackled madly as it tumbled over, smashing buildings as it rolled. The last Exocet failed to identify the target in the turmoil of the other explosions, and it self-destructed.

As smoke and fire filled the sky, jagged bolts of lightning flew from the center of the maelstrom. Two of the French fighters were struck as they retreated. The airplanes vaporized instantly.

With a roar of angry triumph, King Ghidorah spread its massive wings and took to the air.

In response, the Rafales flew in, but their missiles simply bounced off King Ghidorah's hard scales, and the French fighters were swatted out of the sky like so many bugs.

Sensing his chance, the last French pilot stared through his HUD, aiming his nuclear missile at the flying monster. But before he could depress the trigger and launch the Aerospatiale ASMP, one of King Ghidorah's heads spit a bolt of force at his jet.

Desperately, the pilot tried to jink the aircraft to

avoid the blast, but the stream of force seemed to track his fighter.

The Super Etendard, its pilot, and the nuclear missile detonated in a powerful midair explosion.

Radioactive debris mixed with airplane parts as they rained down on the northern suburbs of Paris, and King Ghidorah winged its way toward the English Channel.

The British Tornadoes, despite a valiant effort by their pilots, were no match for King Ghidorah. In a short and fierce aerial battle, nine out of sixteen Tornadoes were downed in minutes. Only a few of the pilots managed to eject into the cold water of the channel, where rescue helicopters hovered, trying to drag the pilots out before they died of cold and exposure.

As darkness descended on England, King Ghidorah flew over the island nation virtually unopposed.

It was nearly midnight on New Year's Eve when the battle group surrounding the carrier *Theodore Roosevelt* was alerted to King Ghidorah's approach. Instantly, pilots were scrambled. In minutes, powerful hydraulic catapults blasted Grumman F-14A Tomcats off the deck and into the dark night sky.

The Tomcats, armed with AIM-54 Phoenix air-to-air missiles, were no match for King Ghidorah's might, but the naval aviators were determined to put up a fight. They all knew that King Ghidorah was heading across the Atlantic Ocean, toward the eastern coast of the United States.

Just before midnight, the G-Force team was notified that King Ghidorah had gotten past the United
States naval blockade and was approaching.

Casualties among the ships were astronomical.
The *Theodore Roosevelt* was sinking, and two
destroyers were already at the bottom of the
Atlantic. In addition, an entire squadron of Tomcats
was lost, the pilots missing and presumed dead.

Even worse, according to radar, King Ghidorah
was heading directly for New York City, and would
arrive sometime after sunrise tomorrow morning—New Year's Day.

In desperation, the president ordered G-Force to
take to the sky at dawn and do battle with the
space monster when it arrived.

The first morning of the new century was cold and
overcast. Low clouds hung over the Manhattan skyline, and snow was predicted for later in the day.

As Raptor-One was wheeled out of a hangar and
onto La Guardia's main runway, the G-Force team
ran system checks inside the cockpit.

Several modifications had been made on the
Raptor and its munitions after the first battle
against Godzilla. Additional heat shielding had
been placed over the missile bays in the wings, and
the depleted-uranium shells for the eight cannons
had been replaced with experimental Teflon-coated shells just developed.

Kip tested and retested the bay doors, because
they didn't always work properly as a result of the
additional weight of the shielding.

Martin oversaw the addition of new software

and avionics packages, and he was reviewing the systems from the co-pilot's seat. Tia had downloaded all the regional maps, railroad maps, and industrial statistics of the entire New York/New Jersey area—the site of the coming battle. Now she was reviewing the data.

Pierce's intense gaze was busy studying those same maps on his HUD. The pilot was not happy about going up against *two* monsters, over a densely crowded urban cityscape—without Lori aboard Raptor-Two to watch their backs. Pierce had come to trust in Lori, and he missed her. Lori's loss weighed on them all.

On the other side of the airport, parked next to the C-130 Hercules, a converted CV-22 Osprey—a copy of the downed Raptor-Two—was also being prepared. Inside the cockpit, Colonel Krupp and General Taggart readied the untested aircraft, and themselves, for the coming battle.

Suddenly, Dr. Birchwood's voice crackled from the cockpit speakers in both aircraft.

"King Ghidorah has been tracked 200 miles off the coast of Long Island," he reported. "The *kaiju* is flying at low speed, but should arrive in the area in the next hour or so…"

General Taggart keyed his mike. "What about Godzilla?" he asked.

"Still approaching along the Hudson," Birchwood replied. "He should arrive in Manhattan at about the same time."

General Taggart nodded. *This is no coincidence,* the general thought. *Poor Lori was right. Something has been guiding Godzilla to this place all along…But for what purpose?* Taggart wondered. *Are they going to destroy each other, or join forces against mankind?*

Taggart keyed his mike. "Prepare for takeoff," he commanded.

News teams from all the major networks were positioned around Manhattan. Nobody was sure where—or even *if*—the monsters would come ashore, so every network affiliate stretched their manpower to the limit, trying to cover the biggest story of the brand-new century.

On the Brooklyn Promenade, a tree-lined public space along the shore of the borough, with a panoramic view of lower Manhattan's towering financial buildings, the news cameras vied for the best positions. Near the entrance to the promenade, Robin Halliday stood facing a camera mounted on a tripod, the skyline of New York City spread out behind her.

Watching the teenage newswoman, Linda Carlisle leaned against the INN satellite truck, her arms folded across her chest. Mike Timko approached the camerawoman.

"What do you think of our star?" he asked, indicating Robin. The teenager was retouching her lipstick.

"I think that if I'd had half her ambition and stamina when *I* was seventeen, I'd be *president* now."

Mike snorted. "You wouldn't want that job. Have you seen that guy lately? He's aged twenty years!"

"Yeah, well, the last few months have been

rough on everybody," Linda said, a shadow of pain behind her eyes.

Mike nodded, remembering Tony Batista, but he said nothing.

"Look at her," Linda observed. "A brush with a monster, a bath in Varan guano, *two* helicopter crashes, and a week in a hospital—and she *still* looks like she just stepped out of the shower on a spring morning—"

Suddenly, a commotion broke out among the camera team next to them, a bunch of losers from one of the Big Three networks. Linda turned around just as one of the network cameramen pointed his lens into the sky. She looked up at the same time as Mike.

"What the hell…?" Mike muttered.

Linda lunged for her camera and pointed it toward the overcast clouds above Manhattan, where something was *definitely* happening!

While there were news teams scattered all *around* Manhattan, only one news crew was actually *in* Manhattan.

Inside the glass-enclosed observation deck of the Empire State Building, a cameraman, a satellite technician, and a lone reporter waited for the monsters to begin their assault on New York City.

"None of this is new to you, eh, Gordon?" the cameraman joked.

Nick Gordon, the award-winning young science reporter whose brush with Godzilla in Tokyo resulted in a best-selling book, shook his head.

"Nope," he said blandly. "Been there, done that."

"What do you think will happen?" the satellite technician asked.

Nick thought about it for a minute. "They'd better fight," he said finally. "A lot of football games have been preempted for this, and these monsters owe it to the fans to provide a good show."

The cameraman and the technician both laughed. Nick turned away from them and gazed out the window at the city below. He remembered the last time he'd witnessed Godzilla's coming, and his thoughts turned melancholy.

"Hey, Nick...what's that?" the satellite man asked, pointing toward the sky. Nick looked up.

The overcast cloud cover was changing, swirling, opening up.

"Yeah..." Nick said. "What *is* that?"

All around the city, people gaped in awe and wonder as the sky above Manhattan began to roll and shift. The low cloud cover seemed to part of its own will, and shafts of sunlight shone through the breaks in the clouds. The brilliant yellow sunlight cut through the gloomy morning like a laser.

"It's beautiful!" Robin Halliday sighed.

As cameras rolled, broadcasting images of the mysterious phenomenon all over the world, the huge hole in the cloud cover widened. The center of the hole was directly over midtown Manhattan and the Empire State Building.

"Something is dropping out of the clouds!" Nick Gordon spoke into his microphone, squinting against the luminous shafts of sunlight that poured through rips in the clouds. The cameraman focused on the sky behind the reporter.

"I think...yes...yes, it is!" Gordon looked into the camera. "It's a parachute, ladies and gentlemen. A parachute is descending through the clouds."

As Nick watched, his eyes widened in amazement. "I think the parachute is coming toward this very building!" he announced. The cameraman turned the camera toward the sky, and the millions of people who were tuned in to INN all over the world watched as a woman in a green flight suit landed on the observation deck of the Empire State Building...right in front of a startled Nick Gordon!

As Nick rushed outside to interview the mysterious woman, the clouds continued to part until the whole island of Manhattan was bathed in luminous sunlight. Then an eerie, penetrating shriek echoed through the canyons of New York.

Nick reached the woman, who had torn off her parachute pack and let it tumble to the streets below. She was watching the sky above intently when the reporter reached her.

"Hello," Nick said. "What's your name? Were you in a military aircraft? Do you have something to do with what's happening in the sky right now?"

As Nick Gordon asked the questions in rapid fire, he shoved the mike into the startled woman's face. She turned and looked right into the camera.

"My name is Lori Angelo," she said. "I'm a member of G-Force—"

"What's happening in the sky, Ms. Angelo?"

Gordon asked. Lori looked up, and a smile tugged the corner of her pretty lips.

"Mothra is coming," she said simply.

Nick Gordon looked puzzled. "Who is Mothra? And why is Mothra coming here?"

Still smiling, Lori stared into the camera and answered. "Mothra is the Protector of the Earth, and she is leading Godzilla to New York to destroy King Ghidorah!"

As the world watched, a vision of wonder and mystery appeared over Manhattan.

With a piercing cry, in a shower of brilliant color and bright, rippling motes of light, a gigantic moth with multicolored wings seemed to float in shafts of sunlight over the very heart of the city.

Mothra seemed delicate and benign, yet everyone who saw the creature could feel her power. The blue, multifaceted eyes seemed imbued with both intelligence and benevolence. Even the most hardened, cynical reporter gasped in awe and wonder as the great winged creature descended from the sky on silken wings.

On the promenade, Linda Carlisle blinked back tears as she watched the being. It seemed like a vision of heaven…an alien creature too wondrous to be on our dirty, insignificant planet.

On top of the Empire State Building, Nick Gordon felt it too. For the first time since the Reyes-Mishra Asteroid Swarm had been discovered, for the first time since Godzilla had returned, Nick felt hope well up inside him.

It felt *good*…

29
THE BATTLE OF
THE MILLENNIUM

Saturday, January 1, 2000, 9:37 A.M.
The cockpit of Raptor-One
In the sky over Manhattan

The G-Force team watched from the cockpit of Raptor-One, hovering over New York City, as Godzilla moved majestically down the Hudson River.

A fleet of military helicopters followed the monster like a score of bridesmaids. Across the frigid, dirty river, on the Jersey City waterfront, hundreds of cameras followed the creature's every ponderous step.

Godzilla waded downriver, his lower legs and writhing, segmented tail submerged in the murky green water. The river was churned by Godzilla's movements, and white froth lapped against his black belly.

High overhead, a military surveillance aircraft left a contrail across the clearing sky. Godzilla lifted his feral head and bellowed a challenge at the passing aircraft. The bell-like roar echoed through Manhattan's canyons of steel and stone.

The Raptor, hovering low among the tall buildings of lower midtown, monitored Godzilla's movement as Toby announced constant updates on King Ghidorah's progress over the radio.

The space monster was expected to land in Manhattan—the estimated time of arrival was less than ten minutes.

High above the tallest towers of the city, the creature that Lori called Mothra circled patiently in the clear blue sky, occasionally emitting shrill, piercing squeaks.

Meteorologists had predicted snow for the afternoon, but the weather, like everything else on this momentous day, was unpredictable.

Except that Lori predicted it, Tia thought sadly. As she watched the data scroll across her monitors, Tia recalled the things Lori confided to her the last time they spoke—before the attack in the Gunnison Forest. Lori told Tia about her dreams and about her belief that Godzilla was being guided by a higher intelligence—an intelligence she called Mothra.

Tia didn't believe her friend that day, suspecting that Lori was suffering from a delusion. Now Mothra hovered over Manhattan, and a creature from deep space was coming to this tiny corner of the solar system at the same time as Godzilla.

It can't be a coincidence, Tia thought grimly. She wondered what it all meant. The headphones crackled inside their helmets, interrupting everyone's tense concentration.

"King Ghidorah has just passed the Coast Guard observation ships," Toby radioed from the mobile command center at La Guardia. The space monster was only minutes away now.

"Roger," Pierce, piloting the Raptor, replied calmly.

"Stay out of sight," General Taggart commanded from Raptor-Two, the V-22 Osprey that hovered above the World Trade Center's twin towers.

Pierce smoothly guided Raptor-One out of visual range. He dropped to an altitude of only a forty feet over Washington Square Park, ducking the aircraft behind a row of high-rise residential buildings that lined Fifth Avenue. The team relied on their electronic surveillance monitors to keep tabs on Godzilla's progress.

"The waiting is the worst part," Martin declared as Pierce locked the aircraft in hover mode. Everyone in the cockpit silently agreed.

King Ghidorah entered United States airspace unopposed.

After arbitrarily destroying a Coast Guard frigate in Long Island Sound with a single bolt from its left head, King Ghidorah banked its massive wings over City Island and swooped down over the Bronx.

Another random blast destroyed an elevated section of the Bruckner Expressway, and the space monster crossed the borough, laying waste to everything in sight.

Bronx Municipal Hospital, Yeshiva University, and the area around West Farms were totally demolished. The animals in the Bronx Zoo could not be evacuated. A single volunteer had remained behind to feed and care for them.

Now the beasts howled, roared, and bellowed in their pens as jagged bolts of pure energy shattered whole sections of the park.

Frightened lions, freed by a smashed wall,

ignored the terrified zoo volunteer and charged down Southern Boulevard.

Flying only a few hundred feet above the city, King Ghidorah continued to level buildings and annihilate streets. The vicious monster left a trail of fire and devastation in its wake.

In the parking lots around Yankee Stadium, the New York National Guard had placed batteries of Patriot missiles. As King Ghidorah approached them, the search radar array targeted the monster.

As one, a half dozen anti-aircraft Patriot missiles leaped from their box-shaped launchers. At Mach 3.0, the deadly missiles streaked toward their target.

The Patriots detonated uselessly against King Ghidorah's golden hide. The space monster replied with an attack of its own. Blasts of energy bolts rained down on the Patriots and on the famed baseball park immortalized by legendary athletes.

In seconds, Yankee Stadium became a cauldron of fire. All around the blazing structure, unlaunched missiles detonated on their trucks, spewing flames and burning fuel among the scrambling crews.

King Ghidorah passed the havoc below, cackling madly as it flew across the Harlem River toward Manhattan's Central Park.

"The Patriots have failed to stop King Ghidorah," General Taggart reported. "The *kaiju* is heading for Central Park...Raptor-One, move toward an intercept position."

Pierce nodded grimly and tightened his grip on the joystick. The engines began to accelerate, and the huge aircraft rose above the high-rise towers. When the Raptor cleared the buildings, the aircraft converted to airplane mode and raced uptown, toward the park and King Ghidorah.

As Raptor-One streaked past the Empire State Building, Lori watched her friends go by, her fingers pressed against the observation deck's window.

"Mothra, protect them..." she whispered.

At Battery Park, on the lower tip of Manhattan, Godzilla thundered ashore. Sea birds scattered into the sky as the monster's booming tread shook the park and splintered concrete sidewalks. National Guardsmen scattered, too. Jumping into their Hummers, they sped away from the scene.

Sirens blared all over the city, alerting the soldiers—posted there to prevent further looting—that Godzilla had entered Manhattan. The soldiers listened, glued to their radios, as reports of destruction streamed in from uptown.

Now *two* monsters moved through one of the greatest cities on Earth. As the world watched, many wondered about humanity's future.

Pierce turned the Raptor over to Kip's control after the aircraft crossed the high-rise-lined street called Central Park South and entered the park itself.

To his right, Kip could see sunlight gleaming off the Pond. Under the belly of the aircraft, the white marble statue of Christopher Columbus shone like a pearl in the morning sun.

Kip slowed the Raptor and locked the aircraft in hover mode. Then he tapped some keys on his weapon's control panel, arming the Raptor's newest offensive weapons.

Under each wing, a modified Tomahawk missile hung from pylons. These two cruise missiles were specially equipped with surgically honed, needle-sharp tips made of Teflon. The missiles were designed to first penetrate the hide of a *kaiju* and then detonate with ship-killing force.

Twin electronic tones signaled that the Toma-hawks were armed and ready for launch. Kip focused the laser-targeting system on the oncom-ing monster. While he watched with surprising detachment, the three-headed monster expanded in the HUD.

Carefully, Kip placed the laser designator on the base of King Ghidorah's central neck.

"You've got tone," Martin announced impatient-ly, letting Kip know he had targeted correctly. Kip ignored the co-pilot, holding back until he felt absolutely certain the missiles would not miss.

Finally, as the creature completely filled the heads-up display, Kip depressed the firing button.

In two bright flashes, the Tomahawks leaped off the wing pylons and lanced forward, toward King Ghidorah. Kip, while still painting the target with his laser designator, prepared to "get out of Dodge" if the missiles failed to stop the space monster.

A second later, both missiles struck King Ghidorah. The first one lost some altitude and hit the monster full on its chest. The missile bounced off King Ghidorah's golden plates and arced down toward 72nd Street. It struck the upper floors of the historic Dakota apartment building, where John Lennon had once lived.

The second missile actually penetrated King Ghidorah's flesh at the base of the center neck. But the warhead failed to detonate.

As Kip dived the Raptor low over Heckscher Playground, King Ghidorah streaked right over them, spitting bolts of energy.

One blast struck the Trump International Hotel at Columbus Circle, cutting the tower in half. The upper portion of the copper-hued skyscraper fell across Broadway, utterly demolishing a smaller office building that housed a religious organization.

As King Ghidorah streaked over the park, a thick golden liquid spilled out of the wound on its neck, spattering huge droplets across the area of Central Park called Strawberry Fields.

A second bolt of force rocked the Raptor. As the aircraft shuddered, Kip fought for control.

"Hull damage!" Martin cried, staring at his engineering board. "Some of the heat-proof tiles have been knocked off." A monitor in front of Kip highlighted the section on a computer-generated schematic.

Kip spun the Raptor on its axis, turning the aircraft 90 degrees and firing cadmium missiles at King Ghidorah's back. The missiles struck the creature without effect.

"Go after him!" Pierce cried.

Kip nodded and pushed the throttle forward, chasing the flying monster toward lower Manhattan's Wall Street—*and* Godzilla.

* * *

On top of the Empire State Building, Nick and Lori watched the opening salvo in the battle of the millennium.

The Raptor had lost the first round. But though G-Force had failed to stop King Ghidorah, they *had* managed to survive.

Now Nick and Lori saw that King Ghidorah was barreling toward them, spitting bolts of energy that arced to the streets, destroying building after building and tearing up great swaths of the pavement.

"Duck!" Nick cried, dropping his microphone and grabbing Lori. As King Ghidorah flashed by, a scarlet bolt of fire shot from its right head, striking the landmark structure.

The thick windows on the observation deck shattered and the Empire State Building shuddered. For a moment, Nick was certain that the upper portion of the building would tumble, dumping them into the street far below.

But miraculously, it remained erect even as King Ghidorah blasted by, rocking the skyscraper with buffeting winds.

"They don't build them like *this* anymore!" Nick cried to no one in particular.

Smoke filled the air all around them, but when the structure stopped quaking, Nick was on his feet again. Lori rose from the floor, too, just in time to see Raptor-One flash by, this time heading downtown.

Lori gasped when she saw the destruction in King Ghidorah's wake. The Chrysler Building's upper floors were blasted away, the silver aluminum facade blackened and melted.

At the Empire State Building, more smoke began gushing into the observation deck, burning their eyes and making them cough. Lori felt a hand on her shoulder. She turned and looked up at Nick.

"The building is burning," he announced. "We've got to get out of here!"

Mothra screeched shrilly and swooped over the Brooklyn Bridge, then banked her wings and turned toward the financial center. The gigantic butterfly was on an intercept course with King Ghidorah.

Godzilla, meanwhile, had slammed his tremendous bulk against the huge glass and steel International Hotel at the base of the World Trade Center's twin towers. Bellowing out a roar that could be heard across the Hudson River in Jersey City, and on the shore of Brooklyn Heights across the East River, Godzilla tore the structure to pieces with his front claws.

Then the mutant reptile turned his feral head to the sky and gazed at Mothra as the gigantic winged creature wheeled gracefully over him.

Mothra screamed out a shrill cry that shattered windows in the surrounding buildings. Godzilla slowed, blinked, and snorted. Then he tilted his head in a gesture of almost human curiosity. Mothra screeched again and again as she circled the sky above Godzilla's head.

On the Jersey City shore, reporters remarked on the obvious. It looked as if Godzilla and the mysterious creature called Mothra were having a conversation!

But the peaceful moment ended abruptly when a jagged bolt of King Ghidorah's lancing rays struck Mothra's furry body in a shower of sparks and fire. Mothra trilled in pain and surprise, then banked away over the Hudson River.

Godzilla's eyes narrowed and his lip curled, baring his long double row of uneven teeth. King Ghidorah dived and slammed into Godzilla with earthshaking force.

The reptile was knocked end over end by the sheer power of King Ghidorah's body blow. Godzilla slammed into the structures behind him.

Number Three World Trade Center, already partially damaged by Godzilla, was completely demolished in a cloud of dust, splintering shards of glass, office furniture, and debris.

But from the center of that maelstrom, electric-blue fire poured forth in a steady stream, smiting King Ghidorah on its golden-scaled chest. The space monster cackled and spit fire as its massive feet crushed the Commodities Exchange Building, across the plaza from the Twin Towers.

His tail flailing madly, Godzilla rose to his feet and bellowed in defiance. King Ghidorah responded by spewing a second blast, which struck Godzilla on the neck and chest, searing his rutted hide.

As the monsters stared at each other from across the ruins of World Trade Center Plaza, Raptor-One arrived.

Even inside the soundproof cockpit, the crew of the Raptor could hear the bellows of rage from the two titans.

Each time King Ghidorah spat bolts of energy, buildings were blasted, sending chunks of steel and concrete into the sky. Flames from a dozen small fires licked at Godzilla's legs as his spine danced with the electrical discharge that preceded a blast of his radioactive breath.

Godzilla roared and spit radioactive fire at King Ghidorah in a stream of force that caused the dinosaur to backstep from his own recoil. When this powerful blast struck King Ghidorah full on its massive chest, the winged creature was blown backward across Church Street.

Helpless against the rays, the space monster slammed into a row of older granite office buildings, which collapsed under the weight like sand castles.

Inside Raptor-One, the headphones crackled in G-Force's helmets. "Stay out of the way!" General Taggart commanded.

Kip slowed the craft and placed it in hover mode. It hung in a stationary position over Broadway, New York's City Hall behind the aircraft, the two monsters in front.

Some emergency service workers had remained in Manhattan. Now fire engines rushed to the scene of the raging inferno that burned in a wide swath from Columbus Circle down to Battery Park. From the river, firefighting boats laid down streams of water on fires that consumed block upon block of waterfront property. Smoke billowed into the air in great black clouds, obscuring the sky and blocking out the sunlight.

*   *   *

Using its forked tail for support, King Ghidorah struggled to its feet. The creature's necks writhed like Medusa's hair, and bolts of force continuously spewed from its three heads. Godzilla roared and stamped his massive feet, shattering buildings and caving in streets and sidewalks.

Then Godzilla pushed between the twin towers, breaking windows on both structures. Glass rained down on what remained of the plaza. With an angry wail, Godzilla lowered his feline head and charged King Ghidorah.

The two mammoth bodies crashed together with a tremendous boom that could be heard for miles. Godzilla's bone-white claws dug into King Ghidorah's flesh as its forearms grappled with the thing. King Ghidorah stumbled backward, but remained on its feet.

Desperately, King Ghidorah's mighty wings beat Godzilla's body, creating a hurricane-force wind that snatched up and carried away debris, abandoned vehicles, and helpless emergency workers. As Godzilla grappled with his enemy, King Ghidorah's central neck looped like a python around Godzilla's exposed throat.

Then King Ghidorah began to squeeze.

Lori wouldn't leave the observation deck, no matter what Nick said or did. So the reporter gave up and sent his cameraman and technician packing, while he stayed behind with this strange woman who had dropped out of the sky and, almost literally, into his lap.

Nick sensed that there was a story here, and he

decided it was worth risking life and limb to get it. But even as he made his decision to stay, visions of his old colleague Max Hulse—who had died when Godzilla destroyed Tokyo Tower—stepped a macabre dance through Nick's head.

To his surprise, the smoke rolling about them soon began to clear, as the sprinkler system was activated inside the bowels of the art deco tower.

Nick rubbed his still-smarting eyes and saw Lori dash out to the exterior observation deck. He ran through the shattered windows to her side.

"What's happening?" he asked. Lori pointed to the sky.

"Mothra is coming back," she announced.

Godzilla's powerful forearms pounded at King Ghidorah's golden chest, but the noose around his neck just grew tighter and tighter, squeezing the life out of him.

Then a familiar shrill keening split the air, and Mothra dived down out of the smoke-filled sky. A thin beam of power crackled from the creature's antennae, striking one of King Ghidorah's horned heads.

King Ghidorah fired back, missing Mothra but taking out a hovering CNN news helicopter. The chopper exploded in a plume of fire, and the burning debris smashed into the Hudson.

Mothra squawked again and circled the two titans, who were still locked in a death grip. Foam flecked Godzilla's gaping mouth as the beast gasped and choked.

Blue lightning arced along his spine, but the

blast never left his constricted throat. Slowly, Godzilla began to weaken, and his reptilian eyes glazed over.

"We have to *do* something," Martin cried. "Godzilla is dying out there!"

Kip, meanwhile, was torn with indecision. Technically, they were still in combat mode, and he was still in command of the Raptor. But Kip wanted nothing more than to turn over command to the older and more experienced Pierce.

"What do I do?" Kip muttered, his fingers tightening on the joystick.

As Godzilla flailed his arms weakly, Mothra hovered over the monsters, beating her wings angrily. But King Ghidorah would not release Godzilla from its death grip.

Suddenly, Kip spotted something dark lodged above King Ghidorah's chest, at the base of the middle neck—the same neck that was slowly strangling the life out of Godzilla. Kip's fingers raced across the control pad, and the HUD magnified the image.

Kip swallowed hard, squinting to make out the contours of the object.

"*Yes!*" he whooped finally, startling the others in the cockpit.

"What is it?" Pierce demanded, his hands locked around his own control stick, waiting for Kip to turn over command to him.

But Kip would do no such thing. Instead, he eased the Raptor forward, closer to the writhing, wrestling titans.

"What are you doing?" Pierce demanded. Kip

ignored the pilot, concentrating, instead, on the battered warhead of the Teflon-tipped cruise missile, which still projected from a wound in King Ghidorah's center neck.

As the others watched, Kip moved the Raptor closer to the brawling monsters. The headphones in his helmet crackled again.

"Pull back!" General Taggart commanded from the other aircraft. "You're too damn close!"

Kip reached up and shut off his radio, then he directed all of his concentration to the heads-up display in front of him. Slowly, he eased the nose of the Raptor down, then switched over to the eight Avenger cannons. Thousands of rounds of Teflon-coated explosive shells were automatically fed into them.

Martin's eyes widened. Then he smiled in comprehension. "Go get him, Kip!" he cried.

When the targeting computer found the spot Kip was aiming for, the sound it made switched from an intermittent beeping to a steady drone.

"You've got tone!" Pierce and Martin said simultaneously.

Kip squeezed the trigger, and the Raptor rocked backward as the eight cannons spit thousands of rounds of ammunition. The shells struck King Ghidorah, exploding in tiny blasts, and tore at the monster's golden plates, splintering some of the scales like glass. Kip danced the stream of bullets up King Ghidorah's body.

The three-headed monster spied the oncoming aircraft, and the two outside heads opened their mouths at the same time.

Bolts of force slammed into the Raptor, blowing out chunks of the hull and pieces of the wing. Still, Kip held the craft steady, not bothering to close the blast doors over the cockpit because he didn't want to risk flying blind for even a split second.

"Pull up!" Martin cried.

"Get away from those blasts!" Pierce commanded. But Kip ignored them both, continuing to pour a steady stream of cannon fire onto the target.

Finally, as bloody foam began to pour from Godzilla's yawning mouth and his eyes rolled up into his head, a single Teflon-coated shell found the target.

With a white-hot blast that rocked the Raptor, the missile's warhead, still lodged in King Ghidorah's flesh, exploded. The force of the blast completely severed the central neck from King Ghidorah's body. A fountain of hot, gleaming golden blood shot into the sky from the terrible wound.

The head and neck dropped into the street below, smashing a kiosk and some abandoned cars.

Godzilla, released from King Ghidorah's grip, dropped backward, slamming into the South Tower of the World Trade Center. The whole building shook, and shattered glass rained down onto him and into the plaza below.

Flailing his tail, Godzilla opened his eyes again. The creature didn't even inhale—he simply let out the most powerful blast of his radioactive breath ever recorded by scientists. But the force wasn't directed at King Ghidorah. The blast tore through the first five floors of the North Tower Building behind the space monster. Glass exploded and steel support beams melted under the intense burst. Suddenly, the North Tower began to tilt, then fall.

Even as the missile exploded, the Raptor was torn apart by King Ghidorah's final blasts. Electrical systems failed all over the ship, and internal fires broke out in the missile bays and near the fuel tanks.

Martin struggled to keep the Raptor in the air, but it was hopeless. The ship lurched to one side, and as Kip fought the controls, the left rotor blades struck the South Tower and broke apart.

"Eject! Eject! Eject!" Pierce cried as the dying Raptor plunged into the street far below...

The full weight of the North Tower slammed down on King Ghidorah, crushing the creature under tons of steel, stone, and glass. Lower Manhattan quaked as the building broke apart over King Ghidorah's back. The space monster cried out in a keening wail of pain. Godzilla, meanwhile, struggled to his feet.

The prehistoric monster stared at the pile of shattered rubble as Mothra circled overhead. Godzilla's eyes narrowed, waiting.

Suddenly, like a phoenix bursting from the fires that consumed it, King Ghidorah leaped out of the debris and into the sky. Wailing, its two remaining necks writhing in fear, the space monster flew toward the Atlantic.

But even as it fled, Godzilla struck its back with

a second tremendous blast of radioactive fire. The creature cried out again and increased speed.

As Godzilla watched, King Ghidorah, minus its center head, flew past Liberty Island and toward the open sea, still spewing golden blood from the terrible, mortal wound.

Mothra, in hot pursuit, streaked over the ocean right behind King Ghidorah.

Godzilla, suddenly alone, blinked, grunted, and flexed his mighty forepaws. Then he lifted his head into the smoke-filled sky.

The monster's final roar of triumph and challenge echoed through the canyons of Manhattan. Then, with a contemptuous flip of his enormous tail, the mighty *kaiju* turned his back on New York City and returned to the banks of the Hudson River.

With a rumbling grunt of satisfaction, Godzilla waded into the cold river and moved ponderously toward the open ocean...his home.

As the entire crew of Raptor-One floated down from the smoke-filled sky on their parachutes, low storm clouds once again rolled over the city.

Before the G-Force team had all landed with a jolt in the middle of Broadway, gentle snowflakes began to fall. Within an hour, a blanket of clean white snow covered the ruined city, smothering the fires and signaling, somehow, that the long, terrible crisis had finally ended.

GODZILLA™

30
AFTERMATH

The United States of America

Late in the afternoon, the G-Force team was extracted by helicopter from the ruins of lower Manhattan. None of them had suffered serious injury in the ejection, though Martin had sprained his ankle when he slipped in the snow.

Toby saw Lori on INN when she landed on top of the Empire State Building. He dispatched an Army Blackhawk helicopter with an extraction crane to pick her up and bring her to La Guardia Airport. The chopper returned with Lori, the INN reporter who interviewed her, and the rest of his news team.

So Nick Gordon got his story, as well as exclusive interviews with the entire G-Force team.

Everyone in G-Force was delighted to find Lori alive and well. Her emotional reunion with her friends was broadcast worldwide. Even General Taggart wiped away a tear when Lori hopped out of the Blackhawk and ran to them.

Lori didn't remember anything that happened to her between the time she ejected over the Gunnison National Forest and the moment she landed on top of the Empire State Building in Manhattan. But she knew that Mothra had helped save her, as she had helped Godzilla save the world.

As the team was debriefed, Pierce could not stop gazing at Lori. And though she was the center of attention, Lori couldn't help but stare at him, too.

Dr. Markham smiled.

This should be interesting, she thought.

Before the sun set on the first full day of the new century, the people of America were taking halting and uncertain steps toward the future.

On the cold, barren, and windswept plains of decimated Kansas, Eleanor Peaster returned to the ruins of her family's farm. It bore little resemblance to the place she grew up in. The house was now rubble, and the barn and silo had vanished. But Eleanor Peaster was determined to begin again.

She didn't know how yet, but she knew she would figure it out eventually.

Hiram and Wanda Roper returned to Kansas, too. They rebuilt their farm with the help of federal disaster relief funds. They adopted Ronette Carry, the little girl who saw her whole family slaughtered by the Kamacuras.

The nine-year-old hadn't spoken yet, but with love and care, the Ropers were hopeful.

Captain Jerry Tilson returned to Pennsylvania, and to his wife, Sandy. She had a little boy in March, and they named him Michael Pederson Tilson.

A decorated war hero in his small town, Tilson was promoted to district manager and dabbled in local politics. He finally resigned his commission in the Air National Guard and stayed home on weekends.

Dr. Craig Westerly published a scholarly paper about his research with the native Alaskans. The dissertation won him a spot on the faculty of Columbia University, though he still spent most of his time in the far north, with the old Native American shaman.

The ancient shaman continued to relate amazing folk tales of his people to the eager anthropologist.

Billy and Zelly Whitman went to college on the money they earned from their story. Billy majored in marketing and girls. Zelly studied art.

Captain Charles Dingle retired and moved to Bermuda, where he sails, fishes, and enjoys his golden years. He doesn't even miss being the skipper of the *Texas Star*.

Not much, anyway.

Dr. Carl Strickler was appointed the director of the Mishra Foundation for Scientific Research, established in honor of the late Dr. Chandra Mishra.

The foundation funds scientific research and higher education for promising students of science.

Linda Carlisle, Mike Timko, and Robin Halliday remained a team. Robin hosts INN's young adult news show, *Teen Beat*. Mike is still her director, and Linda has been promoted to producer.

Before the show's debut, Linda took several months off and filmed a documentary about people in Kansas who were trying to rebuild their lives.

She was nominated for an Academy Award.

Slowly, with time, money, sweat, tears, and tenacity, the nation rebuilt itself. In New York, the World Trade Center was mostly demolished. Only one of the original Twin Towers remained.

George Steinbrenner finally got a new stadium for his Yankees, though he had to pay for it himself.

And Donald Trump built a complex of office towers, highways, and apartment buildings in lower Manhattan. During the project, the developer had to travel a lot, so he hired a former Navy pilot named Kathleen "Dale" Delany to fly his personal helicopter.

They were married six months later.

Oakland, California, after years of neglect, was rebuilt as a shining example of successful urban renewal. The infamous ghettoes vanished overnight. In their place, business and shopping centers were constructed around middle-class, upper middle-class, and luxury housing.

In one tranquil corner of the city, near the rechristened Jack London Square, a lovely little park was built. The peaceful area of shady trees, grassy knolls and playgrounds was named Dennis Flynn Park, after the policeman from San Francisco who crossed the bay with other emergency workers after Godzilla's attack. Flynn died rescuing an entire family trapped in the rubble of their home.

A few weeks after the park's dedication ceremony, a young woman who worked for an ad agency began jogging there. Her name was Annabel Maguire, and for some reason, she really loved Flynn Park.

One Sunday morning, while she was having breakfast under a tree there, Annabel met a charming policeman who'd just been promoted to detective. It was love at first sight.

The couple were married a few months later, under the very same tree where they first met.

Dennis Flynn Park was a happy place that day, and forever after.

Life in America and on planet Earth continued.

COMING IN SPRING 1998

GODZILLA™ AT WORLD'S END

By Marc Cerasini
Cover art by Bob Eggleton

Amid the frigid ice fields of the South Pole, a group
of teenage science students and a team of U.S.
Army Rangers discover an ancient race of crys-
talline beings miles below the surface of Antarctica.

Awakened from their frozen slumber, these
Ancient Ones release an army of virulent monsters
upon the world: the evil, insect-like Megalon;
Gigan, a cyborg; Manda, a gargantuan snake; and
Hedorah, the Smog Monster. As Earth becomes a
battleground of titanic monsters, the young scientists and soldiers at the bottom of the world must
join with Godzilla to become the last line of
defense against a race older than humanity itself.

$5.99 U.S. $7.99 CAN./ISBN 0-679-88827-6

PUBLISHING SPRING 1998